The Long March

RICHARD FOX

Copyright © 2017 Richard Fox

All rights reserved.

ISBN: 154817170C0

ISBN-13: 978-1548171704

CHAPTER 1

Alert sirens blared as Commodore Gage's ship called for battle. The Commodore peered into his holo tank, following the projected course of three pirate cruisers bearing down on the *Orion*. New icons filled the holo as more of his fleet emerged from slip space, all too far and too slow to reach the *Orion* before the pirates.

"Captain Price, give me some good news," he said to his executive officer seated just below his command dais. She swiped through several screens filled with pulsating red status reports.

"Forward batteries are at forty percent strength—" she backtracked on a screen and shook her head "—make that thirty-seven percent; gun nine just went off-line with a hydraulics failure. Port shield emitters are about to flip the breakers. They might take one hit before there's a cascading failure across that flank. Starboard launch bay is still off-line…engines are amber across the board. We can maneuver, at least."

"Helm," Gage raised his voice and pointed to the pale-faced Lieutenant Jellico at the conn, "all ahead flank. Keep our functioning shields toward the enemy and make for the *Ajax*. She'll improve our odds in this fight."

"Aye aye," the ensign said.

Gage watched his ship reorient in the holo tank and felt the deck plates hum beneath his boots as the ship lurched forward. The *Orion* would reach the other Albion vessel's weapon range in fifteen minutes, which left Gage's ship ten very long minutes to deal with the three pirate ships alone.

He tapped the lead pirate ship, the *Carlin,* and glanced over sensor readings; she boasted forward lances built in the Reich and Indus shield emitters. The ship's captain, Loussan, had declared a vendetta against Gage years ago after a skirmish in wild space spoiled a Harlequin raid and sent the pirate away bloodied and empty-handed. Loussan would be eager to strike the *Orion* first, which explained why his ship was creeping ahead of the other two vessels.

At the command of any other battleship, Gage could have made short work of the pirate ships, designed for raiding, not going toe to toe with an Albion ship of the line. But the *Orion* was an older ship, her crew full of sailors fresh from the academies, still recovering from the damaged suffered at the hands of the Daegon mere days before. Against a pirate commander willing to take a few hits…the *Orion*'s situation was in doubt.

Gage looked to the bridge doors, where Thorvald—his Genevan bodyguard—stood against the bulkhead, his face hidden beneath the visor of his semi-sentient armor. Gage lowered one hand to the side of his holo tank and signaled the bodyguard over.

"Prince Aidan may need to abandon ship," Gage said quietly. "Tell Salis I'll get this ship as close to the *Ajax* as possible. The Harlequins may be pirates, but they've a code. In all the years we've dealt with them, they've never fired on an escape pod. I'll send you off once the battle begins."

"My place is here," Thorvald said, "at your side."

"Your place is wherever the hell I tell you it is," Gage sneered. "Loussan is itching for this fight for one reason and one reason only: me. I am the reason Prince Aidan is in danger right now. I am the only one that Loussan's looking to kill and I'll not lose you too, not when the prince needs your protection."

"If I must say it, Prince Aidan stands a better chance if I keep you alive. I have full confidence in Salis, even if she is new in her suit," Thorvald said.

"Commodore," the communications lieutenant waved to Gage, one hand on his headset, "picking up several coded transmissions from Sicani to the pirate ships and between the two ships to the *Carlin*'s flanks."

"And?" Gage asked.

"The *Carlin* hasn't answered a single message," he said. "She's gone dark."

"Enemy ships will enter firing range in two minutes," Captain Price said. "Priority target on the

Carlin or defensive fire?"

Gage traced a circle around the pirate ships inside his holo tank and tapped a knuckle against an icon to bring up the reading from the communication station. The two ships beside the *Carlin* pulsed with new transmissions across several different frequencies. The messages were too encrypted for the *Orion*'s computers to decode, but the ships were broadcasting—that was unmistakable.

The Commodore drummed fingers against the rim of the holo tank, then crossed his arms.

"Launch the ready fighters," Gage said. "All cannons target the *Carlin*, but hold fire."

"I'm sorry," Price twisted around in her seat and looked up at Gage, "did you say not to open fire? We've got range on them for at least three minutes. We let them get closer without so much as poking them in the eye and they'll—"

"I am well aware, Captain," Gage said, "but I think the odds are about to shift."

The two ships flanking Loussan's vessel flashed in the holo tank.

"Cannon fire," said Lieutenant Commander Vashon, the ship's gunnery officer. "Not directed at us...but across the *Carlin*'s bow."

In the tank, the *Carlin* edged forward of the other two ships as bolts of energy flashed across the cruiser's nose.

"Guns," Gage raised a hand, "fire on my mark. Target Loussan." He kept his hand high, watching as the other ships fell back. One struck the rear arc of the *Carlin*'s aft shields—Gage didn't need nearly two decades of service in the Albion Navy to know that last shot was a final warning to Loussan. The *Carlin* adjusted course and speed to match the *Orion*'s, then edged just beyond the ship's effective range.

"Commodore, we're being hailed," the communications officer said.

"Guns, hold fire." Gage lowered his hand. "Send it to my tank."

The holo shifted to Captain Loussan as the pirate removed an ornate helmet and hurled it off camera. Loussan shook out a long mane of blond hair as the helmet ricocheted off bulkheads. He bared his teeth, then brought his visage under control with a deep breath. Loussan's eye twitched as the two captains stared each other down.

"Gage…I doubt your hull bears plasma burns and half your weapons are off-line through negligence on your part," the pirate said. "You were in battle. With who? Where?"

The Commodore stood up straight and clasped his hands behind his back. That the pirate needed to ask these questions made the Harlequin's sudden amicable posture easier for Gage to understand. Steady ships crewed by brave men and women could win most any battle, but information was a formidable power in its own right.

"They call themselves the Daegon. We fought them over Siam before withdrawing."

"An enemy strong enough to send you running…" Loussan wiped the back of his glove across a scar marring one side of an otherwise handsome face. "Do you know what happened to Albion, or did you scurry off after the first broadside?"

Anger simmered in Gage's heart at the insult, but he kept his composure.

"Some personnel escaped Albion and made it to my fleet. I am well aware of what happened on Albion…are you?" Gage asked.

Loussan levelled a finger at Gage. "That is the only reason I haven't blown your ship to pieces and stuck your head on my prow. Against my wishes and the authority my vendetta has over such matters…the Council of Free Sicani hereby offers your ship…parley."

"Parley?" Gage raised an eyebrow.

Loussan glanced down and tapped an unseen screen.

"But I won't have you tread upon Sicani soil if I can help it," Loussan said. "Your ship's transponder has an encryption you use only for Code Vermillion. Send whatever royal you've got hiding in a closet to Derna spaceport. We want someone in authority, not some lowborn sod like you. The Council will send a representative to meet him or her."

Thorvald shifted uneasily, then made his way over to the communication station, his sabaton clinking against the deck. The codes alerting other Albion ships that a member of the royal family was aboard were highly encrypted and buried in normal ship-to-ship traffic. That the Harlequins knew Code Vermillion was in effect was a breach in the Genevans' security plan.

"I will attend the parley," Gage said.

Loussan's eyes twinkled.

"If you refuse the terms offered, then you refuse the protections that come with it. Excellent! Carl, ready the weapons and someone find my helmet." Loussan reached for his console to cut off the transmission.

"Prince Aidan will not attend because he is five years old," Gage said. "By Albion law, I am regent and can serve in his stead for all matters."

Loussan leaned back. Gage waited as the pirate's mental wheels turned.

"These Daegon of yours hit Albion *that* hard?" Loussan asked. Even though the man was a brigand, a thief, and wanted for crimes across civilized space, Gage could not deny that the pirate was perceptive.

"I will discuss it with your Council," Gage said.

"One shuttle, side arms only," Loussan said. "The parley lasts until you've returned to your ship." He cut the transmission and the holo tank reverted to a model of the local system.

Gage let out a sigh.

"Sir, you can't be serious," Price said as she got out of her chair and joined him on the command dais.

"We have to buy time," Gage said, "to get the rest of the fleet assembled in a defensive formation and calculate a slip-space jump to…" He tapped a screen and the tank brought up star charts.

"...Feygold's World. From there we can reach Indus space. We have a mutual defense treaty with them—should have a warmer welcome than what we've found here."

"It could take days before we have a workable jump solution," Price said. "How long can we stall the pirates? They've got a hell of a lot more firepower than just those three cruisers in orbit."

"If they come for a fight, the fleet will make them pay dearly for it," Gage said. "Pirates are raiders, bullies. And it's not just the Harlequins down there." He tapped Sicani's star in the holo and zoomed in on the planet, passing a hand over the ships massed over the North Pole as data fields popped up next to most of the ships. "At least eight different clans, most of whom spend their time fighting each other as much as they do raiding easy targets."

Gage held up his hand, fingers spread wide. "They're like this," he closed his digits into a fist, "not this."

"They could still overwhelm us with sheer numbers," the XO said.

"Not without a mauling. I doubt there's any pirate clan that will volunteer to be the first to charge our guns. Selfless service is rarely profitable," Gage said. "They want us out of here…and before the Daegon follow us from Siam."

Thorvald's helm shifted down from his face and head and slid onto his shoulders.

"If you go to Sicani, they will try to kill you," the Genevan said. "Loussan's vendetta is well-known. You cannot trust this offer of theirs to keep you safe."

"There is…some risk," Gage said.

"'Some'?" Price almost hissed the word. "Do

you remember the stories they told at the Academy about Captain Douglas? She led a punitive expedition against the Gorgon clan at the turn of the last century and wiped out all but maybe a dozen of them. The survivors declared a vendetta, then waited decades before she retired and went on holiday out of Albion space and—"

"And the last Gorgon shot her at the spaceport." Gage nodded. "The Intelligence Ministry reminded me of all this when Loussan's vendetta went out through wild space. For what it's worth, they also told me that there's no part of the pirate's code that isn't open to reinterpretation…to some degree."

"You think they'll let you—an Albion naval officer—just waltz in and out?" Price asked.

"This isn't about me," Gage said. "This is about the fleet. Prince Aidan…home. We need to reach Indus and rally the core worlds to free Albion. Captain Price, you will take command in the event I don't return. You'll have the time to calculate a slipspace jump out of here—that's the least I can accomplish. My intent is clear?"

Price shook her head. "This is practically suicide."

"I'll travel alone and—"

"No," Thorvald growled. "I will be at your side. That is my duty."

Gage looked at the bodyguard and frowned. "Doubt there's any way I could stop you from coming. But if you'll be with me, then…get Tolan up here. I have a mission for our spy."

CHAPTER 2

Tiberian strode through the burnt-out remains of Ludlow as Daegon soldiers led away prisoners, all with their arms bound behind their bodies and pain clamps on the side of their necks. Another Daegon walked two steps behind him, wearing simple armor and carrying no weapon.

The smell of smoke, dead bodies, and spilt blood permeated the air. Tiberian felt almost at home. He spotted a perimeter of honor guard, the onyx lines down their left sides and Tiberian's House crest on their chest. They surrounded a bombed two-story building, one corner collapsed and crumbled into the street.

Tiberian walked toward the guard captain, his pace failing to slow as the captain stepped out of his way.

"Where is Eubulus?" Tiberian asked.

"The Count is interrogating prisoners." The captain made no effort to slow Tiberian as he made his way past the guards. "I am not to disturb him."

"'Interrogation,'" Tiberian huffed. "Such comedy." The bottom floor of the building had collapsed into the basement, so he slid down the bricks and chunks of wall with grace and into the parking garage beneath.

Finding Eubulus wasn't hard. He simply had to follow the screams.

Tiberian dropped down a level, his cape fluttering behind him as he fell and landed next to the bloody corpse of an Albion officer. The unarmed Daegon accompanying him stumbled slightly on his landing and stomped into a puddle of blood.

Eubulus had his back to them. The warrior, massive even by Daegon standards, held an Albian by the throat in each hand, both gasping for air and beating meekly at Eubulus' arms. The one in his left hand passed out and Eubulus snapped his neck with a twist of his wrist. He tossed the body aside and let the still-living Albian fall to the ground where he struggled to breathe.

"He wins again," Eubulus said. "Another!"

A pair of soldiers dragged a man in the tatters of an Albion army uniform into the room and forced him to the floor facedown. One soldier put a boot to the back of his neck.

Looking over his shoulder to Tiberian, Eubulus said, "You wish to play, brother? I find these have excellent fighting spirit, but they lack fortitude. They were at peace too long before we came."

"I am here on Baroness Asaria's writ." Tiberian touched his slate-gray necklace. "I've no time for games."

"Ever the stickler…shame you let the last of the royals escape." Eubulus turned around and cracked his knuckles. His bloodshot eyes and wide jaw made him look like some ancient barbarian raider of myth, not one of the Daegon's premier commanders.

"The Albians still fight you in the streets," Tiberian said. "Both our writs stand unfulfilled."

"This was the last of their military." Eubulus shrugged. "My writ is almost complete. If there are a few that insist on fighting, they will fall to the garrison and the inquisitors soon enough."

"I've come for your 2nd battle group. I need

the ships to hunt down the last Albion fleet and bring their Crown Prince back to the Baroness. Such is her desire," Tiberian said.

"The whole of the 2nd? How many ships slipped away from you?"

"Chasing them down with just enough to win will squander more resources than using overwhelming force. I've come to ask you face-to-face out of respect. Do not drag this out."

Eubulus waved the soldiers off the pinned soldier and the Daegon picked the man up by the scruff of his neck.

"The Albians escaped into ungoverned space. How will you catch them?" Eubulus asked.

"They left a number of their own behind on Siam. I sent them to the racks and received usable information, not a distraction like this." Tiberian sneered at the dead strewn around the room. "They'll try to flee to Indus territory, and the only way is through the Kigeli Nebula."

"You're starting to bore me." Eubulus grabbed the other prisoner and gripped them both by the throat but not tightly enough to choke them.

"I know you lack finesse, but I have a plan to retrieve the Crown Prince alive. Ja'war?"

The unarmed Daegon behind Tiberian raised a hand in front of his face, and the blue-skinned man's face shifted to match Eubulus', then to one of the officers' caught in the commander's grasp.

Eubulus' guards jumped in front of their commander, weapons raised.

"Ha! What toy is this?" Eubulus knocked one of the guards aside.

"A Faceless, a caste of assassins and thieves. We found him in the prison beneath the castle. He's agreed to help us. Knows wild space well. Not as loyal as our specter infiltrators, but the explosive charge I had implanted on his heart will keep him focused and motivated," Tiberian said.

"Clever...clever. Gustavus!" Eubulus raised the two prisoners in his hands up to shoulder height and choked off their air.

A slender Daegon dropped down through a hole in the ceiling and rolled forward, one hand on a sword at his hip.

"Father?" the new arrival said.

"Which, my son, will win?" Eubulus asked. The prisoners gasped for air, their feet kicking.

"The one who survived the game four times already," Gustavus said. "He knows if he passes out first, he dies."

The new prisoner in the tattered uniform slowed down, his face a sickly blue. He went limp and Eubulus broke his neck. He let the other man take a final breath, then killed him too.

"My boy learns fast, doesn't he?" Eubulus asked Tiberian.

"I would not say your lessons are difficult."

"Gustavus will accompany you. Learn from you. That is my only condition," Eubulus said. "Return him and the 2nd battle group from my fleet when you have the Prince. Now be gone."

"May you find glory for the crusade," Tiberian said as he waited for Gustavus to saunter over. The younger officer drew his sword and saluted, the guard raised to just below his eyes.

"Uncle," Gustavus said.

"Come, child. I will teach you how to hunt." Tiberian turned and marched away.

CHAPTER 3

Wisps of super-heated air flitted past the shuttle's view ports as the craft descended into Sicani's atmosphere. Thorvald stood near the cargo ramp, his boots locked to the deck, one hand gripping an empty cargo bin over his head.

He looked over the other passengers—Bertram, Tolan, Wyman, and Gage—as his armor took their heart rate, temperature, and dozens of other biometric readings. The Commodore's physiology was near exhaustion, his state unchanged since the Daegon attack on Siam. The rest read with varying levels of anxiety, with the exception of Tolan.

The spy held a mirror in front of his face, changing his features from one visage to another, his hair growing and shortening, the color altering in waves of different hues. Part of Thorvald detested the Faceless for butchering his God-given form. While Thorvald's body had undergone some enhancement to wear his armor, every implant could be removed. The Genevan doubted Tolan even knew what his own true face looked like anymore.

Thorvald flexed his arms, and the modular plates shifted over his body before locking down and forming a more rigid barrier. He shifted the plates across his body, a pre-battle check he'd done every single day since he first wore his armor nearly two decades ago.

Almost every day. Captain Royce, commander of the Genevan Guard contingent on Albion before his death, had stripped him of his armor before throwing him into the palace's dungeon. Thorvald had plenty of time to consider which aspect of being in prison was worse—the separation from his armor or the humiliation of what he'd done.

Thorvald ran a baseline diagnostic…and the results came back slightly better than marginal. Being in armor that was barely functional was not how he wanted to protect Gage and Prince Aidan.

Turning away from the other passengers, he spoke beneath the roar of engines. "Ticino, our link suffers," Thorvald said to the gestalt within the armor. The artificial intelligence had yet to fully bond with Thorvald since he donned the armor, taking it from Captain Royce's dead body in the middle of the Daegon attack on the Albion palace. The gestalt had yet to share its name with Thorvald, and he could only address it by the name of their Genevan House.

+I hate you,+ pounded into Thorvald's mind.

"I know, Ticino, I know, but the regent will enter a hostile area soon. We must protect him. Stop fighting me."

+Traitor. Oath breaker.+

"No. My oath to Albion remains. I serve to my last dying breath. The same as Captain Royce," Thorvald said as the armor constricted around Thorvald's chest and a sense of grief flowed into Thorvald's mind.

The bond between armor and wearer grew stronger over years, and that gestalt had been bonded to Royce for almost four decades. For Thorvald to abuse the armor's spirit by donning it so quickly after Royce's death would have been forbidden on Geneva, where each House treated their suits as near-priceless relics and forging the AI within the armor took years of work by hundreds of artificers.

+You are not Royce. Traitor.+

"We serve, Ticino. We serve the royal family and Albion. The regent is in danger. I need you to trust me. Deepen our sync for Gage, if nothing else."

+You are not mine. I am not yours.+

The armor loosened slightly around Thorvald's body. The Genevan moved easier, feeling the AI's resistance waning…an improvement Thorvald knew would end the moment they were safely back aboard the *Orion*.

"Thank you. May I have your true name?"

The AI didn't respond.

****

"They'll sell me into slavery," Bertram said. The steward pressed a knuckle against his mouth as his eyes darted from side to side. "I'll spend the rest of my days on some ice ball of a planet, chained to a dozen other stinky, starving men…" He put his hands against his stomach, a hair's breadth away from busting the navy's body-fat limits. "No need to worry about frostbite. I won't last a day when those poor wretches see me. 'Hello, Bertram. Welcome to the salt mines. Step into this lovely bath we've for you. Ignore the bits of carrot and smell of broth.'"

Wyman, sitting to the steward's left, rolled his eyes.

"Ten minutes ago, you were convinced the pirates were going to sell off your organs," the fighter pilot said. "Now you're a main course in a salt mine. What's next?"

"Perhaps I can convince some pirate lord that I can make a good spot of tea." Bertram tapped a fingertip to his lips. "Yes, add a bit of manners to these barbarians. Teach them the wonders of a warm cup at teatime while I woo the captain's daughter to escape with me to some garden world that's not on any star chart."

"For the love of…Tolan, you've been to Sicani," Wyman said. "Will you tell him that nothing's going to happen to us. There's a parley; means we're not to be bothered, right?"

Tolan pulled the skin back on his left cheekbone, twisted his head in his mirror's reflection, then the other side of his face shifted to match.

"The Commodore's protected, not us," Tolan said. "But I doubt anyone will want Bertram's liver."

"There's that," the steward said.

"But the market for Albion blood and marrow is booming," Tolan said. "Our vaccine program is one of the best this far from the core worlds. He'd be a golden goose for years."

"Wait…what?" Bertram went pale.

"Now just a damn minute." Wyman shifted against his restraints. "Bertram and the Commodore have Thorvald to watch over them. I'm supposed to go with you into the city and now you tell me all these pirates wouldn't mind turning me into a blood bank?"

Tolan's skin darkened a few shades and freckles emerged across his nose and beneath his eyes. He set his mirror onto his lap and looked at the pilot.

"Sicani is a free entry world," Tolan said. "No customs to declare or passports checked. So long as you keep your mouth shut—our accents are a bit distinctive—no one will know you're from Albion. We go down there and I'm a malware exporter from Tirana's World. You're my dimwitted hired help."

Wyman looked down at his outfit: worn khakis and a beat-up flak jacket the spy scrounged up from his own ship, the *Joaquim*. The pistol strapped to his thigh had several notches carved into the handle.

"Why do I have to be dimwitted?" Wyman asked. "I still don't even know why the hell you want me with you for this."

"You think I want you with me? You've the field craft of a lumbering ox. The man we're going to see has his own set of rules, ones we have to follow," Tolan said.

"But you've been to Sicani before," Bertram said. "How bad will it be?"

"It's a planet of three billion." Tolan brushed his fingertips through his hair, turning a tuft darker with each stroke. "The murder rate is astronomical compared to home, but I've been to worse places. With so many pirate clans in orbit, Derna will be a powder keg ready to go off—which suits me nicely. Last time I was here, this face took out a few loans that haven't been repaid." The rest of Tolan's hair darkened.

The spy took an injector from a silver case hidden in his coat and pressed it to his throat, then closed his eyes and tilted his head back against the wall. His face twitched for a few seconds before settling down.

"There we are," Tolan said and let out a euphoric sigh.

"You can look like anyone in the galaxy and you pick a face that owes money?" Wyman asked.

"This is the face my contact knows," Tolan said. "Besides, old man Weissgerber is out of the loan-shark game by now. Probably. Maybe. It's been years since the incident and it's not like he was the friendly type that had others willing to carry grudges for him."

"I'm not sure which of us has it worse," Bertram said to Wyman. "Me going with the good Commodore to the belly of the beast or you going to the city's rotting core with that one."

"Do you want to trade?" Wyman nudged Tolan. "Can we trade?"

"No," the spy said. "Only one of you was on Albion when the Daegon attacked." He sat up and blinked at Bertram, his eyes changing color each time. "When you're with Gage, don't eat anything, drink anything, or accept any offer. The parley protects your life. That doesn't mean your hosts won't find some gray areas to tinker in."

"Lovely," the steward said. "Right lovely."

CHAPTER 4

A trio of Daegon fighters ripped overhead. The sonic boom of their passing rattled the crumbling building where James Seaver and his squad hid. He heard the crash of glass up and down the street as remnants of already broken windows came loose or broke apart. After days of fighting, nothing in the city of Ludlow was still whole.

"Why do they keep doing that?" Morton asked as he brushed dust and tiny shards of glass off his uniform. He and Seaver were both nineteen, but after days without sleep and the accretion of dirt and pulverized buildings what youth they had was buried beneath grime and exhaustion.

"To mess with us, I think," Seaver said. "Haven't seen any of our fighters in days. They fly low and loud, telling us they've got command of the air. No one's sleeping through a pass like that." He checked the battery on his rifle. At thirty percent charge, he was better off than most of his squad, but he'd still run out of ammunition before his pulse rifle's power ran out.

Sergeant Hagan came over to Seaver and Morton, staying crouched to keep himself below the line of broken windows.

"Got a signal from our spotters." Hagan wiped grime off his mouth with a shaking hand. "Drone sweep's coming. The lieutenant's getting the civilians ready to move. He wants us to pull any

Daegon away. Standard bait and switch. Single shots. We hit them hard enough to wound a couple, then we fall back before the big guns and show up. Got it?"

"Spotters see any walkers? Or golems?" Morton asked.

"One golem." Hagan swallowed hard. "Bravo squad's got our last anti-armor grenades. Don't waste your shots on them. You know the fallback position?"

"Tech school on Derider Street," Seaver said.

Hagan gave him a quick pat on the shoulder, then hurried over to the next pair of fighters crouched against a broken couch against the wall.

"If there's golems…there's walkers," Morton said. "We should leave now. To hell with the civilians. Not like they can make any difference now. Just sit down there, eating all our food and drinking all our water."

"Shut up." Seaver kicked Morton's shin. "Militia only protect civilians. You want to go run away like the rest of the army did? Should've joined them."

"Did you get a different recruiting pitch than me?" Morton asked. "Seem to remember all of us Youth Corps being told to report to the local constabulary when we got to Ludlow after that giant ship showed up over New Exeter. Then…" He squeezed his eyes shut for a second. "How long ago was that? I don't even know what day it is anymore."

"It's Saturday," Seaver said. "Positive. My mother's birthday. Easy to remember since it's a week after the prism whale festival."

"She's with the fleet, right?" Morton shifted in the spot he'd made amidst the rubble. "Not Home Fleet. Way out system to Caledonia or Usona." Even under the grime, Seaver his friend growing red with embarrassment. Talking about family that were likely dead elsewhere in the war had become a major faux pas in the militia. Nothing of Albion's Home Fleet remained. Seaver had watched it burn through the sky in the first few hours of the Daegon attack.

"She's with the 11th," he said. "Some humanitarian mission on Siam. I was so pissed when she told me. This prism whale holiday was the last time my parents and me were going to be together before I shipped out for boot camp. Guess it worked out okay for her."

"Shit, Siam the vacation planet? All the way out on the edge of wild space? I bet she's fine." Morton fished a tube out of his chest armor and took a sip of water. "You good?"

"Not sure." Seaver stuck his fingertips into the seam of his uniform's outer armored layer and pulled it open. The water tube had come off the clip and wedged into the sweat-soaked layer against his skin. He sucked on the nozzle and got nothing but the taste of salt and grit. He reached to his thigh and touched the water bladder incorporated into the armor on his legs, and found a rip.

"Told you the walls of that last place were too thin to stop anything," Morton said.

"Yeah, figured that out when Janice got killed." He touched his helmet, the only piece of gear the corporal left behind that wasn't shot through or bloodied.

"Here." Morton offered his drinking tube and Seaver took a quick sip. "Ha ha. You drank my pee."

"Yeah, real funny. I know how our uniforms work." Seaver leaned against a desk half buried in the remnants of ceiling tiles and closed his eyes. He felt every cut and bruise over his body, a dull pain that grated against the exhaustion that ran into the depths of his being.

He thought of his father, who was far behind the lines at Camden. The older Seaver hated tourist crowds and had left New Exeter the day before the festival to their family vacation home just off the beach. The Daegon ground assault had overwhelmed the capital city in the first day, then radiated out to the Gable Mountains and to Ludlow, nestled between the mountains and a royal forest preserve.

There'd been no word of other Daegon landings, but information had been spotty. Civilian telecommunications had gone down in the first hour of the Daegon attack, having been functional just long enough to spread word of the attack and whip the entire planet into a panic before shutting down. From what he'd gleaned from the militia officers, they were still in contact with other cities, but Seaver didn't know how.

Not that he wanted all the details. He knew the Daegon took prisoners, had found what was left of them as the battle lines shifted across the city. If he was captured and tortured, the Daegon couldn't tear out anything he didn't know.

His mother...the memory of her in her naval uniform, rank, and doctor's pins glinting in the morning light as she boarded a shuttle was uncannily sharp. She'd tried to warn him away from the service, even as she prepped for a last-minute deployment on the *Orion*.

He'd called her a hypocrite in their last conversation. That she'd joined the navy in the last year only to discourage him from doing the same. But her reasons for joining were different. His father needed extensive care for his Langfei syndrome, the expertise and expense beyond what his mother's skills and the income generated by her medical practice could cover. Seaver had wanted to enlist for the adventure, for the veteran's preference in all aspects of Albion society reserved for the common born.

The whole last few hours he'd spent with her, the bitter arguments, the anger at her leaving before their last family trip…seemed so stupid now. What he wouldn't give to know she was safe, to even talk to either her or his father again.

Morton nudged him with the butt of his rifle.

"Drone sign," he whispered.

Seaver's eyes popped open and a chill spread through his chest as his body dumped adrenaline into his bloodstream. He remained perfectly still as conversations lowered to whispers throughout the room he shared with the other dozen men and women of his militia squad.

Weak red light broke through the window over Seaver's head. The temptation to bolt out of the room and never stop running tugged at his heart, but to do that was suicide. The Daegon trackers picked up motion easily; fleeing would put a giant target on his back.

A steady rustle grew in volume, the rattlesnake-like noise of the drone's repulsor engines. Seaver picked up on a slight discordance in the engine noise and in the angle on the searchlights. The drones always traveled in packs of two.

"Stay chill, James," Morton said.

"No, *you* stay chill. Can practically hear you quaking in your boots," Seaver said.

Sergeant Hagan shushed them both.

"Least it's not our turn to poke the bear," Morton whispered. The angle from the red searchlights changed as the drones floating through the street beyond meandered from side to side.

The snap of rifle shots broke through the air.

Light from a searchlight swept through the windows as the drone carrying it tumbled out of the air. Red vanished from the windows on Seaver's floor and twisted toward the source of the attack.

A smattering of shots filled the air. Seaver heard the *tink* of bullets against armor and the other drone's engine stuttered but stayed alive. A siren began blaring in the street.

"They missed." Seaver rolled onto his knees and popped onto his feet. The drone was a few yards away, its segmented round body and sensor arms giving it an almost crab-like appearance. He brought the holographic sights on top of his rifle level to his eye and shot the drone three times, breaking an armor plate and ripping through the engine.

The siren cut out and the drone went into a tail spin. It bounced against Seaver's building several times before it crashed onto the street.

"Seaver!" Sergeant Hagan dared a look through a window. "What the hell are you thinking?"

"Drone was locked on the other team." Seaver pulled the magazine out of his rifle and pressed new rounds into it. "No way it saw me."

"We need to run," another soldier said. "It sent up our location and—"

Faint thumps carried down the street.

"Incoming!" Hagan fell to the floor and slapped his hands over his helmet.

Seaver did the same. The Daegon artillery was deadly accurate and the next few seconds would tell him if he'd managed to save his squad or doom it.

Explosions ripped through a building a few dozen yards away. The overpressure from the shells shook the floor. Dust and ceiling tiles came loose and filled the air with a thin haze. Seaver stayed pressed to the floor even after the echoes died away. When a second salvo didn't target them, he coughed and shook dirt off of his rifle.

"Think the other squad got out?" Morton asked.

"There was barely a minute from when they took down the first drone to the strike," Seaver said. "Normally takes the Daegon three or four minutes to respond."

"You think they're getting better or that was a fluke?" Morton stood, his shoulder pressed against the wall.

Seaver peeked through the window and caught a flash from a handheld mirror down the block leading toward Daegon lines. He read the code as it came in.

"Enemy infantry coming," he said to Morton. "Ten soldiers…one golem."

Curses rose from the squad; more than one

looked at Sergeant Hagan with fear-filled eyes.

"Stay put," Hagan said. "Enemy's coming for their drones. We open fire *after* the other team uses their grenades. Not the first time we've done this."

Seaver ducked down as the soldier in the observation post down the street stopped flashing his mirror. He heard boots against pavement. The thump…thump…thump of something much larger than a normal soldier.

It had taken time, and a number of lives, before the Albian defenders learned that Daegon weapons were deadly to any non-Daegon that touched them, but the enemy's other equipment could be recovered and studied. Every time a seeker drone was destroyed, the Daegon immediately sent troops to recover it…after they'd pulverized the source of the attack with artillery.

Ambushing the recovery teams had been one

of the few successes in the fight for Ludlow.

He heard the Daegon voices as they spread out around the fallen drones, the commands of a leader close to Seaver's side of the street. He'd shoot that one first.

He gripped his rifle tightly, hoping that the other team opted to spend one of the militia's last anti-armor weapons and let the Daegon retreat with their broken drones. But if they did get into a fight, Seaver and his squad wouldn't have long before Daegon reinforcements arrived. That meant walkers. That meant little to no chance of surviving.

The clomp of massive footsteps grew louder. There was the squeal of metal against the street as the golem picked up a broken drone. Seaver put his finger on the trigger and squeezed his eyes shut.

There was a sharp hiss and a bang that rattled Seaver's teeth.

"Open fire!" Hagan shouted.

Seaver stood up and pointed his rifle out the window. An eight-foot-tall Daegon golem was in the street. Its mound of a head and massive shoulders slouched forward; one arm clutching the remnants of a drone lay in the street, and smoke billowed out of an empty socket.

Enemy soldiers huddled against rubble between them and the other squad—that had launched the anti-armor rocket—their heads down to avoid the sudden onslaught of rifle fire coming at them, leaving them exposed to Seaver and his fellow militia.

Seaver didn't see the leadership stripes running down the arms and legs of the enemy soldiers, and aimed at one furiously pecking at a screen mounted on his forearm. He fired, and the bullet hit the Daegon just above the collar and burst out of the man's back, splattering blood against a wall.

Morton fired quickly, not even using his rifle's sights.

Seaver looked for another target and found the Daegon were rushing straight for his building.

"Climbers!" someone shouted.

"Oh no they don't." Morton leaned out of the window, his rifle pointed straight down.

"No no—" Seaver reached for his friend and grabbed him by the shoulder. He pulled him back as blue bolts from Daegon weapons shot up the side of the building. Morton grunted and collapsed. His chin bounced off the window and he pitched back, a smoking crater where his forehead used to be.

"Grenades!"

Silver disks flew up through the windows, one bouncing off the ceiling near Seaver and wobbling against the floor. Without thinking, he dropped down and grabbed Morton's body. He pulled the corpse over himself as the grenade exploded into a flash of white light and a concussion that knocked his hearing into a high-pitched ring. Searing heat from the device ignited small fires around the room.

Seaver pushed Morton's smoking body off of him, trying not to gag on the smell of burnt hair and singed clothing. Militia who hadn't taken cover in time languished on the floor, exposed skin burnt, clutching at abused eyes and ears.

He saw his rifle just as a Daegon's claw-tipped glove clamped down on the windowsill. Seaver grabbed his weapon, the grip burning his palm and fingers. An enemy soldier's head and shoulders rose into view and Seaver shot him in the face, the sound of his weapon barely coming through the ringing in his ears. The Daegon's head jerked back with a red mist, then he fell back.

Something hit his shoulder and sent him sprawling, another militia man, his stomach a blackened ruin.

Three Daegon had climbed through other windows and were fighting with Sergeant Hagan. Seaver pushed himself free of the dead man and tried to find a clear target through the melee.

Hagan ducked a bayonet swipe and jabbed his rifle into the enemy's chest. He fired twice, knocking his assailant back and to the ground with two neat holes through his breast plate.

A Daegon with yellow stripes running down the length of his arm charged Hagan from behind, light glinting off the blade fixed beneath the enemy's rifle.

Seaver shouted a warning and fired from the hip. His shot missed and the Daegon leader speared Hagan through the spine. The blade ripped through the sergeant's chest. The sergeant looked down at the bloody tip, anger still on his face. The Daegon lifted Hagan off his feet and hoisted him into the air.

The Daegon's war cry pierced through the ring in Seaver's ears. Seaver switched his weapon to full auto and opened fire. The Daegon dropped Hagan and rolled toward the window, evading Seaver's every shot. The leader sprang up and dived out of the window. The others followed him a heartbeat later as what remained of the militia squad fired on them.

The whole building shook and the wall collapsed. Seaver lurched away as it crumbled.

"Golem! Golem, run!"

Seaver made for the stairwell that led to the basement and the maintenance tunnels that would lead to their next rally point. Sergeant Hagan's orders still stood, even if he lay dead.

A massive hand burst through the floor, collapsing a section beneath the feet of a fleeing soldier. The soldier lurched forward and fell onto a sturdy section, his legs and waist hanging over the edge. He reached to Seaver for help. The golem grabbed his quarry by the head, huge fingers closing around his face. The golem crushed the man's skull, sending gray and red viscera and bits of scalp flying through the room.

Seaver tripped over a broken chair and fell against a support beam. The beam shook as the golem one floor below struck it.

"Oh no." He looked up and found a gap in the roof. Seaver jumped forward and landed well short of his goal. He pulled himself forward by his elbows as the golem struck again and broke the beam.

The floor gave way and Seaver fell into dust and darkness as the whole building collapsed.

He tumbled, brick and glass pelting his body as the avalanche of debris carried him away. He came to a stop against a broken wall and a landslide of dust and broken furniture piled on top of him. He had his face next to the crook of one arm, and he could still see and breathe.

Seaver lay still, ignoring the pain in his legs, the blood dripping down his face. He waited, listening for the Daegon, trying to keep his breathing as shallow as possible.

He waited, every bump he felt from the settling building feeling like the approach of an enemy soldier come to finish him off.

He waited until sunset and the sound of gunfire and explosions faded into the distance. Then he worked his way out of the debris. The cloth over his armor plates was ripped and torn, but he'd escaped any serious injury.

Back on the road, members of his squad lay in line, blood from their slit throats mixed into a single pool.

Seaver looked south, to the thick forests just beyond the city's edge, and ran.

CHAPTER 5

Gage paced along the edge of the shuttle's closed ramp and smoothed out the front of his dress uniform. The Commodore's epaulets on his shoulder felt far heavier than usual, and the fleet command pin on his chest dug into his chest. He glanced at his ribbons and medals, most earned fighting pirates across the frontier of wild space. Why Albion's diplomatic corps carried out its business in civilian dress suddenly made perfect sense to him, but even if he'd arrived in mufti, there was no hiding who he was to Loussan or his ilk.

Two bangs sounded against the hull.

Thorvald, standing next to the ramp controls, turned to Gage.

"We should keep the engines running," the Genevan said through his visor.

"You saw the air defense emplacements during our descent," Gage said. "Let's not have any illusions about flying away if our hosts take issue with the idea. Bertram, ready?"

Bertram stood up and buckled a pistol belt around his waist.

"Wish you'd take a shield unit, sir," Bertram said.

"Shields do not convey confidence." Gage drew his pistol and slapped a magazine into the grip.

"We've reason to be confident?" Bertram asked. "I mean, of course we're confident…because…"

"We have Thorvald." Gage nodded to the bodyguard.

Thorvald flicked a switch and the ramp lowered. Hot, humid air blew through the widening gap, triggering memories of Siam and the steaming jungles around the shattered cities. The bodyguard hurried down the ramp, ducking beneath the hull and dropping to the ground before the hydraulics stopped.

On the scorched tarmac, Gage saw a single slate-gray ground car. A slight man in a red-frocked coat opened a rear door, his face severe as light glinted off a single monocle built into his right eye socket.

Thorvald held up a hand and passed his palm across the car. His other hand tapped two fingers against their thumb, a signal the bodyguard had taught him during their flight from Siam—caution.

Gage ignored the warning, strode down the ramp, and nodded to the man holding open the rear door. Skyscrapers surrounded the spaceport, casting long shadows from the setting sun. A few air cars moved between the structures, some linked by enclosed walkways. Holo text in a half-dozen languages wrapped around some of the buildings. An ad for a gun emporium featuring a scantily clad woman wielding a pair of needle pistols played on a loop along the edge of a stadium dome.

"Commodore Gage, I presume," the man in the red coat said. "I'm Derringer, the driver."

"Correct. Is there a problem?" Gage asked Thorvald.

"There's another person in the car," Thorvald said. "Something…off about him."

"He's for your protection," Derringer said as lines of text ran across the driver's monocle.

"I'm all the protection he needs," Thorvald said. "Bring the other man out."

"Lord Moineau and the others are waiting," Derringer said. "I know you're new to Sicani; best not to try their patience."

"Since when do clan lords lend additional protection during a parley?" Gage asked. "The word of a lord carries all the weight of his sword, does it not?"

"Oh, it does, you Albie," the driver said with a sneer. "Just that the whole rock's on edge 'cause your fleet came in out of nowhere. Scared people do stupid things. Lord Moineau would rather not have to rip apart a hab-block looking for whatever down-on-his-luck sod decided that taking a potshot at you was better than living. Derna City has a few desperate types."

Gage looked at the car, then put his hands

behind his back and waited.

"Damn uptight bunch of…" The driver whistled quickly, the front door opened, and a robotic leg stepped onto the tarmac.

Gage edged backwards. His hand clamped down on his pistol, but the weapon remained in the holster. A creature from old nightmares seemed to flow from the car. Light warped slightly around the humanoid figure as it raised over-long arms, the fingers tipped with thin spikes. Gage saw his reflection in the bullet-shaped helm, black as polished obsidian.

A Katar, a cyborg designed for one thing: killing.

Thorvald stepped between Gage and the Katar, the Genevan's armor flowing from his back and redoubling the protection between the pirate Katar and his charge.

"That's right…you tussled with a Katar on Volera II back when Loussan made his play," Derringer huffed.

Gage's heart pounded in his chest, remembering when another Katar had ambushed them in an alleyway and ripped open two of his sailors during a running gun battle though a city under pirate attack. He and the rest of his security team had blown the Katar to pieces…a Katar that looked identical to the one standing before him.

A mechanical croak came from the Katar.

"Says he's never fought a Genevan before," Derringer said.

"Must be why he's still alive," Thorvald said. "Does he want to stay that way?"

The Katar let off a monotone laugh.

"In the interest of time," the driver said, "how about I send Ruprecht here on his way to the dome.

Should be a fine drive, what with the curfew and the roads cleared for you."

"No." Gage dropped his hand from his pistol. "We'll not turn away such a gesture from Lord Moineau. Let's be on our way."

"Sir," Bertram said from behind the Commodore, "if we could *not* have the murder-cyborg in the car with us, I'm sure…Thorvald would appreciate it. Yes, that's the ticket."

"As you like." The driver stepped away from the open door.

Gage grabbed Bertram by the shoulder and guided him toward the car, the steward mumbling as he hurried inside. Gage walked up to Ruprecht and peered into the blank faceplate, his every instinct demanding he shoot or flee from the monstrosity. He made out a skull and a jumble of wires just beneath the dark glass, then got into the car.

Gage's heart pounded in his ears as the smell of spilt blood and echo of screaming men amidst gunfire seeped into his mind. The interior was spacious, sealed off from the driver's compartment. The seats were made of ivory-colored leather and creaked as Gage sat down.

Thorvald followed him in, the bodyguard snapping his fingers with metal clicks.

"No listening devices or cameras," Thorvald said. "Not sure if I should be impressed or insulted they didn't bother to try. My armor's projecting a privacy field. No sound we make will go more than a few feet. We can talk."

Gage rubbed his nose, covering his mouth, and said, "Well done."

"Why bring that abomination with us?" Thorvald asked.

"They sent it just to unnerve me," Gage said.

"If I send it away, I look weak, afraid. If we're attacked without the Katar, Lord Moineau escapes the blame, as we refused his protection."

"Bloody hell…I sometimes wish we were just dealing with the Daegon," Bertram said. "We shoot at them. They shoot at us. None of this intrigue-at-court bollocks."

"Welcome to Sicani," Gage said.

The limousine drove off.

Several minutes later, Tolan and Wyman came down the ramp. Tolan hooked around the shuttle and slapped a hand against the hull twice, signaling the pilots to button up. Tolan made a beeline to an open gap in the fence, where signs flashed in the streets beyond, promising alcohol and other comforts to spacers on shore leave.

"I'm sure we're being watched," Wyman said.

"What part of 'dimwitted-nontalking-help' did

I stutter?" Tolan wagged a finger at Wyman. "Of course we're being watched. Good thing people come to this city just to disappear and I happen to know a few tricks to duck surveillance. Sure hope you remember where we parked, just in case we get separated."

"Why would we—"

"Talking!"

****

The limousine pulled up to a curb just outside the massive dome Gage had seen from the spaceport. A strong breeze blew trash across a muddled red carpet leading to revolving doors flanked by two muscular guards in loose-fitting suits.

Derringer hopped out and a pair of doors on the passenger compartment opened. Thorvald got out first and quickly scanned the area before signaling for Gage and Bertram to follow.

The smell of rotting garbage mixed with the vapors from a broken sewer pipe a block away assaulted Gage's senses as pulsing music thumped through the walls of the domed coliseum amidst scattered cheers.

"Sorry I couldn't take you to the VIP entrance," Derringer said with a shrug. "Boss thinks your pretty uniform might start a riot if the riffraff get a look at you. It is fight night. But he did set up a private party to welcome you. Enjoy." The driver turned a palm up and rubbed his thumb against two fingertips.

"We'll see ourselves in," Gage said, then turned and walked down the carpet, flanked by Thorvald.

Bertram looked at Derringer's hand, then

patted his hips and chest. "Bugger, our pretty uniforms don't have pockets to carry any cash," the steward said.

"Bertram," Gage said over his shoulder.

Bertram toddled over as fast as he could on his bowed legs. "The nerve," Bertram mumbled.

"Do not eat anything. Do not drink anything. Accept no offer," Gage said. "They'll let us leave under our own power and at the time of our choosing, but that's not to say they'll make it easy for us."

"And definitely don't accept free tickets to the ichikiju show if they have it here," Bertram said. Thorvald gave the man a quick look. "I mean, I heard about it after shore leave on La Joya. From a friend. I would never partake in such wild-space deviancy. My friend did and he said—"

Gage raised a hand slightly and silenced his

aide as one of the bouncers touched fingertips just above his eye. "Lord Moineau and the others will see you on the second floor," he rumbled.

The dark glass of the revolving doors shimmered as the trio stepped inside, and the smell changed to a mixture of burning tobacco and spice. Just before they stepped out of the doorway, the doors went semi-opaque.

Inside, a party raged. Women in ostentatious wigs, stiff corsets, and long dresses stood on an upper level, fanning themselves as they watched the chaos of the ground-floor dancers who wore little more than body paint and writhed around a raised stage. Small drones flew drinks over the crowd of dancers clustered near a DJ, his head covered by a holo of a dragon as mirrored balls swirled around him.

"Get you gentlemen a little something?" A topless waitress with a tray full of pills and cigarettes rolled in gaudy colors stopped next to the Albians. "Purest highs this side of the Veil, Lord Moineau's promise." She winked at Bertram, who kept his gaze firmly on her wares.

"Problem," Thorvald said. "Three men in Harlequin colors have taken an interest in us."

"I see them," Gage said, "and they're next to the stairs to the upper level. Surprise, surprise."

"Don't like what you see here?" the waitress asked. "Any of the staff upstairs will see you get what you like." She looked the steward up and down.

"Would be rude to say no to—wait for me, sir," Bertram said as he took another glance at the waitress and hurried after Gage.

The crowd parted as Thorvald led the Commodore to a spiral stairwell. More than one of the pirates spat on the floor as Gage passed. He kept his pace steady and his focus on the stairwell, ignoring the insults that rose from the crowd.

"The hell I will!" One of the Harlequin men pushed another back from the bar. The second man swung a drunken punch at the first and missed terribly. The shouter landed a blow on the other's stomach and sent the pirate stumbling back toward Gage.

Thorvald stepped in front of Gage so fast, Gage could barely react before the Genevan grabbed the off-balance man by the shoulders. Thorvald slapped the man's hand down and across the outside of the pirate's red-and-black checkered pants. There was a yelp of pain and Thorvald shoved him back to his companions.

The man touched a long cut down his pants, where a sliver of bare flesh lay exposed. The pirate wobbled, then collapsed into the other Harlequin's arms.

Thorvald stepped onto the spiral staircase and led Gage higher, Bertram to their rear.

"Gorjira tincture on a fingernail blade," Thorvald said. "Not fatal, but mimics inebriation."

"That was meant for Master Gage," Bertram said. "Why didn't you snap that lout's neck?"

"I believe we have enough problems." Thorvald hurried up the last of the steps and shooed away courtesans that cooed at him from doorways to open bedrooms. Down a hallway, a pair of Katar flanked a vault door covered with crests of pirate clans.

Lines from laser scanners traced down their bodies as they walked to the vault. Gage could almost feel the eyes of Moineau's security apparatus pick them apart detail by detail. One did not become the lord and commander of a wild-space planet by being trusting.

A small portal opened in the floor and a round drone the size of a fist rose up and floated toward Thorvald, an aperture opening in the center as it flew closer. Thorvald smashed the drone to bits with a backhanded swipe.

The two Katar traded guttural words laced with static. One slid a green sword blade out from beneath a wrist but kept it pointed at the plush carpet.

"That toy was expensive," came from a speaker on the sword-bearer's chest, the words fluid and lilting.

"Do you have another scramble drone I can break? EMP emitters and my armor don't mix. But you know that," Thorvald said.

"Genevan protection at Genevan prices," came from the speaker. "Your contract still valid with that, Albie? You could find easy employment out here."

"Open the door," Thorvald said firmly.

The sword retracted into the Katar's arm with a snap, and there was a rumbling of gears in the walls around the vault door as an energy field flickered away with a snap of ozone. The door recessed slightly and slid into the walls. Inside, a single light shone onto an enormous round table.

"Just you," one of the Katar said to Gage.

"Stay here," the Commodore said. Thorvald's hands balled into fists, but he didn't object.

Gage stepped into the room as a constant breeze cast off the lingering scent of the ballroom, and fresh, clean air surrounded him. He stopped in the shadows and waited as the door shut with a mechanical thump behind him.

The light over the table rose, revealing an old man sitting at the far edge on a raised throne. A metal frame bolted to his shoulders, legs and arms ran through a powder-blue jacket lined with gold thread. Liver spots dotted his bald head, and light gleamed off round glasses as he leaned back. He pressed his fingertips into a steeple just below his chin.

"Commodore Gage." The voice came from a small speaker on his jacket disguised as a gaudy medal, the same voice the Albian heard in the hallway. "We've heard all about you. Come, take your place." The old man waved to the far edge of the table, and the support frame bolted to his body whined with the motion.

Gage stepped up to the edge of a table. Stone tiles radiated out of the center, each bearing a pirate clan's crest. Some of the tiles looked fresh; others were worn and pitted with crude carvings of names. Gage's tile was blank.

Men and women stepped out of the darkness and up to the edge of the table. Gage recognized them all, warlords and pirate leaders who were wanted across civilized space for crimes committed over decades. In space, Gage would have gladly blown them and their ships to ashes if they did anything but surrender immediately. What these same men and women would do to him…

Loussan was the last to the table, taking a spot to the throne's right, his lip tugging into a snarl as he glared at Gage.

"Let the table come to order," the old man said. "I'm Moineau. Haven't been off world since before you were born, Albian. Somehow doubt I've ever been on your radar. Not like some of us here."

Chuckles came from some of the captains, but not Loussan or a bald woman with facial tattoos to his right.

"You asked me down here to talk. Let's talk," Gage said.

"We don't want you here, jackboot," said a man with a pulsing red mechanical eye, his words hissing through metal-tipped teeth.

"We want you gone. Gone before whatever doom you called to Siam can follow you," said Kruger, leader of the Totenkopf clan.

Moineau tapped the side of his support frame against his armrest.

"Never in all my years in the void has a banged-up fleet from a prison planet like Albion ever stumbled into free space like yours," he said as he raised skeletal hands up to his shoulders. "Explain."

"They're called the Daegon," Gage said. "Survivors from Albion report they jumped in from beyond the Veil. They have control over slip space far beyond anyone. They came in right on top of our star forts—our fleets at anchor—over our cities. More ships than the Reich or Cathay have in their combined fleets. No demands. No warning. They broke our defenses within an hour."

Gage paused and looked across the pirates. All were silent, some paler than others.

"They followed a refugee ship to Siam, where one of their commanders spoke to me— called me a thrall and demanded instant obedience…and that I turn over the Crown Prince. When I refused, they nuked Siam and gave chase. We destroyed the navy buoy before we entered slip space, which is likely why the Daegon haven't reached you yet," Gage said.

"You think Siam is the only route to wild space, Commodore?" Moineau asked as he leaned forward, canting his head to one side. "You think Albion is the only world these Daegon have attacked?"

A cone of cold spread through Gage's chest. How far had the Daegon marched through the stars?

"Where else?" Gage asked.

Moineau lifted a finger and a star map of the galaxy formed over the table. The image zoomed in to great swaths of stars color-coded to the many states of humankind. Gage found the Kingdom of Albion and saw pulsing red rings around the four stars of her modest borders. More rings sprang up around Nicodemus, Shi Chau, Busan, and another dozen stars. The line of the Daegon advance traced from the Veil…straight toward Earth.

Gage's eyes lingered on one star at the edge of Indus space. Several of their worlds were already under assault by the Daegon. The path for his fleet from Sicani to friendlier territory would be neither short nor simple.

"They spoke to you," Moineau said. "They're…human, at least?"

"Genetically, yes. There have been some

alterations to their genome—blue and green skin, adaptation to a high-radiation environment," Gage said. "Their technology is far more advanced than ours, but is human in origin. There was an issue with infiltrators…"

"That burn into husks when killed." A woman in a naval uniform coat adorned with fleur-de-lis slapped a palm against the table. Genevieve Delacroix, leader of the Wyvern clan, had once been an ensign in the Francia navy. She'd risen through the ranks of the conquered star nation's military after their home world surrendered to the Reich and most of the Frankish ships opted to become pirates instead of surrender.

"I can tell you how we found more sleeper agents," Gage said.

"Well?" Moineau stomped a heel against his throne. "We're waiting."

"That knowledge is all that's keeping my ships and crew safe," Gage said. "I will—"

"The code!" Loussan slammed his palms against the table. "The code is the only reason I haven't gutted you yet. Don't think that just because you managed to run away from the Daegon that you're special. You're of interest to us. For now. And we can figure out on our own what it is you know. I move to strike this parley. I have a vendetta to answer." Loussan took a medallion out from beneath his shirt and tossed it onto the table.

"Anyone else?" Moineau asked. Two other clan leaders tossed medallions next to Loussan's.

"The nays have it," the old man said, "though I'm tempted to invoke host's rights and put an end to all this. Tell me, Gage, anything interesting stand out when you look at my star map?"

"The Daegon haven't moved into wild space,"

Gage said.

"Quite right. The free worlds have stood apart from the power plays in the core worlds—never got involved when one of the Kaiser Washingtons started the Reach War. Never did anything to save the Foster when they went under the waves."

"*Casse-toi*," Delacroix said with a sniff.

"We stand apart," Moineau said, "unless it's to our advantage to cross over and liberate goods for a higher purpose. As such, we're left to our own devices."

"The only reason the civilized worlds never took a torch to wild space is because slip travel from star to star was always too risky," Gage said. "Jump lanes come and go with no pattern, leaving worlds isolated for years at a time. No nation would risk sending a large-scale fleet to end your pillaging once and for all."

The Totenkopf leader let a chuckle. "We bring you into our holy of holies and you have the stones to talk to us like that," Kruger said. "I like it. Given the chance, I'd kill you last."

"Settle down, everyone." Moineau shifted in his seat. "Intervention and interference are not our bailiwick, Albian. The Daegon have left us alone. Why would they go through all the trouble you just mentioned?"

"One of their assassins spoke to me, just after she murdered my Admiral," Gage said. "'*Nobis regiray*'…you will be ruled. We heard it several more times. The Daegon aren't here for territory. They attacked to subjugate every human being. They will come for you. For now, they can afford to ignore you." Gage pointed into the star map. "You see their axis of advance? The Daegon are moving on the Indus core worlds and the Cathay. Their supply lines run through Albion. My world is the linchpin to their offensive. You get me to Indus space and I'll bring more star nations into the fight against the Daegon, cut off their assault before they can crush every free world. Do you really think these monsters will leave you alone if they do occupy every star from Earth to Fallon's World?"

Moineau sat back and drummed his fingers against an armrest. As the other pirates looked to him, he asked, "What do you want?"

"Safe passage to New Madras. You've raided it before, and you either know a few slip lanes to get close or you spent months and years in cryo doing a hard bore through the void to get there," Gage said. "I'll share everything we know with you in return *and then* bring a fleet to Albion that will stop our enemy's advance. Help me, and you'll save yourselves."

Loussan snickered, then broke into full-bore

laughter.

"What's so funny?" Gage asked.

"Quite the bargain you've proposed," Moineau said. "It's just that what you want isn't something all of us can trade."

Loussan's laughter grew louder and he stepped away from the table.

"There's only one clan that knows the lanes to New Madras, Albian. And if the Harlequins don't want to help you," Moineau shrugged, "as we say in free space, you're shit out of luck. I may run Sicani, but when the rest go their separate ways, I've got no pull with them."

"No one else can…" Gage's face flushed as he looked over the map. Any other route to the core worlds was blocked by the Daegon.

"Get back to the table, you dog," Moineau said over his shoulder to Loussan. "We all love a taste of schadenfreude, but you're taking it too far."

Loussan emerged from the darkness, a smile across his face as wide as the conference table.

"Your clan's secrets are yours," the Wyvern said to Loussan, "but if you'd deign to help the jackboots and share what they tell you, my clan would appreciate it."

Shouts of agreement broke out around the table.

Loussan put his hands to his hips. "I'll do it," the pirate said.

Gage remained motionless and waited for the other shoe to drop.

"Take his fleet through the Kigeli Nebula to New Madras safely, share what he tells us. I'll do it…but only after he's dead," the Harlequin said.

"There'll be no cold-blooded murder on my world," Moineau said. "My standards may be low and ill-defined, but I have them."

Gage let the knuckles of one fist fall onto the table. He twisted his hand from side to side, grinding against the stone. There was a way…

"Captain Loussan of the Harlequins," Gage said. "Her name was Ensign Cara Foche. She died on Volera because of you. I demand satisfaction."

Loussan perked up. He set his hands onto the table and stared daggers at Gage.

"You're not a clan captain, jackboot," the Totenkopf said. "Don't think you have those rights out here."

"I'm here under parley," Gage said. "Your code applies to me. Every word of it."

"I move to strike." Krueger took a medallion out of a vest pocket and tossed it into the middle of the table. "Loussan has his rights. This one has none. Send the pig back to his ship and let the Harlequins deal with them. Should be fun to watch."

"Opposed." Delacroix slid a medallion between the other captain and her. "Let Loussan try and answer his blood oath in an arena. Doesn't matter which of them dies. The Harlequin has a lieutenant that can get these Albians out of our stars and the jackboot has a lackey that knows everything he knows."

"Throw," Moineau said, waving at the table. Clan leaders tossed their votes onto the table. Within a few seconds, the pile in favor of the Totenkopf's motion to end the parley and send Gage back to the *Orion* was larger.

Loussan held his medallion tightly, then tossed it to Delacroix's stack. Even with that last vote, the Totenkopf won.

Moineau leaned forward, then lifted his spectacles up. He squinted hard, then tried looking with just one eye.

"Delacroix's motion carries. Send them to an arena," the old man said.

"Are you blind!" The Totenkopf kicked the table. "It's obvious my motion carried, you old—"

Several of the other pirates suddenly cleared their throats.

"—and wise, and generous host of hosts." The Totenkopf punched his fists together. "Perhaps someone else could take count."

"Fair enough." Moineau reached down and tapped Loussan on the shoulder. "Which pile's larger, my boy?"

"The arena," Loussan said.

"There we are—confirmation." Moineau rubbed his hands together. "Oh, Commodore Gage, you did say you'd share how to find Daegon infiltrators with all of us before you—or your designated survivor—leaves orbit, yes? Wouldn't want the Harlequins to forget to share all that with us, what with all the goings-on."

"That's...what I meant to say." Gage lowered his head slightly.

"Then we've a matter of honor to settle. Loussan and Gage, as your host, I'll have you both at the Diamond Auditorium here in my coliseum. Duel begins in four hours," Moineau said.

"Four hours?" Loussan asked. "Why can't I just kill him in the hallway right now?"

"Because I'm going to sell tickets, son," the old man said with a cackle. "You know what price free men will pay to see a jackboot take a pigsticker to the gut? Or see your pretty head kicked around a stage? A fortune! Gage is still under my protection, and don't any of you forget it. Now all of you get out of my sight."

CHAPTER 6

Tolan stepped around a food stand offering boiled grubs on skewers and hopped over a small puddle of blood glistening in the waning sunlight, Wyman following a few steps behind. Both wore different clothes from what they arrived in, and Wyman's face was darkened with soot smeared across his brow. Tolan kept a hood over his head as he continued down a tenement street.

"If you ever eat the hawk-fly larva, make sure it's well done," Tolan said, wagging a finger at Wyman. "They tend to go dormant when exposed to heat. Sometimes the cook will be in a rush and serve not-quite-dead larva…which then wake up in your digestive tract and they're more agitated when that happens. But you get them with teriyaki sauce and…" Tolan kissed his fingertips, then stopped on a corner and looked around the ground-level shops selling clothes, firearms, and more than one body shop promising secondhand augmentations.

"There we are…see that red mountain painted on the stairwell? Faylun's still in business." The spy crossed the street and ducked into the stairwell.

Sitting near the top of the stairs, wrapped in layers of clothing, was a woman, her skin dark with grime.

"Hey, nana," Tolan said to her. "You hungry? Bite bite?"

"Not so empty as to give you the look," she

said, huddling closer to the wall.

"There still a pubby house two blocks away? Cot and a sponge for some silver?" Tolan wiggled two fingers, then flicked his wrist and a small rectangle of embossed silver appeared between his fingertips.

"Some pincher out of the Ryukus bought it last month. Price doubled." She looked at the money and licked her lips.

Tolan flicked his wrist and offered twice as much. She snatched the money from him and hurried down the steps.

Wyman put a hand to his nose as she passed. "Why does everything in this city smell so bad?" the pilot asked.

"This city is all about freedom. No taxes means little in the way of public services, unless you want to pay for it out of your own pocket. The poor may want it, but they won't get it. And what did I tell you about talking?" Tolan walked up to a white door, the paint peeling away, and held his hands up to his forehead. He pressed his thumbs and forefingers into a triangle and waited.

And waited.

"You look ridiculous," Wyman said.

"You ever met a Martian, knuckles?" Tolan held the symbol up a little bit higher.

"A…Martian? I thought they couldn't survive off Mars. You mean one's here? In this dump?"

"Faylun likes the weather," Tolan said.

A small panel flipped open on the doorframe and a camera-tipped metal arm slid out and flexed, reaching toward the spy's face. Tolan kept still as the camera went from eye to eye and around his face. When Tolan opened his mouth, the camera took a good look at his teeth. The arm retracted.

"New rules," Tolan said as he dropped his hands. "You can look. You can talk. But do not touch."

"You know I'm not an idiot, right?"

"No touching."

"No touching—fine. Just tell me it'll smell better in there."

The door split down the middle and rolled open. Just inside, blue light filled a small compartment with plastic walls just big enough for the two men.

"Go." Tolan pushed into the cramped space and got Wyman's shoulder against his face as the larger man struggled to fit. The door rolled shut and white fog filled the compartment.

"Hey, what is this?" Wyman asked.

"Sanitizing," Tolan said. The entire box filled with the fog that carried a hint of iodine. There was a faint chime, and a fan kicked on. The compartment sides fell down and Tolan wafted away the last of the fog.

Faylun's store was several rows of glass cases full of specimen jars, bits of old computer cores, and more than one rack of assault weapons. The far wall was made up of wooden cabinets all labeled in Chinese symbols. A metal bar and stools separated the cabinets from the rest of the store.

"Ah…" Tolan took a deep sniff. "Hasn't changed a bit."

"How does this work? There's no one here. You just take stuff, drop money on the counter, and hope he lets you back in later on?" Wyman reached up to a model of a red three-winged airplane.

Tolan slapped the pilot's hand.

"It's a lot worse than 'you break it, you bought it' in here," Tolan said.

"It is you…" came from behind the cabinets, the words slow and just above a whisper.

A hunched figure entered behind the bar, a bright yellow cloth draped over his back and head. He walked slowly, feet stomping into the floor from a brace that circled his waist and extended to his feet. A grill covered Faylun's mouth and lower jaw, and wisps of vapor escaped with each exhalation. Lenses, embedded in his eye sockets, magnified his irises to almost bug-like proportions. The Martian's limbs were overlong, as if stretched in some torture device for years on end.

"May the sun greet you each day and life be pure," Tolan said and then touched two fingers to a temple, to the side of his neck, then over his heart.

"Don't mock my soil, Tolan," the Martian said. "Had I known you were going after Ja'war, I would have never directed you to that butcher. That the Black One didn't torture you to death and come for everyone that helped you is a miracle. Imagine my surprise when I heard Ja'war was off the market."

"He didn't go down easy, if that makes you feel any better. And that hack you sent me to get the job done," Tolan said.

"Amateur. I can see cracks in your matrix already. What are you using to compensate?"

"Bliss; keeps the edge off."

"I might have something better. Come." Twig-like fingers motioned the spy closer.

"That's not why we're here." Tolan opened his coat, withdrew a vacuum-packed item, and gently set it on the bar. "We need you to consult your data core."

Faylun snapped his gaze to Tolan, then to Wyman.

"You know I can't do that. Exposing that

information without Conclave approval will mean a recall to the red. Footy season is about to start, can't miss that…" The Martian gave a weak chuckle and inched back to the doorway.

"It will concern Mars eventually. I have a witness." Tolan stepped aside and pointed to Wyman. "I am the second."

Faylun fidgeted for a moment, the rasping through his grill growing faster.

"I will listen…but promise nothing after that," the frail man said.

"Wyman, tell him what happened to Albion. All of it," Tolan said.

Wyman gave a slow, stumbling retelling of his time on the *Excelsior* just before the first contact with the Daegon through their escape to the Sicani system. Faylun listened quietly, his eyes locked on the pilot.

"His biometrics read true to all of it…some

details omitted about his transit to Siam, but he doesn't consider that important to these Daegon. And your testimony?" Faylun asked the spy.

Tolan drew a combat knife off the small of his back and ran the tip down the length of the package. He removed a Daegon armored gauntlet and set it before the Martian, the fingers cracked and broken. The smell of dried blood and burnt meat rose from the blue metal.

"We know little of our enemy," Tolan said, "but I suspect you might know more."

"Curious…" Faylun poked at the piece of armor, like it was a sleeping animal that might jump up and bite if startled. "The construction is…odd. How much time do you have?"

"We need answers sooner than later."

"I can disassemble it, destroy it in the process…"

"We have more aboard the *Orion*." Tolan crossed his arms over his chest.

Faylun reached under the bar and took out a shallow metal bowl.

"I'll not touch it again…who knows where it's been?" Faylun wiggled his thin fingers at Tolan. The spy moved the gauntlet into the shallow bowl and stepped back.

Faylun raised his arms, then snapped his hands to either side of the bowl with a pop of overworked joints. A blue-white field filled the bowl and the gauntlet rose a few inches. Text swarmed across the Martian's eye lenses.

"Bio-neural interface…almost familiar," Faylun said. Metal strips pulled away from the gauntlet and orbited around the armor. "Why didn't you bring the cortex implant? There's no other way this system could operate."

"Autopsy found slagged devices at the base of the Daegon's neck, C7 vertebrae. Docs say they self-destructed once their hosts died. None of the boarders survived the attack," Tolan said.

"That tells me something." Faylun's fingers twitched inhumanly fast and the rest of the armor stripped away, leaving a skeletal frame behind. "DNA shows human…extensive gene modding…were they blue-skinned? Perhaps green?"

Tolan nodded.

The armor strips reassembled on the frame, changing their configuration to different styles. Tolan recognized a medieval knight's gauntlet, a simple exo-suit, then back to the original shape.

"Almost Genevan," Faylun said. "The technology shares a lineage. This was bent from the core programming, functions poorly compared to the gestalts. Wearing this would be somewhat painful.

Long-term nervous-system damage is certain…but no gestalt needed to function."

"The Daegon are Genevans?" Wyman asked. "Like Thorvald and Salis?"

"The armor bears some similarity," Faylun said, "like comparing a sword forged by a master blacksmith, then comparing it to the work of a later generation that carried on the master's technique. And…ah…what's this? A code fragment in a biometric buffer? Don't mind if I do."

Red lines rose from the gauntlet's wrist and traced text in front of the Martian's eyes.

"Can you read it?" Tolan asked. "If we can learn their coding, we can hack their systems, reverse engineer—"

"There's a kernel here," Faylun said. He leaned closer to the gauntlet and squinted with one eye. "Not in any language I've ever encountered, but then there's this…" He leaned back and an image materialized over the Daegon artifact, a crest spinning slowly in the air. A double-headed eagle behind a shield, the claws grasping a segment of a castle wall and the other had talons embedded into a fish. In the center of the shield, a sun blazed.

"Why is that in the code?" Tolan asked.

"It's the encryption firewall," Faylun said. "They're using a 4-D tier to mask the base code, an old technique I've only ever seen used in post-Cataclysm information systems. Odd."

"Can you crack it?" Wyman asked.

"My data core might have an old source code…" Faylun pulled his hands away and the gauntlet settled into the bowl.

"Then what are you waiting for?" Tolan asked. "You'll have to go back to Mars anyway, show this to the others. The free nations will need Martian help. You all can't stay under your mountains forever."

"We've done quite well for ourselves under our mountains, thank you very much." Faylun raked his fingertips through the air. "We helped Earth reach the stars again after civilization collapsed with the express understanding that the rest of you stunties would leave us the hell alone in return."

"I somehow doubt the Daegon are part of the Non-Interference Treaty with Mars." The left side of Tolan's face started twitching, and he pressed a hand to his mouth and stomped a foot against the wooden floor.

"Extraordinary times, extraordinary measures," Faylun said. "The one you brought, he's but a child. No idea what a show he's about to see." The Martian touched his fingertips to his sternum and bowed his head.

"Yeah, I'm just chopped liver back here," Wyman said. "What do you mean, 'a show'?" he asked Faylun.

"He won't answer right now," Tolan said. "Last time a Martian accessed his data core was over a hundred years ago, sent all the major powers' intelligence services into a frenzy, trying to figure out what was uncovered. They still teach it at the academy. Assassinations, bombings, sudden slip-engine failure between the stars. There was a shadow war for years."

"What's so special about these data cores?"

"Sum total of all Martian knowledge stored in a quantum lattice. Pre-Cataclysm information, everything the Martians have worked out since the first colonies back in the twenty-first century. Mars has a few scholars like Faylun spread across unaligned worlds to collect more information, bring it back to the red planet every decade or so. They're information junkies, in case you haven't noticed," Tolan said.

"If this data core is such a big deal, why hasn't anyone in this cesspit of a planet ever tried to take it from him?" Wyman asked.

"That the cores even exist is a state secret, and if a Martian is ever harmed on a planet, that planet tends to suffer cataclysmic events: the computers that maintain infrastructure slag, leaders' air cars fall out of the sky for no apparent reason. An entire planet's banking records go up in smoke."

"The Martians do that?"

"No, I'm sure it's just a coincidence." Tolan rolled his eyes.

The right half of Faylun's chest hinged open. The Martian opened the false flesh exterior, revealing a mechanical lung and a glowing cube situated close to the centerline on his chest.

Wyman tried to back away, but Tolan grabbed him by the elbow and kept him close to the bar.

Faylun held the cube between his narrow fingertips. Red lines traced down the sides.

"So much information…" Faylun muttered. The eagle crest appeared on his eye lenses, then vanished in a cloud of static. "Nothing…nothing to decrypt the Daegon code."

Tolan bashed a fist against the bar.

"But there is something…a partial hit on unverified data…" The cube powered down and Faylun returned it to his chest. "Mount Edziza erupted and sent Earth back into the Stone Age in 2109, no forewarning. Billions died in the ensuing ice age, but there were rumors that some on Earth knew the event was coming."

Faylun twisted a hand over and a small

projector on the back of his wrist lit up. A single image of a massive spacecraft being built on the dark side of the moon, with Earth in the background, appeared. Faylun tapped a finger to his palm and the image zoomed in to the side of the vessel. On the hull, half-obscured by construction scaffolding, was the same crest Faylun found in the Daegon armor.

"When was this picture taken?" Tolan asked.

"Eighty-four days before Mount Edziza erupted and choked the sky with ash," Faylun said. "This image was taken by a satellite that was hacked and redirected by a team of scientists in the Alamos biodome. After this, all contact between Earth and Mars ended. The official reason was a 'solar event,' which never actually occurred."

"The ship looks like an early colony ark," Wyman said, "just like the *Britannia* that brought the first settlers to Albion…but none of those ships left

Earth for centuries after the eruption."

"They knew." Tolan tugged at his bottom lip. "The Daegon knew Earth was about to be wrecked and they kept it secret. Earth had an extensive information-sharing network at the time. Who the hell had that kind of power to keep a ship that size secret?"

"Who says they did?" Wyman asked. "Maybe that knowledge was lost in the ice age. They're still digging stuff out of the museums in London and New York City."

"Something tells me if every human being knew a ship full of colonists had escaped, it would've entered the collective subconscious like the story of Noah's Ark," Tolan said. "Mars know of any colony ship like this?" he asked Faylun.

"No. We were a few hundred strong when Earth fell. None of the Originals ever spoke of a colony ship in their memoirs." Faylun shrugged.

"So what are we supposed to tell the Commodore?" Wyman asked.

"The Daegon have a link to Earth, very powerful people on Earth from before the Fall," Tolan said. "We have a starting point, which is better than the basically nothing we had before we came in here."

"I'll arrange passage back to Mars." Faylun gave the bowl with the gauntlet a gentle shake. "If the Daegon are returning to the home world, Mars will be in danger. The Conclave must know of this. Perhaps I'll learn more there. It's been decades since my last core sync."

"You can keep that," Tolan said, motioning to the Daegon armor. The spy leaned slightly over the bar. "Don't suppose you have anything better than Bliss. I get these tremors and maybe some

Dizorphomene or Xera's Kiss…"

"He's a drug dealer?" Wyman asked and Tolan's lips squeezed into a thin line.

"I prefer 'apothecary.'" Faylun opened a cabinet and removed a glass jar full of neon-green bark. "Dealing in remedies for all ailments caused by injuries both physical and or mental. Tolan is a bit of both."

"You know why I became Faceless," Tolan said. "For justice."

"Bliss was not your only option." Faylun brought out a corked jar with a spiked slug clinging to the inside. The Martian reached into another cabinet, then froze. "You have a problem."

"It's not because I like Bliss. It's because I don't want lose coherency and walk around with a face and body that looks like wet clay," Tolan said testily.

"No, not that," Faylun said. Holo screens formed flat against the bar. Images of small groups of men and women in gang colors moving through the nearby streets played on the screens. Icons tracing side arms hidden beneath their jackets and coats popped up.

"Oh look, White Knives," Tolan said.

"You still owe Weissgerber money?" Faylun asked.

"What happened, Mr. 'We'll duck surveillance—no one can find me unless I want them to'?" Wyman drew a pistol from his coat and reloaded the magazine.

"I thought he'd be dead by now…" Tolan hissed through his teeth.

"This is their territory. As my hosts, they have certain expectations I have to meet," the Martian said. "I may be part machine, but I can still feel pain."

"We'll leave." Wyman turned away.

"Not out the front door," Tolan said, shaking his head before giving Faylun a knowing glance.

"I can fabricate my video logs, show you leaving soon after you arrived." The Martian traced a word onto the bar top and a glass case moved to one side, revealing a narrow staircase.

"Just get us a head start." Tolan pulled out his own pistol and started for the stairs, then caught himself and half-twisted around. "Have you got anything off the shelf? You know, for the effort."

Faylun plucked a bottle full of black and white flecks and tossed it to the spy.

"Dizorphomene. The abusers call it Dizzy. It's strong, be careful," the Martian said.

Tolan gave the bottle a quick shake and stuffed it into his coat.

****

Wyman kept one hand against a slimy wall in a tunnel lit by a flickering glow strips every few yards. The passage was so narrow, he had to almost walk sideways to keep his broad shoulders from scraping against god-knew-what on the bricks. He adjusted the grip on his pistol and kept his focus on a green light off in the distance.

"Thanks for not turning into a babbling lump of tears like when we made our exit from Albion," Tolan said from just ahead of him. The smaller man had a much easier time navigating the narrow confines than the pilot.

"Cockpits are tight, enclosed spaces," Wyman said. "Not that different from this…but I've never been in a Typhoon that smells so bad. Everything about this pirate crap hole of a planet makes my skin crawl. And so what if I don't like being exposed to raw slip space? You know many people that do?"

"Once dated a girl that liked to meditate outside the hull during slip travel. Said it made her feel 'closer to oneness with the universe.'" Tolan stopped Wyman with a hand to his chest. The tunnel rumbled as a heavy vehicle passed overheard.

"I know where we are," the spy said. "Faylun has a couple different bolt holes across the city. He's rather paranoid, a trait I can get behind. So unless the zoning commission decided to tear down the neighborhood's penultimate strip club…"

Wyman heard Tolan tapping against the side of the tunnel with the butt of his pistol until the taps changed to a hollow thunk.

"Ha! Still got it." Tolan stepped back, then bumped his shoulder into the wall with no effect. He tried again, then breathed a curse. "Knuckles, if you please." He backed down the tunnel a few steps.

"You've got a funny way of asking for favors." Wyman found the spot Tolan had tried to force open, braced himself against the ground, and pushed against the wall. There was a creak of stone on stone, then a narrow door swung outward. Air that stank of tobacco and spilt beer blew past Wyman, a welcome respite from the mildew and sewage.

Inside, a ladder was bolted to the wall of a small chamber. A square panel just large enough for Wyman to squeeze through lit up on the ceiling above the ladder.

"Finally," Wyman said, holstering his pistol and climbing up the ladder. He reached for a latch on the panel when Tolan pulled him back by the edge of his coat.

"Hold on," the spy said. "Before you go rushing face-first into a titty bar, activate the cameras

Faylun's got watching our exit. He's paranoid, remember? Just tap the panel."

Wyman pressed his fingerprints within the lit edges and holo screens popped up along the ceiling.

Inside the bar, groups of men in matching gang colors clustered around tables littered with bottles. Strobe lights and laser-effect beams flashed across the stage featuring dancers with moving tattoos and shimmering body paint.

"Damn it," Tolan said. "Tables next to the exit and the backroom entrance. What do you see?"

"Bunch of thugs…that aren't drinking and aren't watching the girls," Wyman said.

"And…" Tolan zoomed in on one table and moved the camera from brute to brute. "They're all packing HK-999s. Very expensive side arms. Very rare out here. They aren't White Knives. They're someone else."

"Is there anyone on this planet that you haven't pissed off?" Wyman hopped off the ladder.

"Nice thing about being Faceless is that I needn't suffer from a bad reputation." Tolan took a small injector from his coat and pressed it to his throat. His face went slack, almost drooping from his skull. He pressed the blades of his hands against the sides of his nose and stretched his skin back. It sprang into place, puffier and several shades lighter than a moment ago. He tugged on his nose, bending the bridge to one side like an old boxer's.

"Yeah? Good?" Tolan's voice modulated, ending slightly higher.

"Does that…hurt?"

"You have no idea. Too bad we can't do much for you…who they'll be looking for, not me," Tolan said.

"If these guys are pros, won't they be

watching every exit?" Wyman asked.

"They will, which is both a problem and an opportunity." Tolan reached into his coat and took out a puck slightly smaller than the palm of his hand.

"What's that?"

"Explosive cord. Never leave home without it. Amazing what a little boom-boom can accomplish when you're in a pinch." Tolan pressed a button on the puck and drew out a length of yellow and black cord. "I'll make us an exit through the roof out onto the street. Random explosions aren't too unusual in this part of town."

"What about people up there? What if some kid's walking by and you—"

"It's a high-speed route, automated drivers only. No one will be on the road and I'll use a cutting charge. Mostly safe. If we go charging through an exit covered by the local muscle, there will be bystanders hurt in the crossfire. We rarely get perfect choices in this line of work. Best we can do is pick the least bad option."

"Flying fighters has a hell of a lot less guesswork, just so you know. What else do you have on you?"

"Eight types of currency, two cameras with full-spectrum passive collection, a hazmat mask with its own air supply, two pistols, dazzler grenades, quick-clot spray, and five—no six—knives. I'm traveling light. What did you bring?"

"Some…extra bullets and beef jerky," Wyman said.

"Amateur hour down here." Tolan drew a length of the explosive cord from the puck and ducked into the outer hallway. "Bit of a risk that the overpressure will kill us," the spy called out, "but we'll be inside our little cubbyhole."

"'They want either you or me to go down with Tolan,'" Wyman said, mimicking Ivor's feminine voice. "'It'll be fun. Besides, I just got off ready flight and I'm so tired. Would you *please* go?' I am such a sucker."

Tolan closed the door and Wyman was treated to another round of limited personal space as the spy nuzzled against him so they could both fit.

"Hold me." Tolan looked up at the pilot and batted his eyes.

"If I break your face, can you fix it yourself?"

"Your chivalry only goes so far, eh? Cover your ears and hope for the best." Tolan raised his arm holding the explosives case and clicked a button.

The blast sent a tremor through the chamber, flexing the door against the frame. Wyman's ears popped. Muffled shouts came through the panel as panic broke out in the club overhead.

"That's enough of that." Tolan pulled away from Wyman and grabbed the door handle. He gave it a pull, and the door groaned.

"Uh oh…" Tolan pulled with both arms, but the door remained fast. The spy banged a fist against the frame, then kicked the door.

"What have you done?" Wyman asked.

"Look, Sicani isn't exactly known for its quality workmanship. I'd wager the doorframe bent when part of the tunnel collapsed. Thing's jammed shut."

"You'd 'wager'? So we're trapped in this tiny coffin until we die?"

"No, the locals will eventually come down and find the door, bust it open, and kill us." Tolan pointed to the panel leading into the club. "We have a new less bad option."

"This is the last time I ever leave the *Orion*. To

hell with shore leave," Wyman said as he climbed up the ladder and pulled the handle. The panel sprang up on a hinge. Dim, off-white light beckoned to him.

He got his head and shoulder through the opening and found himself beneath a desk. A meandering line of stools ran parallel to more desks. He saw the bare legs of women as they scurried past. Some ducked down to pick up clothes as the legs moved toward one end of the line of desks.

Wyman pulled himself up and crawled into the dressing room, pistol in hand. Fixed to the desks were tall mirrors surrounded by mostly functioning lights and piles of makeup and sprays.

A dancer with a half-shaved head looked up as she stepped into a set of overalls and frowned at Wyman.

"Gang war or not, this room's off-limits to customers," she said.

"Good to know." He got to his feet and moved his pistol behind his back. "There an emergency exit?"

"Carl, our idiot bouncer, locked it again." She zipped up her overalls and pointed to a gaggle of angry dancers gathered near a doorway. One yanked against the handlebar and shouted a curse in a foreign tongue.

"Faylun, you dog," Tolan said, crawling out and smoothing the front of his jacket.

The dancer leaned to the side and got a look at their entrance.

"I didn't see anything," she said.

"Smart." Tolan winked at her.

One of the dancers turned to the hallway leading out to the stage and put her hands on her hips. "Hey," she said to someone Wyman couldn't see, "get back out there before Carl breaks your legs."

A brute of a man stepped into view, a snub machine gun clenched in one hand. He did a double take at Wyman, then swung his weapon up as the dancers broke into screams.

Wyman froze. Fighter combat came with a certain distance. He never saw the enemy pilots he shot down, only their ships. Facing off against a steely-eyed killer did not rouse the same instincts as when he was in the cockpit of his Typhoon.

Shots sounded from just behind Wyman and the thug crumpled to the ground, two splatters of blood dribbling down the wall behind him.

The dancers screamed louder and pounded at the rear exit.

Tolan pushed past the stunned Wyman and shouted, "Out the front! Now!" He pointed his pistol down the hallway and stomped toward the panicking women. A pair skipped over the dead man and ran, and the rest followed within seconds.

"Hurry." Tolan went down the line of desks and glanced down the hallway. "More trouble's on the way. Get the door open."

"I-I…" Wyman stared at the corpse as pools of blood and urine seeped out from beneath the body.

Tolan snatched up a lipstick case and hurled it at Wyman's face. The pilot ducked aside and gave Tolan a dirty look.

"The. Door." Tolan jerked his head at their escape.

"Right." Wyman pushed against the handle and felt the door jiggle slightly. "Well, I can—"

A shot rang out and part of the door level with the pilot's head burst into splinters. Tolan fired as Wyman ducked down. Screams and shouts echoed down the hallway.

Wyman stood up and slammed his boot into the door. The lock ripped out of the decaying wood and the door swung open.

"Moving." Tolan fired two more shots. "Moving, yes?"

Wyman waved to the dancer that saw them earlier and ran out the door into an alley full of rotting garbage.

"I don't know you," the dancer said as she followed on Wyman's heels, Tolan just a step behind. "I don't want to know you. Just leave me alone, okay?"

"Fine by me." Tolan ducked as a bullet sprang off the wall just over his head. "Move a little fa—" His foot caught the side of a trash bag and he stumbled forward.

Shots rattled out from the dressing room and the dancer shrieked, then pitched forward into

Wyman's arms. He felt hot blood beneath his hands as he dragged her out of the alleyway and onto a sidewalk running along a backstreet.

The dancer looked into Wyman's eyes, her face wrought with pain as she coughed up blood that covered her mouth. Droplets sprinkled across Wyman's face.

"You'll be okay," he said. "Get you to a doctor and—"

An explosion rocked the club, sending a gout of dust down the alley and into the air. The blast shattered windows and led to several beat-up cars crashing into each other in the confusion.

Tolan crawled out of the dust and smoke.

"We're out…of explosives," he said.

"Help me with her." Wyman looked down and into the dancer's lifeless eyes. Her head lolled to one side, but the blood kept oozing from the bullet holes in her back.

"No, stay with me," he said, tapping her on the cheek with bloody fingers, leaving a red smear down her face.

"She's gone." Tolan looked around, then pointed down a street. "There's a market down there. We can slip away and then get back to the Commodore. Let's go."

Wyman laid the woman down on the sidewalk as gently as he could.

"It's not fair," he said. "She just wanted to—"

"Down!" Tolan pointed at a shadow in the smoke and shoved Wyman to the side. A blue bolt sliced through the air where Wyman had just been and struck the sidewalk with a sizzle of fat hitting a hot pan.

The shadow jumped high, far higher than Wyman would have ever thought possible for a normal human, and landed in a crouch a few yards from the two Albians. A slender man with slicked-back hair and a leather coat popped to his feet and threw two small razor blades, both crackling with energy. One hit Tolan in the arm and he seized up, limbs rictus, and fell next to the dead woman.

The blade meant for Wyman nicked his thigh. Pain shot through his leg, leaving it numb. Wyman stumbled over his dead leg and fell against a car. The man in the leather coat pointed a strange-looking pistol at him.

"Where is the Martian?" the man asked, his face neutral. "What did you tell him?"

Wyman fell back onto his elbows, one leg spasming uncontrollably.

"You're one of them, a Daegon," the pilot said.

"This can kill you," the man said and the

pistol in his hand emanated a red light from the barrel, "or it can set your every nerve-ending on fire. Talk, and you'll live."

"He's not allowed to talk," Tolan said. Wyman and the Daegon looked aside. Tolan held a knife by the tip, reached back, and hurled it into the Daegon's chest. It hit just below the collarbone and sank into his flesh.

The man yelped and dropped his pistol.

Wyman kicked the Daegon in the knee, buckling his legs. The pilot picked up a hunk of brick blasted out of the club walls and rose onto one knee. He smashed the brick against his enemy's face. Then again. And again. The Daegon's body began smoldering and Wyman rolled away before it immolated into charred meat.

Wyman slapped a hand against his cut thigh. Feeling was coming back, but slowly.

"Nice job, kid. Can you walk?" Tolan asked through fat lips. One half of his face drooped; the other seemed frozen in place.

"Yeah." Wyman got up, leaning against a car for support. "You took one of those knives clean to your arm. How are you moving at all?"

"Rolled onto the unfortunate miss," Tolan said, waving a hand toward the dead dancer. "Blade stuck in her. Seems it doesn't work on the dead."

Wyman wiped a sleeve across his face and saw the Daegon's pistol on the ground.

"We could use that," he said.

"Don't touch it. Daegon weapons are booby-trapped."

Wyman hefted the hunk of masonry he used to kill the Daegon and slammed it onto the dead man's pistol. It shattered into a thousand pieces.

"You want to hang around here? See if he had

friends?" Tolan asked.

"No." Wyman helped the spy up, and as the two shuffled away, Wyman took a final glance over his shoulder to the dead woman. She'd been alive mere minutes ago. Now she was just a body on the roadside, and Wyman never caught her name. He looked away, the image burned into his mind forever.

CHAPTER 7

Gage shrugged off his coat and handed it to Bertram. A small dome of energy-shielding surrounded the Commodore, his steward, and his bodyguard, and a wide dueling strip of white rubberized flooring ran from beneath Gage's feet out of the shield to where his opponent waited without his own dome. Sound from a chanting crowd pulsed through the shielding.

Old bloodstains marred the dueling strip. Black volcanic sand formed a perimeter around the strip, not a single grain touching the alabaster surface of Gage's forthcoming duel. That the pirates would leave a fighter's spilled essence but sweep away the sand told him something about the pirate's culture: Honor remains.

Gage stripped off his undershirt as he turned and went to a rack of melee weapons at the edge the white strip.

"Sir, this is madness," Bertram said as he carefully folded the coat, brushing dust off the Commodore's St. Michael's medal, awarded for destroying an enemy ship in combat. "You can't trust these brigands to keep their word. They'll kill you no matter what happens, send me to change out the chamber pots in a house of ill repute for the rest of my days…and who knows what they'll do to Thorvald."

"They will not take me alive," the Genevan

said.

"You won't even try to get me back to the fleet safely. Perhaps if I was taller and a lovely lady with flashing blue eyes and an ample—"

"You are not the principal," Thorvald said. "If Gage loses…" he cocked his head to one side as pain flitted across his face, "if Gage loses, then I must return to Prince Aidan."

"Are you all right?" Gage asked.

"My gestalt, sir, it's giving me some difficulty. The crowd…the duel…everything screams danger to my suit and it wants me to get you out of here," Thorvald said.

"Well, then why didn't the voices in your head make you throw the good Commodore over your shoulder and hustle him away *before* we came into the fighting pit?" Bertram asked.

Thorvald reached out to the smaller man very

slowly and put an armored hand on one of his shoulders. Thorvald's grip tightened slowly, stopping just on the edge of causing discomfort to the steward.

"If this goes poorly," Gage said, running his fingers along the handles to various swords, flails, and maces, "fleet command goes to Price. She knows the mission."

"Be positive, sir." Bertram tried to shrug off the Genevan's grip but failed. "You could win—will win! Ow."

"I've already won." Gage drew a saber with a beat-up hilt and tested the weight. "The Harlequins will lead the fleet to New Madras no matter the outcome."

"You have too much trust in those with no honor," Thorvald said, lifting his hand off Bertram.

"Loussan—and by extension, his entire organization—made a promise in the open, in the presence of other clan leaders. If they fail to follow through, they'll be the wrong kind of disreputable. Planets across wild space will turn them away…no using buoy data to travel from star to star quickly, no trade. They burn us and every last one of them in the red and black will wither on the vine." Gage swung the blade from side to side, then made a quick circle eight with the tip.

"You put your life at risk for the sake of the fleet." Thorvald tapped a fist to his chest. "My gestalt is sated…somewhat. Let me see your weapon." He held out his hand, taking the saber by the hilt.

Running his palm down the length of the blade, he frowned.

"This weapon is defective," he said. "Poorly constructed or sabotaged, a solid blow and it will crack at the hilt."

"Still think we should trust these pirates, sir?"

Bertram asked.

"They won't interfere during a match," Gage said, "but before…can you fix it? I doubt the other weapons are any better."

Thorvald pinched the hilt between his thumb and forefinger. Segments of armor shuffled down his arm and onto his hand; there was a squeal of metal as he squeezed the hilt against the blade. He passed the weapon back to the Commodore.

"What do you know of this Loussan's fighting style?" Thorvald asked.

"Duels aren't common for the lower-ranked pirates, but among officers and ship captains, they're almost expected whenever a raid fails or turns unprofitable due to a mistake. So either a pirate knows how to duel…or he'd best never make a mistake," Gage said. "They fight with single weapons until one is dead or yields."

"Then just yield the moment the fight starts," Bertram said. "Loussan will win, no one—particularly you—gets stabbed, and we can leave."

"Loussan is under no obligation to accept a yield. If I drop my weapon, he won't hesitate to kill me," Gage said.

"And what does your opponent know of your ability with swords?" Thorvald asked.

"That academy graduates are taught to fence is common knowledge. It trains us to use a weapon that's an extension of our body, meant to build aggression, not see our ships as tools separate from our will. Granted, I doubt he knows I fenced epee, not with sabers."

Green lights pulsed along the edge of the white strip.

Gage put his free hand behind his back, turned his rear foot perpendicular to his body, and bent both knees slightly, a fencer's stance.

"Your enemy thinks he knows you," Thorvald said. "Use that against him."

"Sir, I know you're a gentleman," Bertram's face fell, "but do kill this piece of human filth as fast as you can. King's rules needn't apply."

"Seconds out," Moineau's voice sounded through the shield.

The two men stepped through the shield, leaving Gage alone.

A holo of the elderly pirate's head appeared eye level with the Commodore.

"You understand the rules, Albian?"

"I do," he said, giving his repaired weapon a quick shake. "All too well."

"For a jackboot, I rather like you. I suggest you stay on the dueling pitch. The crowd's awful worked up due to your fleet being in town. Would hate to think what they'd do to you if you're out of bounds."

"Why're you helping?"

"It's the odds, son! You think I'm making money off just tickets and booze? I'm the house. You want to guess what the bookies have for your chance to win? If your fight lasts more than two minutes, I'm deep in the black for the year. After that, I don't really care who wins. Fight starts in thirty seconds."

The old man's holo morphed into descending numbers.

Gage ground his rear heel into the pitch. The dueling field was a good deal wider than the mats he'd trained on. He thought back to his days at the academy, remembering his fencing instructor's advice to keep his skills up as a matter of health and warrior ethos…and regretting that he spent his time with pistols and boxing instead. That he might end up in an honor duel with a pirate had never come up during his time as a midshipman.

As the timer ran down to zero, the force field pulled in and stopped at the edges of the dueling pitch. The field blocking his view down the white strip faded away, and he saw Loussan ten yards away. The pirate was also shirtless, his hair pulled into a tight bun on the back of his head. He swung his saber back and forth across his black and red breeches, then raised his arms high as the crowd's cheering rose to a crescendo.

With the bright lights bearing down on them, Gage couldn't see more than a few rows of spectators to either side of the volcanic sand extending a few feet from the pitch. But he heard the crowd, thousands and thousands of voices chanting a single name.

Loussan.

A bottle came tumbling out of the darkness and bounced off the force field running along the edge of the pitch. Gage swung the tip of his blade to one side, and it passed through without even a tug at the weapon. Spaceships used similar force fields in their air locks. The field would keep the spectators from interfering but would let either combatant pass through it so long as they were partially inside the pitch.

"I've waited a long time for this, jackboot!" Loussan pointed his sword at Gage and marched forward.

Gage raised his hilt up to his face in salute, then lowered his guard.

"You have any idea what I went through after Volera? My first ship and you forced me to dump my cargo. I lost half my crew, then three of my mates—men I'd served with since I was old enough to stand a watch—called me out. Three blood duels in three days, three times I had to kill my friends. And every time I ended them, all I could think about was seeing you on the end of my blade." Loussan stopped two sword lengths from Gage and held his sword up to a high guard.

"The only reason I didn't fight a fourth duel, against my own sister, was because I declared vendetta against you," Loussan said.

"You talk too much," Gage said and lunged forward, driving the sword point at the pirate's heart.

Loussan parried the stab to one side and flicked his blade toward Gage's face. He heard air sing over the edge as it flashed across his vision, missing his nose by an inch. Gage pulled back quickly, his sword held straight from his shoulder.

"I just want you to know why I won't make this quick." Loussan slashed his sword down, the tip angled toward Gage's extended forearm. Gage jerked his arm to one side. Loussan lunged forward, driving the strike toward Gage's knee.

The deft blow should have plunged through his thigh and to the bone. Instead, the blade caught on the vac-suit lining, designed to withstand minor damage during a space battle, and turned to one side. Loussan's hit ripped through the pants' outer layers and managed only a shallow cut to the outside of Gage's thigh.

Gage swiped at Loussan, but the pirate danced back and raised his blade overhead, showing the crowd that he'd drawn first blood.

"Not impressed," Loussan said as Gage tested his weight against his injured leg. "These people paid for a show. At least have the courtesy to give them one before you die. I thought Albion officers were all about proper manners."

Loussan put a hand behind his back, mimicking Gage's stance. He trotted back, then skipped forward, laughing as he twirled his blade tip in a circle. Loussan brought his forward knee up, telegraphing a lunge from a mile away, then stabbed forward.

Gage lowered his blade and caught the strike against his hilt, pushing the lunge to one side, the naked steel of their weapons hissing at each other. Gage sidestepped the pirate as he rushed past him. The Commodore twisted his weapon over and slashed at the back of Loussan's head. He felt the blade connect, then the pirate tumbled forward.

Loussan turned the fall into a roll and sprang up onto his feet as his mane of hair came loose and fell around his face.

The crowd went wild as Loussan removed a broken gold hair clip caught in his locks. He tossed it through the force field, then swiped his weapon around as Gage approached.

"That's the spirit," Loussan said as he leapt at Gage, surprising him with a midair thrust aimed at the Albian's neck. Gage batted the blow aside, raising his arm up and across his face.

He didn't see Loussan's kick, but he felt it when it slammed into his side.

Gage stumbled back…and fell through the force field. He landed on his back, the black sand falling into his mouth and eyes. He spat and rolled onto his hands and knees.

In the front row of the audience and right in front of Gage, a long-bearded, burly pirate in Totenkopf colors rose to his feet and fumbled with a knife sheathed on his chest just beneath his beard. Gage glanced back and saw his feet still inside the force field and Loussan screaming threats at the

Totenkopf pirate.

Gage pushed himself back and into a roll, falling onto his haunches just as the man in the audience hurled his knife at him. The blade bounced off the force field as a mix of boos and cheers ran through the crowd.

A shadow passed over Gage. He swung blindly up and caught Loussan's swing, turning the blade flat against his. The side of the pirate's sword smacked against the top of his head, hard as any blow he'd ever taken in the boxing ring.

Gage kicked out and connected with Loussan's knee, earning a shout of pain, then scrambled back to his feet, trying to shake away the effects of Loussan's last blow.

Loussan braced his knee with one hand, his sword tip scraping against the white pitch as he moved backwards.

"All right, a minute to rest?" Loussan asked.

Gage went back into his fencer's stance, his guard low and ready.

"Didn't think so." Loussan shifted forward onto his "bad" leg and slashed his sword up at Gage, who got his blade beneath the pirate's and tried to deflect it up. Loussan stretched out and sliced into the outside of Gage's exposed shoulder.

The crowd roared as bright blood spilled onto the white dueling pitch.

The Commodore's sword arm dropped to his side as blood streamed down his flesh and onto the hilt. Gage could feel the cut, the hot blood, his sluggish arm, all dampened by adrenaline coursing through his system. He realized he had only seconds before the real pain broke through.

Loussan brought his sword back, the blade pointed at Gage's heart, and lunged forward with a killing blow. Gage stepped to the side, blocking his opponent's view of his other hand as he brought it out from behind his back.

Loussan recovered from the lunge just as Gage hooked a fist into his jaw. The pirate's head snapped to one side, his hair whipping into the air. Gage kicked the pirate's legs open, then punted him in the crotch, lifting him off his feet with the impact.

The crowd gasped.

Loussan fell to the ground, retching. Gage kicked the pirate's sword through the force field, then grabbed his own sword with his good hand. He reversed the grip, raised it high as the crowd went into a frenzy, then rammed it down.

The point sank into the pitch a half inch from Loussan's throat. Gage grabbed the pirate by the hair and yanked his head toward the sword, pushing his bare throat against the blade, coming perilously close to cutting the flesh.

"Her name was Ensign Cara Foche," Gage spat.

Loussan's eyes were wide, locked on the blade that was about to end his life.

"Her death demands justice…" Gage grabbed Loussan's head with both hands as blood ran down his injured arm steadily, staining Loussan's mane and dripping onto his face. "But my fleet needs you."

Loussan called out for help.

"Murdering savage or not," Gage said, moving the pirate's neck a bit closer and into the blade, drawing a line of blood along the edge, "you know the routes. If you'll keep your word and get us to New Madras, I'll let you yield."

Loussan's eyes snapped toward Gage, then to the blade, then back at Gage. He nodded quickly, his chin barely moving.

"Say it!"

"I yield!" Loussan called out.

Gage let him go and stumbled back. He went down, one hand pressed against the cut on his shoulder.

There was a snap of air and the force field around them powered off.

Ruprecht rushed out of the darkness, thin blades held in each hand. The cyborg moved with the same fluid grace that plagued Gage's nightmares of the battle on Volera. Gage stared down the assassin and spat on the mat.

Thorvald jumped between Gage and Loussan, a dueling mace in each hand.

The Katar skidded to a stop next to the pirate and retracted its swords back into its forearms. It knelt over Loussan and pressed a hand to the cut on the man's neck.

When Thorvald moved Gage's hand off his injured shoulder, a gout of blood spat out.

"Your circumflex humeral arteries are damaged," Thorvald said. He raised one hand and the armor around two fingertips morphed into tiny surgical instruments.

"I need you to hold still." The bodyguard brought his hand just beneath the one covering his wound. "On three. One…"

Thorvald poked his fingers into the gash and Gage's shoulder exploded in pain. He growled and bashed a fist against the ground.

"Not bad." Moineau floated over on a hover chair. He kicked a battered-looking first-aid kit to Thorvald, who picked up a compression bandage as it fell out of the case and rolled toward them.

Moineau lifted his head up and cocked his ear to the grumbling crowd.

"Bread and circuses normally keep everyone in line," the old pirate said. "Losing money when you bet against a jackboot tends to make everyone grumpy. Get back to your ship. Now. I'll send Loussan up to guide you out soon as I can. Don't ever think you can come back here, Gage."

"I'm not planning on it," the Commodore said.

Moineau's chair spun around and he floated off after Loussan as his Katar helped him off the far end of the stage.

"What do you think of my plan now?" Gage asked Thorvald.

"Your footwork is terrible. You missed at least four opportunities to land a fatal blow and you've lost over a liter of blood. Other than that, it went as you predicted."

Gage rocked back and forth slightly and

blinked hard.

"Spinning…" he said.

"That's the blood loss. Let's get you someplace moderately safer for a transfusion." Thorvald pulled Gage up onto his feet.

"Sir! Sir!" Bertram ran up the steps and waved them toward an open door. "Car's here for us and…Commodore, look what they've done to you. I don't know if I can mend those pants and you know how poorly the laundry does with bloodstains."

"Can I crush his head?" Thorvald asked Gage.

"Maybe…later," Gage mumbled.

CHAPTER 8

Gage stepped out of the car parked near his shuttle. His injured leg buckled before he made it to the base of the ramp, and Thorvald caught him under his good arm and kept him mostly upright. He felt blood ooze down the gash beneath the bandages on his forearm. Pain stabbed through his side with every breath.

"I'll do a proper suture once we've taken off," the Genevan said.

"While the shuttle's bouncing through turbulence?" Gage asked through gritted teeth.

"It's a minor procedure, very easy."

"Why didn't you do it in the car? Can't say I care if there's a bit of blood on their upholstery."

"Too much risk of an attack on you. I can guard your life and treat your wounds, but I can't do both effectively at the same time."

Gage made his way up the ramp slowly as Bertram hurried past him.

"I'll get tea and sandwiches ready," the steward said.

"And a few pain relievers if you don't mind," Gage grunted.

Shouts carried across the tarmac. From the gatehouse along the perimeter, two men burst through the doors and sprinted toward the Albion shuttle.

Gage looked up into the open, empty cargo bay, then to Thorvald.

"That them?"

A lens flipped over the bodyguard's eye from the edge of his helm.

"Different clothes…faces are filthy, but that's Wyman and Tolan."

A trio of armed guards ran after the spy and the pilot. One drew a pistol and fired into the air. Thorvald stepped between the Commodore and the new danger.

"Derringer," Gage waved to the driver with his good arm, "they're with us."

Derringer nodded and turned away, fingertips to an ear. The pursuing guards slowed and stopped, two of them beating nightsticks against their palms.

Wyman won the footrace and stopped at the base of the ramp. He leaned forward, elbows to knees as he breathed hard.

"Daegon…in the city…" Wyman said

between heaving inhalations.

"I have no reason to stay in this city and you come with another reason to leave sooner rather than later, Lieutenant," Gage said. "Get aboard."

Wyman nodded furiously and made his way past Gage.

The Commodore did his best to ignore the rank stench coming off the pilot as he waited for Tolan. The spy wiped sweat off his brow as he stepped onto the ramp, relieved as if he'd just crossed a finish line.

"Well?" Gage asked.

"Found out what we could," Tolan said. "A few complications along the way, but I'm paid for my ends, not my methods."

Gage started back up the ramp.

"We heard there were a number of explosions in the city," Gage said. "That was you?"

"Complications." Tolan waved a dismissive hand in the air. "A little larceny here and there, some major property damage, killed a Daegon infiltrator and a few of his unwitting local muscle. Looks like you had less fun than we did. Did flyboy mention that we should leave? Now?"

Gage crossed the threshold into the cargo bay and sank into his seat. Thorvald undid the sling holding the Commodore's arm and unwrapped the bandages as the engines roared to life.

****

Wyman tilted his head back against the bulkhead as the shuttle cleared Sicani's atmosphere. His skin crawled from the filth that soaked through his boots and clothes. He felt the warmth from growing bruises over his body, but his mind stayed fixed not on his physical discomfort, but on the dancer that died in his arms.

Wyman leaned forward and looked at Tolan sitting next to him. The spy removed a small mirror from his jacket and held it close to his face. The man's features adjusted, morphing to the countenance Wyman was used to.

"I heard you talking to the Commodore," Wyman said.

"Mm-hmm," Tolan hummed.

"You didn't mention the dead woman. The innocent bystanders that were hurt. Why?"

Tolan lowered the mirror and sighed at the pilot.

"She doesn't matter."

"Doesn't matter? She's dead, you bastard. Dead because of us."

"Now now, we weren't the ones that shot her.

Weren't the ones that decided to put the locals in danger by gunning after us. You can find all the reasons you want to make yourself responsible for what happened to her, and it'll never bring you a moment's peace. What's done is done. Get over it and move on to the next mission."

"If we hadn't screwed up, if we'd made it in and out of the Martian's place without being seen, she'd still be alive. Don't tell me your conscience is clean."

"Listen, my boy, I killed my conscience a long time ago. It was of no use to me. In all my years poking around wild space, I learned the hard way that survival depends on a very highly refined sense of selfishness. Empathy and compassion get intelligence operatives killed. You think my ship, the *Joaquim*, was meant for a single person? I had a team. They're all dead because one of us decided to make a choice between the harder right and an easier wrong. You've got emotions over one civilian casualty? Get over it. Take responsibility only for your actions. We got what we went down there for. We won."

Tolan picked up his mirror and tugged at his eyebrows.

"It gets easier with time and practice," the spy said. "Which is a good thing…and a bad thing. Used to have a few faces in my dreams…now they all blend together. At least you've got your fighter to go back to. What we just went through is my life."

"I'm not sure if I should feel sorry for you or sick that we need people like you." Wyman looked away.

"Neither matters to me, Wyman. What does matter is seeing Albion free once more. And what price won't you pay to see that happen?"

Wyman raised a finger, his mind searching for

a retort...but no answer came to him.

****

Gage sat on his bed, naked from the waist up. A metal tray with medical instruments and a wad of bloody bandages sat next to him. He looked away from Dr. Naomi Seaver as she ran a sterilizer wand over a thin scar on Gage's shoulder.

"We should be doing this in my med bay," she picked up a scanner and ran it down his arm. "Any loss of feeling? Tingling?"

"It's fine," Gage raised his arm and winced.

"It may not be 'fine' if the grafts in your deltoid just broke," Seaver clicked her tongue and thumbed a different setting on her scanner. "I would have no doubt as to your treatment if we were doing this in med bay. Where I have all my best equipment.

Not just a field kit."

"I do appreciate you doing this," Gage kept his eyes turned away as she picked up an endoscope and pressed the point against the top of his shoulder.

"And why are we doing this in here, Commodore?" she clicked a button on the scope and there was a slight hiss as pain killers went through Gage's skin.

"I don't want the crew to think I was badly injured on Sicani," he said. "They see me wheeled into med bay and word will spread like wild fire. And sailors have a tendency to exaggerate."

"You could have walked out of med bay fit as a fiddle in less than ten minutes. Is this hassle really worth a hiccup in your reputation?"

"Yes. I may not be an admiral but I'm still the commander of this fleet. Our sailors must know I am strong, in charge, alert. I am the keel of the 11th Fleet and—nnh! There's that pinch you mentioned."

Dr. Seaver lifted the endoscope away and set it into a kidney-shaped tray next to Gage.

"Better now?" she asked.

Gage slowly lifted his arm and nodded.

"The flight deck crew saw you get off the shuttle with your bloody uniform and your arm in a sling," she said. "No one would think you weak for seeking proper treatment. You're only human."

"I am the commodore," he said.

"All well and good," she picked up the tray and stepped away from Gage's bed. "Commodore…did you learn anything of Albion while you were down there? Any news?"

"Nothing more than we already know. I'm sorry." Gage slipped on an undershirt then picked up a new uniform top. An incoming call chimed on a data slate propped up next to the bed.

"Let me know if the shoulder gives you any bother," she left the room.

Gage swiped a hand across the slate and a full body hologram of Captain Michael Barlow of the *Retribution*, projected into the room.

"Great Scott," Barlow looked over Gage, "I heard you'd been stabbed!"

"It was more of a slice," Gage gingerly put his uniform on.

"I thought you were going down there to cut a deal with the pirates, not get into a bar room brawl like a sailor on shore leave. Tell me there was a woman involved, at least," Barlow said.

Gage gave him a quick rundown of the events on Sicani.

"And you think Loussan—the pirate who's had a vendetta against you for years and who you just humiliated in front of his peers—is going to keep his word and get us to Indus space?" Barlow ran a hand down his face.

"The deal was with the pirates as a whole. You've dealt with them long enough to know oaths made in public are a serious matter. Their standards may be low and ill-defined for most things, but those they have they enforce mercilessly," Gage said.

"Here—on our private channel—I'll tell you you're a bloody idiot. When you present this to the fleet I'll pretend it's brilliant then turn to," Barlow picked up a data slate and began tapping at the screen.

"You think I'm in for some push back from the other captains?" Gage asked.

"I can't say I'm brimming with better ideas," Barlow slapped the slate against his thigh. "You know no one's ever charted the Kigali Nebula before, right?"

"No one in the core worlds."

"So we just trust the Harlequins…and yes, some of the other captains may object a bit more politely than I have," Barlow said.

"'Some' and 'may', you don't seem that confident."

Barlow sighed. "The cruiser captains have become very polite in their dealings with me. They know you and I are friends and don't seem interested in letting anything untoward slip to me. The destroyer and frigate chaps are behind you. That the divide falls along where the captains went to school, and the amount of noble blood in their veins, doesn't surprise me."

Gage straightened his uniform and rolled his injured shoulder back and forth.

"The welfare of this fleet and Prince Aiden are my responsibility, not pats on the back from the good old boy network," Gage said.

"You're the commodore and the regent. Those bunch of prima donnas don't have the admiralty to back them...that's actually a dreadful thing to say in light of our circumstances. Sorry."

"One problem at a time. I doubt any of the captains will break their ships out of formation and petition to join the pirate clans. Not yet, at least."

"Thought you said the pirates had standards? An Albion ship flying with the Totenkopfs? I know our world's under occupation by an enemy we've never heard of until recently, but let's stay realistic."

Gage chuckled and a rare smile crossed his lips.

"Your birthday's a few weeks off," Barlow raised an eyebrow. "I've got a little something special in my locker for you. A spirit you're rather fond of. Meant to break it out after the business on Siam, but here we are."

"A few weeks…I barely know what'll happen in the next few hours."

"The bottle will keep. Let's get the fleet someplace safe so we can enjoy it properly, yes?" Barlow asked.

"Fair enough. Time to plan the next phase."

"It will be brilliant. I've no doubt." Barlow reached to one side and his hologram flickered away.

CHAPTER 9

The King's forest outside of Ludlow was once a place of fond memories for Seaver. Hikes along manicured trails. Fires and stargazing with his parents. The occasional glimpse of raccoons and the native shlandeera lizards with their chameleon scales that flashed the full spectrum of the rainbow whenever they attacked their prey.

Now, running through the forest in the dead of night, the reality of his situation was far removed from his childhood memories. A glow from the burning city mixed with pale light from the full moons. The smell of death and smoke assaulted him with every breath, and Seaver wasn't sure if the foul air clung to him or if it flowed from the city.

He stopped next to a tree, panting. The dull ache from scrapes and bruises grew more intense as he rested. He looked over his shoulder, every rustle of trees or branches bending to the wind brought the fear of pursuit. He went on, following the constellations toward the southwest.

Eventually, he would come to the highway marking the outer boundary of the forest preserve. A highway leading to Corinth where the Albion Army had a training facility for their reserves. If he could make it there, he could still keep fighting.

Seaver slowed and looked up at the stars. A cloud obscured the Cross of Saint George constellation, which pointed east. He considered stopping, as guessing his direction would lead to zigzagging through the forest and would only serve to exhaust him even further and slow his travel through the forest.

"Come on," he muttered.

His toe clipped a rock and he stumbled forward. With his eyes off the sky, he saw the sudden cut off of a ravine right in front of him. He fell onto the ledge and the loose dirt gave way. He grabbed at thin roots jutting from the soil and tumbled down the slope a few yards until he came to a stop in a creek with a splash.

Seaver sputtered in the cold water and pulled himself out. Cold seeped into his uniform and boots. Not only was he wounded, hungry, and terrified…and now he was wet.

He sat on the muddy bank for a moment and ran his fingers through his hair. Water ran down the back of his neck and into his collar. He buried his face in his hands and felt his resolve start to crack.

The call of a blue jay snapped him out of his

near-moment of self-pity. He reached for his lost rifle and looked across the creek at a soldier in camouflage, aiming a battle rifle at Seaver's chest.

"Who won the last blitz ball championship?" the soldier asked.

"Leeds over Utica, 30 to 19," Seaver said.

The soldier lowered his rifle.

"What unit you with? Where from?"

"Ludlow militia. City's overrun. I…I…" He looked back up the slope to where he'd come from, unsure how to explain it all.

"Come on." The soldier motioned for him to follow. "Got a hideout with a couple other stragglers. Guess the Daegon aren't on your heels, not like you made it hard for anyone to find you."

"There are others?" Seaver sloshed through the creek, no longer caring how wet his socks became.

"I'm O'Reilly. Best stay quiet from here out."

"Seaver." He followed the soldier, an older man that moved with a practiced grace through the forest.

After a few minutes, O'Reilly pointed to the base of a tree-covered hill. Seaver made out a camouflage tarp covering a doorway.

"Food. Water." O'Reilly cradled his rifle across the front of his chest, then took a small data slate out of a pocket. He typed in a command and Seaver heard the snap of bolts unlocking. "I'm going to keep an eye out for more like you. Go make yourself comfortable; I'll get you to Corinth tomorrow after sunset."

"How many others?"

The soldier slipped back into the woods.

"Okay, then." Seaver moved the tarp aside and stepped into an arched doorway made of plastic. On a recessed door was a faded emblem for the

King's Conservation Corps. It opened before Seaver could knock and a hand beckoned him inside.

He squeezed around the opening and found a round room lit by light green glow sticks. He heard breathing and the rustle of boots against a hardwood floor. The door shut behind him and a light flipped on.

Three men and a woman shared the room with him, all in uniforms the same disheveled state as Seaver. One man wore civilian clothes.

"Hey." The female soldier, a private named Powell by her rank insignia, tossed him a bottle of water.

"Where are we?" Seaver took a greedy sip from the bottle.

"Ranger way station," she said. "That O'Reilly fellow found us all in the woods and dropped us off. Think he's a ranger or something that was on duty when everything hit the fan. Where you from?"

Seaver cracked open his uniform and let fresh air wash over his chest. He sat in a beat-up plastic chair and began unstrapping his boots.

"Ludlow…" He laid out the last failed ambush and his flight through the woods.

"You were lucky to get away from that golem," another soldier named Inez said. He wore an infantryman's field uniform, but was missing the strap on armor plates, with private stripes on his sleeves. "Two of them killed my entire company outside New Exeter."

"Walkers got my squad in Ludlow," Powell said.

"O'Reilly said he'd get us to Corinth. What's going on over there?" Seaver asked.

"Smith knows." Inez motioned at the civilian. "Tell him."

The civilian, who'd sat against the wall staring at his own shoes without saying a word until that moment, looked at Inez and rolled his eyes.

"Not again," Smith said.

"Come on, man, share the good news. New guy here's had a hell of a time," Inez said.

Smith sighed.

"Some of our leadership made it out of New Exeter," Smith said. "Few generals and admirals, couple intelligence guys. They're in Corinth, organizing resistance cells across the planet. Don't know why, but the Daegon aren't burning out every city like they did with New Exeter and Brighton."

"Just get to the good part," Inez said.

"I shouldn't have said anything. It may not be true." Smith looked away.

"What?" Seaver pulled a foot out of his boot and the air against his bare skin felt incredible.

"The Daegon are on every frequency, every broadcast, and wire channel," Smith said. "Giving new orders, demanding obedience…and they're showing pics of the royal family. All dead. All but one of them. Prince Aidan."

"The prince is just a kid," Seaver said. "They wouldn't…"

"They got Prince Jarred and his whole family." Smith shuddered in disgust.

"But Prince Aidan might be alive?" Seaver rubbed warmth back into his foot.

"I don't believe it," Powell said. "The Daegon are all over New Exeter and nothing got out of there during the attack."

"Not true," the last occupant spoke up. He'd sat against a small desk, his knees pulled to his chest and head down since Seaver arrived. The man wore a torn navy uniform, one side of his head and an eye were covered in fresh bandages. "I worked traffic control at the space port. A ship made it out of a hangar hidden in the cliffs."

"Not supposed to talk about those," Smith said firmly.

"Piss off, not like the Daegon don't know about them by now," the sailor, named Allen, said. "I sent two fighters to protect the ship. All three made it into orbit. I bet that's how Prince Aidan got away."

"Makes sense, right?" Inez asked. "Those bastards aren't showing his body. Ship gets away from the palace."

"You get people's hopes up and you know how bad it'll be if you're wrong?" Powell asked.

"But what if we're right?" Inez asked. "Prince Aidan lives. The royal family is still a part of Albion. I'll take that hope over the Daegon boot, thank you very much."

"Who else knows about this?" Seaver asked.

"The Intelligence Ministry," Smith said. "They've been spreading it through their networks. I believe it, but I also think it could be a ploy to keep the nobles from surrendering completely to the Daegon, from going full collaborator."

"That's why Smith here dragged me out of New Exeter," Allen said to Seaver. "They want me on camera telling the story."

"Are you with the Intelligence Ministry?" Seaver asked Smith.

"No, kid, I'm just a patriot." Smith opened a drawer and tossed Seaver a pack of food vacuum sealed in plastic. "Eat up and go to sleep. Who knows when you'll ever get another chance like this."

Seaver ran his hands across the food pack, never more excited to eat cheese tortellini in his entire life.

There was a shuffle just outside the door.

Smith pulled a small pistol out of a vest.

"O'Reilly's supposed to cut the lights before he sends someone through," Inez said.

"Maybe someone else found the place on their own." Powell licked her lips nervously.

The door opened a few inches and Smith leveled his pistol at the opening as he moved to put himself between the door and Allen.

Five silver balls rolled into the room. One veered toward each occupant and bounced into the air. Seaver kicked at the object, but it bounded over his foot. Spider legs snapped out from the ball and clamped down on his shin. Prongs bit into his skin and electricity arched down the legs and into his body.

His body seized up and his mouth locked open, a scream frozen in his chest.

CHAPTER 10

Gage ran his hand up the flap of his tunic. The stiffness in his shoulder had almost faded away. Dr. Seaver had spent a good half hour doting over him in the med bay, and her few comments about Thorvald's field dressing and minor surgery gave Gage a good deal more confidence in the Genevan's abilities.

The Commodore checked his uniform in a mirror. He didn't see the battered and bruised man that came back from Sicani. That was not the look of a leader that needed his captains to believe in him, to follow him on a damned fool's crusade.

"Sir," Bertram said as he stuck his head into the Commodore's ready room, adjacent to the *Orion's* bridge, "all ships online and ready for you."

Gage glanced at a clock.

"What ship was last to check in?" Gage asked.

"Captain Arlyss on the *Renown*. Just now."

Arlyss on the *Renown*. Admiral Sartorius once told Gage that making oneself available just minutes before the commander's call was tantamount to insubordination in the Albion Navy. Arlyss, the scion of a wealthy noble house on the home world, had not taken well to Gage taking command of the fleet after Sartorius' death. If the reason sprang from Gage's common birth, that he went to a less prestigious academy, or that Arlyss had been on the short list to be Sartorius' aide-de-camp and should have inherited the command, Gage wasn't sure. Any and all the potential gripes Arlyss—or any of the other noble-born officers—could have were reasonable explanations.

"Bertram...does the crew know what happened on Sicani?" Gage asked.

"Know...what exactly?" The steward's eyes darted from side to side. "Certainly your negotiations with the pirates were no one's business but yours. Do you think Thorvald's been talking up a storm again? Spreading scuttlebutt to the lower decks where—"

"The fight with Loussan. Has word got out to the crew?"

"I may have shared the high points with Grisham on the flight deck, Paolo in the galley. Then there's that cute med tech with the blue eyes and—"

"Who's the steward on the *Renown*?"

"Petty Officer Norville, sir."

Gage turned away from the mirror and raised an eyebrow at Bertram.

"Who should hear the story in all its glory, yes sir." Bertram straightened up and clicked his heels together. "Do believe I understand, sir."

"You're a good man, Bertram." Gage walked toward the door to the bridge. Mutinies relied on a significant portion of a crew acting together. When given the choice between a Commodore that beat a pirate lord in a sword fight to save the fleet, or an abrasive captain with a chip on his shoulder, Gage was certain the crew of the *Renown* would choose wisely. Arlyss was many things, but not a fool.

Gage strode out onto the bridge and made for the raised command dais in the center. Crew nodded respectfully to Gage as he passed, more than one gaze lingering on his now-healed shoulder.

Captain Price stood back from the command dais as Gage went up the stairs.

"Sir, good to see you all in one piece," she said.

"Not a place for shore leave," Gage said. He

scanned the data in the holo tank, his gaze stopping on his fleet, the vessels arrayed in a diamond shape with the *Orion* at the center. He touched a keypad and a wire diagram of the *Retribution*, Barlow's ship, came up. Her engines and power plant flashed amber.

"Fusion core's running at sixty percent efficiency," Price said. "She was supposed to go into dry dock for servicing but was kept flying for the mission to Siam. Battle damage during our last fight with the Daegon made whatever problem she's having even worse. The *Retribution*'s having the least amount of engine trouble in the fleet. I tasked a team of engineers to augment the *Retribution*'s repair crews. Status report due in an hour."

"Well done, XO," Gage said. He swiped a hand through the holo and dismissed the *Retribution*. He zoomed out and found a single pirate ship on a convergence course with his fleet. He touched the

Carlin's icon and changed it from "threat" to "neutral."

Price sucked air in through her teeth.

"Bless me…I never thought I'd see the day," she said.

"Politics makes for strange bedfellows. War…stranger still." Gage flipped a switch at the top of his control panel and holos of the captains of each of the 11th Fleet's ships came up in the tank.

"Ladies and gentlemen, let's begin," Gage said. "I have negotiated safe passage for the fleet through wild space to the Indus world of New Madras. We've already received grav-buoy data for the jump to…by our star charts CX-12722, the locals refer to it as Gilgara. From there, we will be escorted to Indus space."

"Does this escort have anything to do with the Harlequin ship on an intercept course?" Arlyss asked.

"It does. The…locals were not willing to share jump data all the way to New Madras. Instead, they will guide us the rest of the way once we reach Gilgara. Captain Loussan—"

Gage kept his mask of command steady as the captains recoiled slightly at the name and more than once tried to interject their disagreement.

"Captain Loussan," Gage continued, "has rescinded his vendetta against me after some intense negotiations." He felt his injured shoulder twitch. "His is the only pirate clan that can get us to Indus space. The Daegon have advanced toward the core worlds, and we lack the supplies and power to do a hard bore to friendly territory."

"You want us to trust a pirate?" Captain Arlyss asked. "One who wanted to kill you—and by extension, all of us—until just recently? One who's been indicted on a litany of charges in civilized space? You think he's actually going to keep his word and not leave us stranded in the Kigeli Nebula to rot? With all due respect, sir, I think you've—"

Gage cut Arlyss off with a tap to his screens.

"Loussan agreed to do this in exchange for information we'll provide to all the clans. They will hold him accountable if he manages to escape. In the meantime, if he does try to cross us, we'll blow him out of space. He will either deliver or be killed by us or his fellow pirates. That's sufficient leverage for me to trust—no, never trust—be reasonably certain he'll follow through. All ships will maintain a constant firing solution on his ship. Now, for our guide."

Gage double-tapped the *Carlin*'s icon with his thumb and forefinger to open a hail, then tossed a small window that popped up into the center of the tank.

Loussan appeared a moment later. The pirate looked from one side of the Albion captains to the other. He brushed hair off his shoulders, revealing a pink scar along one side of his neck.

"Don't everyone thank me at once," Loussan said.

"Captain, please explain how you'll guide us to New Madras," Gage said.

"The path is rather dangerous, especially for so many large and cumbersome jackbo—Albion ships such as yours. I wouldn't take this route with anything larger than my *Carlin*, but this is what you want, so you'll get it," the pirate said. "Once we arrive at Gilgara, I will access my clan's grav buoys and share the jump solution with you all. From there, we will jump to the Kigeli Nebula and make our next jump to a star with a strong slip connection to Madras. I will leave you there, as I seem to be *persona non grata* with the Indus for some minor incident years ago."

"You robbed a medical transport heading for the civil war on Peshawar," Price said dryly.

Loussan rolled his eyes. "The medical supplies still made it to Peshawar. The belligerents just paid a little more for them."

"And how the hell will we get through the Kigeli Nebula?" Barlow asked. "It's a stellar nursery eight light-years across. Parts of it are protostar systems. Dust and rock halos nearly a thousand AUs from the stars. No one's ever navigated through it before."

"At least one of you has an appreciation for the finer points of slip-space travel," Loussan said. "To correct—Barlow, is it?—your misconceptions, no one from the core worlds has ever navigated the Kigeli Nebula. We know a relatively safe route, one that's become worse over the years and cut off fat worlds from our attention, but it can be done."

"Curious that you've kept it secret for this long," Gage said.

"The Harlequin clan set up the route at great expense. We set up a few surprises along the way, obstacles only ships' captains know how to get around. Lowers the risk of crew changing their colors and sharing trade secrets," Loussan said. "And don't think you'll ever be able to navigate it without me."

"How long will this journey take?" Gage asked.

"A few days…give or take. The gravity lanes can be a bit temperamental."

"Maneuver the *Carlin* to here." Gage dragged the pirate ship's icon to just ahead of his fleet formation. "We'll send over a tight beam transponder and communications system once you're in place."

"That's awful close to your ships." Loussan

tugged at his collar.

"Yes, well within our close-range weapon systems. You try to sneak off and the rest of our guns will open fire," Gage said evenly.

Loussan opened his mouth, then snapped it shut with a click of teeth.

"Given the circumstances, I can't say I blame you." Loussan raised his nose slightly.

"All ships, you have your instructions. Make ready for slip space once the *Carlin* is in formation." Gage ended the conference call.

****

The *Orion* snapped out of slip space. A barren, asteroid-pummeled world lay in the distance, swamped by the light of a blue star, as a pair of overly large moons alive with volcanoes and lava flows circled the world.

The rest of the 11th Fleet appeared, scattershot around the *Orion* for dozens of miles.

On the ship's bridge, Gage unbuckled himself from his chair and pulled off his helmet as he made for the holo tank.

"Conn, status," Price said.

"All ships report in. Ship dispersion is way above normal. There's a graviton anomaly somewhere in the system that must have thrown us off a bit as we hit the stars' outer gravity well," the lieutenant said.

"Scope is clear, sir," the gunnery officer said. "Nothing on passive sensors coming off the planet either."

"CX—" Price shook her head slightly, "—Gilgara's nothing but a ball of rock. No metal core to mine. Radiation is absurd. The moons make the surface unlivable. Not hard to believe this system was never settled."

"Where's Loussan?" Gage asked. "Where's the *Carlin*?"

The pirate ship materialized within the holo tank just behind and below the *Orion*. It coasted ahead, pulling amidships with the Albion battleship.

"Guns, work up a firing solution," Gage said.

"Aye aye, practically point-blank," the lieutenant commander said.

Loussan appeared in the holo tank.

"Ahh, no one here to greet us. Thanks for checking on that. So sorry we were a bit tardy. Did I mention the graviton lensing from the Wicked Sisters?" Loussan asked. "Tends to futz with anyone entering the system."

"Every time you withhold something, my trigger finger gets a little itchier," Gage said.

"You have any idea how to get out of this

system?" Loussan asked. "The Sisters make calculating a jump solution back to Sicani rather difficult, but if you want to set up a colony on Gilgara, you're more than welcome to. The fire and brimstone rain only lasts most of the year."

"What's our next step, Loussan?" Gage asked.

"Down to business, finally." The pirate looked away and gave curt orders to his bridge crew. A course plot came from the *Carlin*, one that took them within the nearer moon's orbit.

"We need to weigh anchor at this Lagrange point between Gilgara and Susan. From there, I'll provide the jump formula to the Kigeli Nebula. I suggest you raise your shields. Susan's and Natalie's volcanoes throw up a good deal of rock while Gilgara's gravity cleans it out."

"Curious names for moons you call Wicked Sisters," Gage said.

"The first Harlequin's ex-wives. Yes, sisters; he was a different sort. Now will there be anything else or should I go back and fret while you keep a knife at my back?"

Gage cut the transmission.

"XO?" Gage asked.

"Course plots true to the Lagrange point," she said from the conn station. "He's right about shields. The ejecta will chew our hulls up if we pass through at march velocity. We have to raise shields right as we begin deceleration. This will be a slow trip."

"Keep the fleet on yellow alert. Two flights of ready fighters at all times with the rest of the Typhoons ready to launch in less than ten minutes. We're staying on our toes." A message flashed on Gage's control panel and his lips pulled into a slight frown.

"There's an issue I need to address. Price, you

have the bridge."

****

The pair of armsmen outside Prince Aidan's quarters snapped against the bulkhead as Gage came round the corner, Thorvald just behind him. Gage walked up to the door, expecting it to open automatically, and almost bumped into it.

"Genevan changed the door protocols," one of the armsmen said. "My apologies, Commodore."

Gage knocked hard, and the sound of a child bawling carried through the door. The armsmen inched away.

The door opened and Gage found himself face-to-face with Salis, a young Genevan woman in armor but for her exposed face and head. On her chest was a smear of mashed sweet potatoes, corn, and green beans.

Aidan's bawling intensified amidst Bertram's attempts to calm the child.

Salis stood aside.

"I take it he still doesn't want to wear his vacsuit," Gage said and entered, the door sliding shut behind him.

"I had to threaten to sedate him before Bertram could lock the helmet down," Salis said. "I would have done it for the sake of the Prince's safety, which would have only made my duties that much more difficult in the future."

"He's a child on a warship, Salis. This environment is not meant for him, no matter what we do to make him comfortable," Gage said.

"And I am not—" She bit her lip and the armor plates on her shoulder slid down her arms, then back up. "Forgive me, Commodore. I was not trained in matters of child-rearing. Wish me to plan full-proof security for delegations from warring factions? Done. Find the vantage points for counter-sniping teams? Simple. Defend you from a half-dozen armed assailants? With ease. But taking care of a child, especially one who's gone through such recent trauma…"

"It is beyond your purview, I understand."

"My oath is to protect the Albion royal family. Nothing is beyond my purview…though some things are beyond my skill set."

"You're doing better than I could manage, Salis."

Gage walked through Admiral Sartorius' old quarters and into the main bedroom. Toys manufactured in the *Orion*'s fabrication shops were strewn across the room. On the bed, Aidan lay under the covers, sobbing. Bertram held a tray, the meal spilled across the metal and onto the steward's sleeves.

"This menu isn't to his liking," Bertram said sheepishly. Gage motioned to the door and Bertram hurried out.

Gage sat on the bed and rested his forearms against his knees. He ran a hand through his hair and felt exhaustion taking hold, like he was a windup toy and the key in his back was slowing down.

"Go 'way!" Aidan said.

"Hello, my Prince," Gage said.

Aidan yanked the covers off his head and rubbed tears away. The five-year-old crawled out and latched on to Gage's arm. He wore a smaller version of Gage's own vac-suit, the Albion royal crest sewn onto his chest.

"I was scared," the Prince said.

"That's all right. Everyone on the *Orion* gets

scared when it's time for battle stations." Gage winced at the last two words.

"Not Salis. She's only mean."

"She has the most important job on the ship—protecting you. She doesn't have time to be anything but very serious."

"I don't like her. Send her somewhere else."

"Would you rather Thorvald stay with you?"

Aidan was quiet for a moment, then very quietly said, "No."

"Why not?"

"He doesn't like me."

"That's not true. Just last night, he…he told me how proud he is of you. That you're very brave and will grow up to be a great king."

Aidan looked up and wiped his nose.

"We can go home soon?"

"We will go home. I swear, on my honor and

my life, that we will return to Albion…I just don't know when. Yet."

"I miss everyone. I miss my room. I want to play outside again."

"So do I, my Prince. So do I." Gage leaned over and picked up a thin book from the floor. "Can I read you a story?"

"Yes. But do the voices. Mr. Berty doesn't do them right at all."

****

Captain Price sat in her command chair, drumming her fingers against her armrest while watching the *Orion*'s shields flicker through the forward viewports. Volcanic ejecta from the Wicked Sisters had grated against the ship's shields for hours, causing waves of energy that flowed across the shields like the auroras that stretched down from Albion's poles every solstice.

"Guns, what's your read on our emitters?" she asked.

"They're holding...for now," Vashon said. "Repair crews got our port shields up to ninety percent before we left Sicani, but the work-around they used was meant to stand up to pirate guns, the occasional big hit. Not this sandpaper fog we're flying through."

"What's our worst-case scenario if the emitters fail?"

"Hull pitting. Micro-punctures to outer decks. Might lose some antennae. Real problem is mass accretion. If we lose port shields, every bit of rock that comes in will bounce around in the interior shield wall and stay there—like walking around in a rainstorm with a bucket. The bucket gets heavier the longer you're out there. It'll slow us down."

"We could invert if we lose shields," the conn officer said over his shoulder. "Turn the ship over and move the open section away from the direction of the moons. Should decrease the mass accretion significantly."

"An option," Price said as she pulled up a screen from the side of her chair and checked the fleet's formation. Several of the destroyers on the edge of the diamond had drifted, distorting the neat shape the fleet had before they passed within the moons' orbits. The lasers the fleet normally used to exchange ship-to-ship telemetry data were badly degraded in the fog of ash and rock particles flowing down to Gilgara. Radio broadcasts would cut through, but they would also serve as a beacon to anyone listening, which was why the fleet was under silent running conditions.

One of the wayward destroyers, the *Fairbarn*, edged back into place. For a moment, an unidentified contact appeared on her screen, just inside the outer cordon of destroyers. Then it appeared again, deeper within the fleet's formation.

"Sensors, what do you make of that?" Price asked.

"Ejecta colliding," Lieutenant Jellico said from her station. "Our passives are almost overwhelmed with random thermal plumes from here to the planet's surface."

"On the surface? Show me," Price said. A moment later, an image of one of the many coal-black craters along the equator came up on her screen. Time stamps from almost fifteen minutes ago appeared next to small heat readings as they appeared along the rim. All had an altitude of a few dozen to several hundred meters above the surface.

The sensor ghost appeared again, closer to the *Orion*.

"Jellico, Gilgara doesn't have much of an atmosphere," Price said. "How is anything burning up so close to the planet?"

"I…that's a good question, ma'am," she said as logs of sensor data came up around her workstation. Another brief return pinged on her screen, the largest one yet and even closer to the *Orion*.

"Ma'am," Vashon said, "suggest we direct the gun crews to do a visual sweep of that sector."

"Conn, how much longer until we're at the jump point?" Price asked.

"Twenty minutes at current speed," Jellico said. "We still don't have the jump equation from the *Carlin*."

"Hail those criminals and tell them to

disseminate it," Price said. "No point waiting around if it isn't absolutely necessary."

Price drew a quick plot from the far side of the two moons and the barren planet and bit her lip. If a hostile fleet was out there, it would have just enough time to catch up to the 11th before it could jump away.

"Sensors, I want a directed radar pulse across sectors seven through nineteen. Something's off," Price said.

"Ma'am, Commodore Gage ordered silent running. The pulse energy needed to cut through all the noise will—"

"Did I stutter?"

"No, ma'am. Sensor pulse from seven to nineteen. Aye aye."

Price swiped a fingertip across a pad and brought up the emergency contact screen. She double-tapped Gage's icon.

"Commodore to the bridge," she said quietly.

"By the king!" Vashon called out.

Price's head shot up.

"Got hostile contacts on an intercept course. Return is fuzzy, but they read as Daegon boarding shuttles," Vashon said.

Price angled her chair screen up. The enemy was well within their perimeter…and only minutes away from the *Orion*. Dread welled up inside her and flooded her body. She lunged out of her seat, her body moving far slower than her mind as she jumped onto the command dais.

"Red alert! All ships to battle stations!" Price shouted. "I want a full sensor sweep, now. Guns, can you intercept those shuttles?"

"Flak turrets are spinning up," Vashon said, "but the targets went to full afterburners once the radar sweep hit them."

"Damn it," she said. The holo tank flared to life…and dozens more Daegon assault ships appeared just beyond the fleet's perimeter. More enemy ships appeared over the horizon of the outer moon, a Daegon force of capital ships that grew larger by the second.

"The Harlequins set us up," Price said to herself.

****

Gage ran his fingertips down the page of a thin book he held in his hands and glanced at Prince Aidan, where the boy lay curled up next to him on a couch.

"'You are a bird and you are my mother,'"

Gage read. "The end."

"I like the story." Aidan rubbed an eye with his fist.

"It's a very, very old story from Earth," Gage said. "My mother used to read it to me before bedtime."

Aidan pushed himself up and dangled his feet over the edge, knocking his heels against the couch.

"I'm like that little bird," the Prince said. "I want to go home and find my mother. When can we go back?"

Gage set the book to one side.

"That's hard to say, my Prince. It won't be soon, I'm sorry to say."

"Before my birthday?"

Gage's brow furrowed. He didn't know that date. The King's and Queen's birthdays were public holidays on Albion, not so for their children.

"We'll see. But before then, will you be nicer to Ms. Salis?"

"No," Aidan snapped. "I don't like her."

"Well, she ca—"

Battle stations sounded. Aidan shrieked and buried his head against Gage's side. Salis burst into the room, her armor sliding over her face and head.

"Aidan, your special clothes," Salis said as she opened a locker next to the door and pulled out a bespoke vac-suit and helmet.

The boy began sobbing.

"Get him to his quarters." Gage tried to pick the boy up, but he squirmed away.

"I've got him, sir." Salis unzipped the vac-suit and tossed it on the couch.

Gage got up to leave, but Aidan clawed at his arm.

"No leave!"

"My place is on the bridge. Salis will take care of you." Gage pulled the boy's hands away as Salis wedged herself between the two of them.

Gage rushed out of the room and found Thorvald waiting with a pistol in one hand, a void helmet in the other. Aidan's cries carried through the bulkhead.

"This is no place for children," Gage said, taking the helmet from Thorvald and putting it on. A mechanism in the base of the helmet connected to his shipboard uniform and a puff of stale air filled his visor. He pulled on a pair of gloves as he and Thorvald ran for the nearest elevator.

"Commodore, it's an ambush," Price said through his helmet once it connected to the ship's network. *"Dozens of Daegon assault boats. They were waiting for us on the planet's surface. We missed their approach in all the noise. It's my own damn fault. Permission to open fire on the*

Carlin."

"Belay that. Do we have the jump solution yet?"

"Negative. Daegon fleet, currently scanning fifty-nine cruiser analogs and one battleship on an intercept course."

Gage bit back a curse. He turned down a hallway, feeling the deck shake as the nearby point defense battery opened fire.

"Best speed to the jump nexus. This is not the time or place for a last stand," Gage said.

A groan of metal filled the passageway. Thorvald grabbed Gage by the shoulder and jerked him back just as the hull ripped inward and a Daegon boarding torpedo broke through the *Orion*'s defenses.

Air whipped around Gage as it rushed to the open vacuum. Lights flickered and all sound beyond Gage's suit vanished. The gale pulled Gage off his feet, and only Thorvald's iron grip kept him from sailing into the void.

The Daegon torpedo's fire-scorched hull rotated on its axis, grinding out sparks against the *Orion*'s superstructure.

"Down." Thorvald pushed Gage to the deck a heartbeat before a side panel blew off and sliced over their heads.

Daegon soldiers clambered to get out of the opening as light from passing energy bolts of the *Orion*'s weapons passed over their blue armor and glinted off their rifles' bayonets. Thorvald flicked a switch on his pistol and braced it with both hands. The weapon fired on full auto, shredding the tightly packed Daegon as they fought to break out of the boarding torpedo.

One soldier managed a hip shot that glanced off the Genevan's shoulder, pulling the last of his rounds wide.

Thorvald's armor shifted into a round shield on a forearm and he charged forward. A Daegon shot bounced off the shield and into the ceiling. A second caught the bodyguard in the ankle.

Thorvald jumped forward and smashed the edge of shield into a soldier struggling over the body of a comrade. The blow snapped the man's neck, leaving his head dangling at an angle that turned Gage's stomach.

Thorvald slapped away a clumsy stab from the last Daegon, then grabbed him by the face, tearing the front of the soldier's helmet. Air spilled into the vacuum and the blue-skinned Daegon dropped his weapon and pawed at his mouth and nose. Thorvald grabbed a fallen rifle by the barrel and clubbed the Daegon against the side of his head.

Blood spattered to the deck and boiled off almost instantly.

"I can't get you through here," Thorvald said. "The closest lift to the bridge is on deck nineteen."

A squad of *Orion* Marines ran around the corner and drew down on Thorvald.

"Stop!" Gage yelled.

"Sorry, Commodore," the lead sergeant said. "His armor looks a bit like theirs."

"Is the maintenance hatch to deck four still intact?" Gage asked.

"Yes, sir, just went past it," the sergeant said.

"The Crown Prince is in room 11-Alpha. Escort him and his Genevan to the Admiral's quarters," Gage said.

"But what about you?" the sergeant asked.

"Are you insulting me?" Thorvald asked as he came back from the boarding torpedo.

The ship rocked as an explosion reverberated through the decks.

"Get moving," Gage said.

****

Petty Officer Challons ran up to a vent spewing flames. He felt the heat through his helmet and gloves as he unsnapped a hose from his leg and aimed the nozzle at the vent. The fire blackened and the warped gate hung from a single hinge. Two more sailors stopped behind him, both holding carbines and crowbars.

"Deck Officer, this is damage control team three," Challons said as he sent a quick burst of foam into the opening and the fire sputtered. "Got a ruptured air line somewhere between the antennae array station and the magazine on deck two."

He opened the aperture on his nozzle and

flooded the vent, coating pipes and cables with foam. The foam hardened, then exploded as the flames reconquered the space and hardened foam bounced off his helmet and shoulders.

"Deck Officer, team three, we got a fire line here. Suggest we go full vacuum on the deck. If this gets worse, the main transmitters will be at risk…Deck Officer?" Challons tapped the side of his helmet.

There was a flash of light and one of his teammates pitched forward, a smoking hole in his chest, as three Daegon soldiers rushed at them from behind. One rammed a bayonet into a sailor's chest and raised him into the air, skewered at the end of the weapon.

Challons fumbled for a pistol locked in its holster. One of the Daegon grabbed his arm and flung him against the bulkhead. The sailor bounced off and fell to the deck, stunned. A Daegon stripped his pistol away, then hauled him up onto his knees. He pinned Challons' arms back and held him as the sailor struggled.

A man in an Albion Navy vac-suit walked around a corner. The Daegon soldiers ignored him as he put his hands on the side of his helmet and lifted it up. Beneath was a man made of matte obsidian. Every bit of his head was pure darkness—even the flicker of firelight seemed to melt into his skin.

"I need to see him," Ja'war the Black said.

One of the Daegon unsnapped Challons' helmet and tossed it aside.

"What is—what is this? Deck Officer? Deck—"

Ja'war darted forward and grabbed Challons by the throat, choking him.

The Faceless pressed a finger to his dark lips.

"Deck Officer," Ja'war said in a singsong voice and an electric shock snapped through Challons' throat as he gagged.

"Deck Officer," Ja'war said again…in Challons' voice as the black skin lightened to match the Albian sailor's. Skin pulled taut around the eyes and Ja'war's features morphed, like there were fingers pressing against the inside of his face.

Darkness pressed around Challons' vision as Ja'war became a perfect replica of him.

"Thank you for this gift," Ja'war said and then snapped the sailor's neck with a quick twist.

"Now what?" one of the Daegon asked.

Ja'war edged his toe beneath one of the carbines of the dead sailors and kicked it up. He caught the weapon and gripped the handle.

"Now you're of no use to me." Ja'war jammed the muzzle into the nearest Daegon's chest and shot him though the heart, pulling the corpse against him and using it as a shield to deflect the hasty stab from the next boarder's bayonet. Ja'war shot him through the throat, then ducked and spun around to shoot the last of his escorts.

The Faceless picked up Challons' helmet and put it on, then took an explosive charge off his belt and tossed it against the bulkhead near the raging vent. Ja'war hurried down the hallway and ducked around a corner, flipping off the Daegon jammer on his belt.

"—the hell are you, team three?" came over Challons' intercom.

"It's gonna blow!" Ja'war clicked a button on his gauntlet and a fireball roared down the passageway, singeing his vac-suit. With all the evidence disposed of, Ja'war brushed himself off and made his way to the *Orion*'s communication nexus.

CHAPTER 11

Gage rushed out of the lift and made straight for the bridge's holo tank.

"Send reserve platoon alpha to deck eight," Price said to a battle-armored Marine's image in the tank. "We cannot lose the fusion plants if we ever want to make it out of here."

Gage slapped a panel on his side of the tank and his fleet materialized. He spent a few seconds analyzing the data before saying, "Price, what's the status on boarders?"

"Breaches all across our starboard. They

coalesced into three teams—two of which we eliminated—and we've got the last one pinned down near bay seven, quartermaster's stores," she said.

A diagram of the *Orion* came up, hull breaches pulsing like bleeding wounds. Red lines traced the boarders' advance through the ship.

"Going for our power plants this time, not for the Prince," Gage said.

"Commodore, priority message from the *Carlin*," the communications officer called out.

"Have them stand by," Gage said. "Price, you have the counter-boarder fight."

"Aye aye," she said.

Gage swiped through the holo tank and his fleet appeared. Tiny icons of Typhoon fighters danced around Daegon assault ships, destroying one every few seconds. His walls of destroyers and cruisers closest to the planet kept up a steady stream of fire, annihilating the few Daegon ships racing toward the 11th.

From everything he could see, the fight was going their way. The Daegon had attacked with assault craft unsupported by larger ships and committed them to the battle piecemeal, and the Albion guns were defeating them in detail.

"Amateur effort," Gage said. "Not like the Daegon at all…"

"Sir, the *Carlin* is transmitting a distress call," Price said.

Gage zoomed in on the pirate ship and found it listing in space. Three Daegon boarding torpedoes stuck from her hull like embedded crossbow bolts.

"Conn, do we have the jump solution out of here?" Gage asked.

"Negative, sir," the pale-faced lieutenant said.

The *Carlin*'s engines exploded, cracking the

ship down her keel and sending the halves tumbling away from each other.

Price made an undisciplined gasp and covered her mouth. Silence fell across the bridge.

Gage did a quick mental calculation for a return jump back to Sicani and quickly concluded that there was no way to get to the nexus without going through the much larger Daegon fleet.

"Sir?" The communications lieutenant peered down at his status board. "We're still being hailed by the *Carlin*."

"Send it," Gage said.

A scared, tired-looking Loussan appeared in the holo tank.

"That is the *second* ship you've cost me, Gage," the pirate said. In the battle space within the tank, life pods appeared near where the *Carlin* exploded. "The Harlequins are normally the ones boarding ships.

Seems we weren't quite ready for swarms of blue-skinned monsters to come rampaging through our decks."

"Loussan, do you have the jump solution?" Gage asked.

"Of course I have it." Loussan rolled his eyes and held up a data rod. "Recover me and my crew and I'll give it to you."

Gage pointed at Price out of the pirate's view and shook his hand back and forth. Price nodded in acknowledgement and began ordering the *Orion*'s fighters to converge on the life pods.

"We don't have time to waste. Send me the solution now," Gage said.

"First, if I transmit it to you in the open like this, the Daegon can use the same data to jump right after us. Second, if you have the jump solution, you don't need me anymore, do you? You're under no obligation to help me out of here."

Gage seethed for a moment, then found reason behind Loussan's first excuse.

"We may never trust each other, which is fine by me," Gage said, "but I need that data to get out of here alive and your options are to land on Gilgara or take your chances with the Daegon. Redirect your pods toward the *Orion*. Land in bay three."

"Have you ever seen a life pod 'land' before, Gage?" Loussan asked. "I saved my coin for top-of-the-line weapons and engines…I picked these life pods up from a wholesaler not known for her warranties."

The life-pod tracks within the battle space angled toward Gage's ship.

"Do the best you can," Gage said.

"Does the Albion Space Navy have a 'you break it, you bought it' policy?" Loussan asked.

Gage cut the transmission.

"I hate pirates," he muttered. "Thorvald, Jellico, go to bay three and get the jump data the instant he crawls out of that pod and broadcast it to the rest of the fleet."

"My place is here," Thorvald said from his usual spot against the bulkhead.

"We don't have time for games. If he sees you, he'll know you're willing to rip his fingers off to get at the data," Gage said.

Thorvald canted his head slightly, then nodded.

"Jellico—" Gage gave the young officer a look.

"I can set up a remote station down there," he said as he hurried out of his seat. "The rod he had looks like Reich tech. Our readers can pull the data from that."

"Alpha flight will rendezvous with the life pods in two minutes," Price said. "Daegon fighters and assault ships down to ten percent strength."

One of the Albion frigates, the *Retribution*, Barlow's ship, flashed amber. The vessel fell out of formation, slowing rapidly.

Gage pounded a fist against the holo tank.

****

Tiberian sat on his throne, chin to his hand, his concentration so evident that his command team knew better than to disturb him with anything but the most critical of information.

The semi-opaque image of thrall-crewed destroyers flanking his battleship shone through his bridge walls, lesser wolves struggling to keep pace with the alpha. Some commanders preferred to see the battle space in a holo sphere; others used physical models held aloft by anti-grav repulsors and chose to direct ships by hand. Tiberian enjoyed the true scale of feeling his ships around him; it heightened the emotions of the hunt—the rush of adrenaline, the spike of ecstasy as his guns drew first blood.

But now…now he felt nothing but bitterness and anger.

"Seems this Faceless one played you for a fool," Gustavus said. He walked up the three tiered steps around Tiberian's throne and leaned his shoulder against the Daegon commander's seat.

Tiberian's hand tightened into a fist. Anyone else that disrespected him in such a way would have died after hours of agony. But Gustavus was blood…and suffering a few verbal barbs along the way to returning to the Baroness' favor was a small price to pay.

"Your assessment is shortsighted," Tiberian said. "Normal for one so young as you."

"Hardly." Gustavus raised a hand toward the distant Albion fleet. "Ja'war told you to hide the fleet on the far side of the outer moon, swore that was the route the *sclavi* would take. He claimed to know this part of space, yet they charted a course closer to the planet. We were caught far out of position and now we may not even stop the *Orion* from escaping with your prize."

"The boarding parties…"

"Yes, I can't wait to see you explain that to Father. A battalion of *themata* soldiers lost with nothing to show for it. A battalion you put under command of the Faceless." Gustavus shook his head.

"You defeated them on their home world. How well did they fight?"

Gustavus snorted. "With passion but without skill. We've taken significantly fewer new thralls from that world than others during the crusade."

"Do you think they'll surrender the last of their royal family, the boy?" Tiberian asked.

Gustavus put his hand on the hilt of the sword hanging from his belt.

"Given your last—and failed—attempt, I would say not."

"The Faceless is wise, and knows these stars and the ferals better than we do," Tiberian said. "If I kill the boy, the Baroness will be satisfied. If I bring him back and use him to crush the resistance on Albion, I may return to my place by her side. I want the boy alive—my asset knows this. If we push them into a corner, they will fight to the death. The Faceless insisted on being given command of the assault battalion…and kept his plan a secret from all but me. Kept your father's soldiers ignorant and desperate."

"What plan? Why haven't you sent the signal to blow his heart out of his chest yet? He's obviously failed." Gustavus' violet cheeks darkened.

Tiberian rose and strode down to the forward edge of the bridge. He reached out and made a fist, and the *Retribution* appeared before the Daegon commander.

"Have you ever hunted dune wolves on Caelius?" Tiberian asked.

"No, it's suicide," Gustavus said.

"To face the entire pack is folly. But a patient hunter can separate them, lower the intelligence of their hive mind, and make the kill. While we strip away the layers around the *Orion*, the Faceless will eat away at its heart. We've looked the fools until now, time to complete the performance before the next act."

Tiberian chopped an X through the *Retribution*.

"Just that one? The ley lines are difficult in this system. How will you track the rest of them when they jump?"

"You should have faith in your betters, child. Care to wet your blade?" he asked Gustavus.

"You have to ask?"

****

"We have the jump solution," Price said. "Nine minutes before we can make a coordinated jump. Three if ships transit solo."

"I highly encourage you to make a coordinated jump and cut your velocity the instant you make translation within the Kigeli Nebula," Loussan said from inside the holo tank. "The margin for error is very slim, as you'll see when—maybe if—we arrive."

Gage had his eyes on the *Retribution* and watched as it fell farther and farther behind.

"Sir, your orders?" Price asked.

Gage's mouth went dry as he weighed options. The Daegon fleet continued to close, vectoring straight for the *Retribution*. The math was simple, the conclusion inescapable. There was no way the *Retribution* could reach the nexus before being overwhelmed by the enemy. If the enemy chose to bypass the *Retribution*, they could engage the frigates *Remorseless* and *Perilous* and a good third of his destroyers, stopping them from escaping.

Gage lifted a hand, then set it back down, unable to control its trembling.

"Open a command channel to the *Retribution*," he said softly.

Barlow appeared in the tank. He looked at Gage, then removed his helmet. He straightened up and cleared his throat quickly.

"Sir," Barlow said.

"Michael…as your commanding officer, I'm ordering the *Retribution* to perform a rearguard action. Delay the enemy for as long as possible, then make your way to the rendezvous point in Kigeli," Gage said, forcing himself to look his old friend in the eye.

"Funny, I was just going to call and suggest the same thing. No need for that second set of instructions. I'm quite sure how this ends," Barlow said.

"I can't find the answer to bring you with us," Gage said. "This fleet has a mission and—"

"—and that mission is a single person.

There's no fear or shame in what we're asked to do. Bring Prince Aidan back to Albion, Thomas. He is all that matters. On behalf of my crew, see the name *Retribution* entered onto the Hall of Honor. I daresay we'll earn it in the next few minutes. Albion's light burns, old chap. The torch is yours."

The transmission cut out and the *Retribution* slowly banked to one side, readying a broadside for the oncoming enemy. Plasma batteries lashed out, obliterating a half-dozen Daegon fighters and ripping through the fore of a cruiser.

Gage looked up and found Price staring at him through the holo. She gave him a slow nod.

The Commodore watched the jump timer as the *Retribution* fired again, hating himself as the seconds ticked down.

CHAPTER 12

Barlow gripped his armrests as another blast shook his ship like a ship at the mercy of an ocean wave. Another hit flung Barlow against his restraints. The deck near his conn exploded upward, sending shrapnel of twisted metal into Ensign Malone and his station.

The ensign cried out and slumped against his seat.

"Bollocks," Barlow said, getting out of his chair and going to the man. Blood poured down a gash across his chest and onto his lap. His vitals flashed on his visor: flatlined. Sparks erupted from the wrecked workstation.

"XO, transfer conn to—"

The deck lurched and sent Barlow tumbling across the bridge. He came to a sudden, painful stop next to his executive officer's station.

The lights dimmed, then the jaundice yellow of emergency lighting came over the bridge.

"We've lost main power, sir," his XO called out.

The ship lurched backwards and Barlow's helmet bounced against his XO's leg.

"What do we have left?" Barlow asked as he scrambled back to his seat.

"Weapons off-line. Life support failing. Hull breaches on…all decks, engines are off-line," his XO said.

Barlow pressed a hand against the side of his

chair and felt a slight vibration.

"We should be dead in space. How are we moving?" he asked. He flipped up a screen from the other side of his seat and pulled down a menu of every camera on his ship's hull. All but two were washed out in static. One gave him nothing but the vast emptiness of the void…the other held the underside of the Daegon battleship, and his ship was moving into a massive open hangar.

"They must have us in a tractor beam," his XO said.

"Engine room, can we manage one last shot from the lance?" Barlow asked into the command intercom but got nothing except the hiss of an open line in response.

"Engine room took a direct hit," his XO said. "Not reading any movement on internal sensors."

"What I wouldn't give to have a few

torpedoes right now," Barlow sighed.

The ship jerked as docking clamps trapped his ship within the Daegon vessel. A surge of electricity snapped across the still-working stations. Blue-white electricity arced from the XO's screens and onto his hands.

The man went into spasms then fell against his station.

"Damn it all to hell." Barlow touched his screen, but it was dead. He tapped a pad on the back of his left hand to activate the PA system but got error buzzers instead.

"Mateer, Bruce, help me." Barlow got up and grabbed a lever flush with the deck just beside his chair. He pulled a second lever, then pushed his chair over. The glow of the *Retribution*'s computer core filled the bridge.

"How did they manage to fry everything but

that?" Mateer asked.

"Best not to assume the enemy is stupid until proven otherwise," Barlow said as he grabbed an oblong metal ring on one side of the core. "Even then, never assume he'll stay stupid. Grab and heave on my go."

The sound of weapons fire echoed down the corridor. Shouts and dragged-out screams triggered a deep, primal fear in Barlow's heart.

"Rest of you hold the door. If the bastards get this core, they'll get the jump coordinates the *Orion* just sent us. This is our last service to the kingdom—make it count."

Barlow, Mateer, and Bruce pulled the top of the computer core partway up when it jerked to a halt. Weak blue light filled the bridge from the still-functional core.

The last eight living sailors on his bridge drew

their pistols and formed a cordon around their captain. One, Donnelly, Barlow's steward since his days as a senior lieutenant, went to the bridge's sliding door and opened a panel that held a yellow and black striped handle.

The bridge doors opened slightly just as Donnelly pulled the handle. The emergency lock, designed to seal the door in the event of a hull breach, stuck halfway down. Donnelly pressed his weight on top of the handle, but it didn't move.

Blue armored fingers wrapped around the edge of the open door and gripped the metal.

"Novis regiray!" sounded on the other side of the door.

Barlow grabbed his pistol and drew down on the boarder, snapping off a shot that sprang against the edge of the doorway and ricocheted into the hallway beyond. The fingers pulled back.

"Seal the door! Seal the door!" Barlow tapped two of his sailors on the back and sent them forward. They grabbed the vertical handle on the door and started pushing.

"Almost got it," Donnelly said as the emergency lock inched downward.

A blast of energy ripped through the door and into Donnelly. He pitched back and slid against the deck, his chest a smoking ruin.

A sword pierced the door and impaled one of the Albians. The point emerged from the back of his neck, blood sizzling as the blade grew white-hot, then the blade withdrew and the sailor crumpled to the ground, smoke and bloody steam rising from his neck.

"Lift, you dogs." Barlow grabbed the core's handle again and heaved upward.

The bridge door buckled as a blow smashed it

from the other side. After a second blow, the door collapsed and Tiberian charged into the room. His white-hot blade cleaved into Barlow's navigator, slicing her from shoulder to hip. Punch spikes on Tiberian's fist popped out as he swung at Mateer's face. The blow shattered his helmet and caved in the front of his skull.

Ignoring the panicked screams of his crew as Tiberian tore them apart, Barlow jammed his pistol into the gap between the core's top and the deck and fired as fast as he could pull the trigger.

Tiberian grabbed Bruce by the face and snapped his neck with a quick jerk to one side and then hurled Bruce's body into two crewmen with bone-crushing force. The *Retribution*'s executive officer shot the Daegon commander in the side. The first two hits fizzled against Tiberian's energy shield; the third hit him in the ribs and marred the armor.

The blow seemed only to enrage Tiberian. He rammed his blade into the XO's sternum, sinking it to the hilt and raising the man off his feet as he kicked and screamed ever so briefly.

Barlow fumbled with a new magazine as Tiberian swung his blade to one side and sent the XO's corpse rolling across the deck.

"No, please…" The last crewman dropped his pistol and fell to his knees, hands up.

"*Miserum*." Tiberian backhanded the begging sailor. The blow demolished his helmet and sent a spray of blood across Barlow's visor as he finally got the new magazine loaded.

Barlow backpedaled and aimed, catching a glimpse of white light as Tiberian swung his simmering blade up. Barlow felt a tug on his wrist as he fired, but his pistol remained silent. He watched as his hand slid off his arm at the wrist and fell to the floor. For a moment, Barlow felt the weight of the pistol, the feel of the handle through his glove. Then a spike of pain shot up his arm.

Tiberian surged forward and slammed a meaty paw against Barlow's chest, gripping him by the front of his vac-suit and lifting him into the air with ease. Tiberian's visor pulled off his face, revealing the blue-skinned man with hate-filled eyes within.

"Barlow," Tiberian said, "I know this ship from Siam. I expected better from you."

"You'll get nothing from me, you monster. Nothing!" Barlow tried to kick the Daegon, but he was as helpless as a mouse in the jaws of a wolf.

Tiberian jammed the tip of his sword into the deck, embedding it a few inches and leaving the handle swaying slightly. Tiberian removed a cuff from off his back and held it up for Barlow to see.

"You will be ruled and you will serve."

Tiberian slapped the cuff around Barlow's neck as the metal stretched out and locked tight. The Daegon dropped the *Retribution*'s captain and smiled as Barlow went stiff as electric shocks from the collar coursed through his body. The pain torque was an old tool, but one that worked to teach new thralls their station.

The Daegon commander walked over to the smoking computer core and gave it a kick.

"Too slow, uncle," Gustavus said from the doorway. The younger man pointed his blood-slick sword at the destroyed computer core. "So much for seizing their jump solution and following them."

"You know so little of our quarry, Gustavus." Tiberian waved a hand over Barlow and the pain torque lessened its assault. "The brigands that transit this system use a grav buoy to calculate their jumps into slip space—one we located the moment it transmitted to the Harlequin ship. It will be ours within the hour, then the hunt continues."

Gustavus' mouth twisted into a snarl.

"Why keep that from me? Then why bother with this?"

"To see if you were clever enough to realize the enemy's mistake. You disappoint, as ever. I came here for this one." Tiberian gave Barlow a kick to the stomach that doubled him over.

"He will prove most useful."

CHAPTER 13

Wyman jumped into his cockpit and strapped himself in as the launch bay doors opened ahead of him. He did a double take at the lava flows on one of the nearby moons.

His crew chief tapped him on the top of the head twice and his canopy lowered. Wyman threw his helmet on and sealed it shut.

"They want us to fly through that?" Ivor said through his helmet. "The brass understand that fighters moving at high velocity hitting all that crap in the void is a bad thing, right?"

"Set forward heat shields to maximum. That'll clear out most of it." Wyman's hands danced across his control panels and brought his fighter online and ready to launch.

"'Most' being the operative word," Ivor said.

"Cobras," the squadron commander, call sign Marksman, came on the air. "Daegon assault ships are within the fleet's perimeter. Weapons free. Negative on fighters, but stay frosty out there."

A crewman raised a pair of lit batons in front of Wyman and his Typhoon rattled as the catapult locked onto his landing gear. He braced himself against his seat and the electronic rails beneath his fighter shot him forward and out into the void.

Firing up his engines, he sped forward, feeling the impacts of tiny particles against his wings. A spider web crack the size of his palm appeared at the edge of his canopy.

"Like flying through a hailstorm." He powered up his forward heat shields and the rattling stopped, just before his canopy HUD went berserk, threat icons appearing and disappearing all around him, and an error message flashed.

"Freak, did your HUD just shit the bed?" Ivor asked.

"Roger, Briar, too much interference for the computers to handle. We're going to have to do this by eye." Wyman deactivated his HUD.

"I take back everything I said about Marksman when he sent us through the sims to do analog drills," Ivor said. "Bogies to our three o'clock. Four by my count, moving on the *Orion*."

"I see them." Wyman flicked the safety off his cannons. "Engaging."

****

Wyman dove behind a Daegon assault craft, and it jinked from side to side, throwing off his shot. He did a barrel roll to dodge the ship's rear cannons and dove down, the prow of the enemy ship snapping open into four pincers as it closed on the *Ajax*'s hull.

Retro thrusters fired from the assault ship and it slowed down as it began final approach on the Albion warship, where it would latch on and disgorge its payload of Marines into the battle cruiser. Wyman pulled up and opened fire.

His cannons stitched across the void and hit the Daegon ship just ahead of the engines. The tail kicked up and it went tumbling end over end…heading right for the *Ajax*.

Ivor cut across Wyman's nose and hit the assault ship twice, blowing it into an expanding cloud of hull fragments and tumbling bodies.

"Mine," she said.

Wyman banked aside and watched as what was left of the vessel spattered against the *Ajax*.

"Freak, Briar," Marksman came over his helmet. "Got a priority-one mission from the *Orion*. Find the life pods from the *Carlin* and escort them to bay alpha. How copy?"

"Order received." Wyman looped over and saw the remains of the *Carlin*. Flipping a switch on his commo panel, his fighter cycled through known distress frequencies. "Come on...damn pirates."

"You got them?" Ivor asked.

"Negative. I don't know if they're not broadcasting a mayday because they're surrounded by Albion ships and are used to hiding, or if they think the Daegon will shoot them even though they're in life pods."

"Maybe both. We can—wait—two o'clock by

five. I think I see them," she said.

Wyman changed course and cut his velocity as he looked around, careful to check his six in case any of the Daegon had lost their narrow focus on boarding the Albion ships. Ahead, he caught a glimpse of maneuver thrusters.

Seconds later, he'd pulled alongside a painfully slow escape pod just ahead of another pair. The pods were long and narrow, like oversized torpedoes. Wyman wagged his wings next to the cockpit and waved to the pirate in the glass-covered nose.

The pirate looked at Wyman and extended the middle digit of his hand.

"Positive contact made." Wyman made an exaggerated gesture toward the *Orion*. The pirate switched his upward finger to his thumb.

"Never thought we'd see the day." Ivor fell in on the other side of the leading escape pod. "Please come aboard my warship, you pillaging, murdering bunch of Harlequin bastards. Hungry?"

"Pay attention now, implications later. Maybe they'll be so grateful, they won't steal everything they touch."

"You going to leave your footlocker open?"

"Nope."

They crossed the distance to the *Orion* in minutes.

"Freak Show, this is landing control," came from the Orion. *"Had an emergency landing just now. Have the escape pods slow."*

"Control, this is Freak Show. I don't have radio coms with them. How long until the pad is clear?"

"Unknown, have them loop around and await further instructions."

"Negative, control, they—crap." The lead pod

accelerated forward as the finish line of the open bay came within reach. Wyman sped his fighter forward, waving frantically at the pilot, who kept his eyes glued on the bay. He wagged his wings again but got no response.

"I tried yelling at them on every freq, no joy," Ivor said.

"I'm done being polite." Wyman fired across the nose of the leading escape pod.

The pirate at the controls gave Ivor a glance but didn't slow. Another pirate, a woman with a felt cloth across her forehead and small coins attached to the edges, stuck her head into the cockpit and started yelling at the pilot.

"Freak Show, the pad has emergency personnel all over it. Abort landing! Abort!"

"Damn pirates." Wyman sped ahead of the escape pod and cut his velocity. Keeping a hand on his throttle, he looked over his shoulder, watching the wide-eyed pirate as he got closer and closer.

"Freak, what the hell are you—"

The escape pod veered to the side.

"Other one! Other one!" Ivor shouted.

Wyman steered his fighter out of the way as the second and third life pods bore down on him, their landing thrusters blazing. He danced out of the way and the two pods slipped into the hangar. They slammed against the deck and came to a screeching halt, sparks flying.

Inside, the emergency crews cowered next to the bulkheads and against a fighter crumpled against the back.

"Well done, Freak Show," control sent. *"Got the crews clear. Have the last one land, then return to base."*

"Control, request alternate landing assignment." Wyman flew back to the last void-born escape pod and directed it back to the *Orion*. Several pirates were looking at him from the cockpit, and none seemed pleased to see him.

"Roger, Freak Show…bay two."

****

Gage stood on the periphery of a group of sailors clustered around a half-wrecked Typhoon wedged against the outer bulkhead. Two engineers stood on either side of the canopy, cutting away at the edges with circular saws. One raised a hand and a gap opened for a pair of medics with a stretcher.

The canopy fell away and the pilot crawled out with—Gage noted—an acute sense of urgency.

"Back!" The pilot fell off the side of the cockpit and landed on a tool chest, scattering items across the deck. There was a whine from the cockpit and a snap as the ejection system malfunctioned. Sailors fell in around Gage as the seat launched up and jammed against the bent frame of the Typhoon, the seat sticking up from the wreck like a sore thumb. Sparks fountained off one side for a few seconds.

The pilot got to his feet, turned to the crowd, and bowed. The sailors broke into applause and Gage turned away, shaking his head. Normally, he'd accept the loss of the fighter in stride so long as the pilot survived. Before the Daegon invasion, equipment could be replaced. Lives could not. Now, hurtling through the farther reaches of wild space and with no supply lines to support them, every piece of damaged equipment inflicted a wound on the 11th that would not heal.

A cordon of Marines separated the far edge of the flight deck from the rest of the ship. All faced the blast doors; all were armed and tense.

Gage picked out Thorvald just on the other side of the line of Marines and heard shouting, which only grew louder as he approached.

"—demand to see him now. Not when we're in the nebula. Now!" Loussan shouted.

Gage tapped a Marine on the shoulder and moved past him.

Thorvald faced off against the shorter pirate, Loussan's Katar standing a few feet behind the captain. Four dinged and scratched escape pods sat on the edge of the flight line with almost two dozen of the *Carlin* crew. The only semblance of a uniform any of them had was some article of clothing in red and black stripes or checkers.

"There," Loussan raised a hand at Gage, "you can deliver." Loussan took a step toward Gage, but Thorvald stepped in front of him.

Ruprecht let off a rattle that could have come

from a snake's tail. Marines raised rifles to their shoulders.

"That's enough." Gage removed his gloves and stopped beside Thorvald.

"This is how you treat all your guests who save your precious backside from the Daegon?" Loussan asked with an incredulous look.

"You were tried in absentia by the Albion Court of Interstellar Justice for nineteen capital offenses," Gage said, "and found guilty of all of them. This ship is Albion territory, and by regulation, I should consign you—and the rest of your crew, if they're known to the justice system—to the void."

Loussan crossed his arms over his chest and rolled his eyes.

"But as serving regent, I have some latitude in carrying out sentences," Gage said.

"I'm not in the habit of thanking people for

not killing me," Loussan said, "especially when I'm their only hope of survival. So how about we drop the pretense and get down to brass tacks, eh?"

Gage worked his jaw for a moment but didn't respond.

"You want to get through the Kigeli Nebula and on to Indus space? You need me. I know the route and the stand-down codes for the variety of surprises along the way. I'll guide you through, then you'll give me one of your ships once it's time to part ways."

Thorvald, of all people, laughed.

"He's a liar," said one of the pirates as he rose from beside an escape pod. The burly man with a singed beard that stretched to his belt stomped toward them. "He doesn't know the way through. He's going to get us all killed!"

"Thank you, Mr. Onoro." Loussan half-turned and brandished a finger at the man. "Feel free to sit down and shut up."

"No one's been through Kigeli in decades," Onoro said. "This con can't go on anymore. Tell him the truth!"

Loussan looked at Gage and put a hand to the side of his mouth.

"I know the way through," the pirate whispered and added a wink.

"There's a route back to Harlequin space from the Anchor," Onoro said, his fists shaking and his face red with anger. "We all know it. You've already killed most of our crew and lost everything we spent years building. I'm not going to let you end it all for me too."

"Onoro, you are embarrassing me in front of this jackboot and if you think this little tantrum of yours will—"

Onoro jabbed the straight index and middle finger on one hand at Loussan. As he did, the fingers swung open at the knuckle, revealing a pair of muzzles.

Ruprecht moved like lightning, a blade sliding out from his forearm and spearing Onoro right between the eyes. The pirate's arms and legs went slack. He hung from the blade piercing his skull, limbs jerking, then Ruprecht let him fall to the ground.

Loussan turned to the rest of his crew and shouted, "Anyone else feeling froggy? I want shit from any of you, I'll have Ruprecht squeeze your head."

The pirate spat on the deck, then spoke to Gage. "Sorry you had to see that. A number of failures came to light when the Daegon boarded my ship. There are no review boards or courts of inquiry on a free people's ship. There is only the captain's authority and the code. As for Onoro, can't say I ever liked him. Sorry about the mess."

"There's another way back to wild space?" Gage asked.

"Naturally. One way in or out of any system is three too few." Loussan smiled. "You could cast your lot against the clans, doubt you'd last that long."

"I ask, as I'm curious who else might be waiting for us at this Anchor your man mentioned. We're going to Indus space, Loussan. Indus," Gage said.

"As was promised. Now, as for the ship you owe me, I think one of the cruisers will—"

"You'll spend the rest of this voyage in the brig," Gage said. "My Marines will escort you and your crew there. Resist, and I'll remember to start checking our database for wanted criminals."

"The brig?" Loussan's face lost some of its color. "We are your honored guests…the law of the void requires you to…" He raised a finger and glanced over Gage's shoulder to the wall of Marines, then pressed the finger to his lips. "Come to think of it, my crew is known for larceny and hell-raising. The brig would be the best place for us. For your protection. And mine. Mostly mine."

Ruprecht made a series of clicks.

"Yes, of course, old friend," Loussan said. "He stays with me. And we get our own cell."

"Fine. We break out of slip space in a few hours. I'll speak to you then," Gage said.

Loussan turned back to his crew and clapped his hands twice.

"Good news, everyone! I've secured us berthing and food. On your feet and keep your hands to yourself."

CHAPTER 14

Petty Officer Sarah Foster sat down on a locker-room bench. She ran a towel through her wet hair, the silence of the otherwise empty facility a respite from the last few hours of nonstop work in the engine room.

Having the showers all to herself was one of the few chances for solitude she ever found aboard the *Orion*. After a double shift of working to isolate a fault in the fusion engine core and stopping a cascade failure from frying the dorsal shield emitters, Lieutenant Derschowitz had finally let her and her team off for five hours for sleep, food, and hygiene.

The showers on deck seven had a smell to them, but Foster knew they'd be free during the gun crew shift change, and that meant some quiet time.

She pressed her towel against her face and took a deep breath that threatened to turn into a sob. With her first chance to unwind after the last brush with the Daegon, her mind turned to Mateer aboard the *Retribution*. With no news from Albion, her old friend from boot camp was the closest thing to family she had.

"Maybe they got away," she said. "Maybe the Daegon don't murder their prisoners."

"Not from what I've seen," someone said.

Foster jerked the towel off her face. A woman, still in her coveralls, leaned against a locker, staring at Foster.

"Sorry, thought I was alone," Foster said. She

hoisted the towel wrapped around her midsection up a bit and frowned. "You're leaning on my locker."

"I know," the woman said in a different voice...in Foster's voice.

Ja'war's hand snapped out and he pressed a tiny injector against Foster's throat before she could react. Her eyes rolled back and she went limp as Ja'war's venom knocked her unconscious. The Faceless grabbed her by the chin and arm, holding her upright as he took in her appearance. His skin changed color, hair lengthened, and bones cracked as they realigned to mirror Foster's frame.

A door on the opposite side of the locker room opened and Ja'war heard several people talking as they stopped at the towel rack around the privacy wall. Ja'war opened a locker and stuffed Foster inside, then removed a small, obsidian case from a pocket and opened a corner with a flick of his thumb. He opened Foster's mouth and flicked a pill into it, then shut the door as quietly as he could.

Ja'war put his hands to the side of his face and grimaced as he forced his new face out of place and bent his nose into an ugly hump. He grabbed Foster's uniform and boots from her locker just as three sailors came into the locker room, all dirty and weary-eyed.

"This isn't your assigned shower," one said.

"Mine's on deck eleven and got wrecked in the last fight. Catch as catch can, hope you don't mind," Ja'war said. He stepped around the sailors and made for the exit.

One of the women huffed. "Saw her stripes on her uniform," she said. "Would've given her more shit about using our water ration, but she's a non-comm."

"Who was she?" the second asked. "Never

seen her before."

"Maybe someone cross-leveled from another ship? Who knows…she shows again, we'll get the senior chiefs involved. You don't screw with another section's shower time. Just not done." The first woman sniffed the air. "Ugh, what is that?"

Dark smoke wafted through the edges of the locker where Ja'war had hidden Foster.

"Christ, not another fire," a sailor said.

"Why's there no heat?" One touched the locker, shrugged, then opened the door.

Foster's desiccated body fell out and landed against the bench, her flesh breaking apart and flying into the air like fine ash.

****

Tolan floated in a haze, the sensation of his body fading in and out as brilliant colors swirled across his vision. A slight tingle danced across his skin, then the sensation lifted up and he felt the colors playing against each other.

Faylun was right. The Dizzy was strong.

He felt a cold breeze waft over his being, then a shadow darkened the colors.

"Tolan," his name echoed through his mind.

"Not now, Mr. Panda," Tolan said. "I'm waiting for the elephants."

"You are under the influence of narcotics," the voice said.

"You don't sound…like a panda," Tolan slurred.

The shadow loomed over him, and he felt a sharp pain on his arm. The haze from the drug the Martian gave him collapsed, replaced by Thorvald's unfriendly face.

"What the hell did you…" Tolan gagged, then sat bolt upright. "You—" Tolan vomited between his knees and all over his sheets. The spy groaned and rolled onto the floor with a thump as a cold sweat emerged all over his body.

"I injected you with a purge compound. On Geneva, we call it *dasiert*," Thorvald said.

Tolan dry-heaved and pushed himself up on his hands and knees.

"You could have…dragged me to the bathroom first, you buzz-killing asshole," Tolan said.

"I could have."

"This better be good. Real good. Like enough reason for me *not* to lock up your shell and play drums on that empty head of yours." Tolan wiped a hand across his mouth.

"There's been an apparent homicide." The

Genevan handed Tolan a data slate. "The Commodore wants your opinion. No one on the ship's seen anything like this before."

Tolan snatched the slate away and swiped across the screen. He stared at the image of Foster's bones in a pile of ash, then the next image of her skull crumbling away, then the last of a gray swath on the locker-room floor.

Tolan looked up at Thorvald. A ripple passed down the Faceless spy's body and he said, "We need to lock the ship down. Now."

****

Gage stalked into his quarters and slapped a hand on the control panel, locking himself away from the rest of his ship. The burning pit of despair next to his heart blossomed and he stumbled against his bed. He sat on the floor, his head buried in his hands.

Barlow. The *Retribution*. He'd left them behind. Condemned his friend and all the souls aboard to the Daegon.

He'd lost sailors before, had them die fighting besides him…but ordering Barlow, his friends since their days at the Academy felt like he'd been run through the heart with a poisoned needle.

"Was there another choice?" he half-whispered. "Could I…No. I am the commodore. I am responsible. I am responsible."

Gage lifted a foot and kicked his nightstand and sent it rolling across the deck. Data slates, paper bound books and a framed photo spilled out. There was a crack of breaking glass as the frame bounced off the wall.

The commodore tamped down on the emotions raging in his body and mind, then picked up the picture: his mother and father on their wedding day. His father wore his navy uniform and new ensign bars, his mother looked radiant in her alabaster dress. A crack ran through the glass over his father.

In a way, he'd never met either of them. His father died in battle before Gage was born. His every memory of his mother was that of a despondent woman that never recovered from her grief. She'd sent him away to boarding school at a young age and barely kept in contact with him. She'd passed away while Gage was in his teens.

"Must carry on," Gage said, echoing his mother every time he'd shared a problem. "I bear the mantle of command. I break and the fleet will fall apart."

A chime sounded over his door. Gage glanced at a screen on his forearm, didn't see any urgent or life threatening messages, and ignored the visitor.

A fist pounded on the door.

"I bet he's drunk," Tolan's voice carried through the door. "I bet he's drunk and you don't have the balls to hit him with that same bullshit you gave me." Tolan knocked again, louder.

"You know this is important, override the door," Tolan said to someone on the other side.

"There is no immediate danger," Thorvald grumbled. "I must give him another four minutes before I open the door. That is protocol."

"You think there's no immediate danger? I thought we paid you to be paranoid. Does that tin can of yours come with a stick that you…"

Gage righted the nightstand and stowed away the mess as the bickering continued just outside his door.

"Enter," Gage said, his mask of command back in place.

****

"It's called nihilum in the Faceless trade," Tolan said as he tossed the data slate with Foster's final picture onto the deactivated holo tank. Gage, Price, and Thorvald stood around the circle with the spy. "They use it to cover their tracks during an infiltration. Stops anyone from bumping into themselves, which tends to make carrying out a contract that much more difficult."

"Is that the only explanation?" Price swallowed hard.

"I'm certain of it," Tolan said. "I've seen this too many times to mistake it for anything else."

"Then we have an infiltrator," Gage said. "The ship is under combat conditions. Every air lock is sealed. Section chiefs are under instruction to keep their sailors in sight at all times, travel in three-man teams when necessary. Which doesn't strike me as a permanent solution."

"It will slow him down," Tolan said, "but it's hard to tell how much damage he's already done."

"Must have come aboard with the Harlequins," Price said.

"No." Tolan shook his head. "Operating as a Faceless is expensive. Someone has to pay for a contract and there's no one on Sicani that would shell out that sort of coin to hurt us—we were leaving. The problem of our presence was solved. Also, Faceless don't take suicide missions. There are far cheaper options for that sort of wet work."

"What are you getting at?" Thorvald asked.

"Faceless will go after someone if it's personal, and that's what we've got here." Tolan tapped at a screen and a mug shot appeared in the holo tank. The face changed several more times before stopping at a man's head and shoulders so black they were almost a silhouette.

"Ja'war the Black," Tolan said. "Responsible for the Reuilly bombing way back when, a fact we only learned a few years ago. Ormond sent me and a team to wild space to hunt him down, which was a lot like looking for a needle in a haystack made out of needles."

"But you caught him," Gage said.

"I did. And I brought him back to Albion in irons and threw him in the dungeon," Tolan gave Thorvald a quick look, "before the brief trial he didn't deserve. Where the Daegon must have found him and realized he's useful."

"He's here for you?" Thorvald asked.

"No. He came aboard with the Daegon assault torpedoes. Which means he's had the run of the place for several hours. If he wanted me dead, he would have come for me first. The Daegon turned him loose for another purpose."

"Prince Aidan." Gage shook his head.

"Salis and Bertram," Thorvald almost growled the steward's name, "are with the Prince. No one's been in or out of the Prince's quarters since before the first assault ship attacked us on Gilgara."

"He's safe for now," Tolan said. "Ja'war won't make a move until he has an escape route and he doesn't have that while we're in slip space."

"How can you be so certain?" Price asked.

"Ja'war was our obsession for years. The team and I studied every contract he ever carried out. We played cat and mouse with him on more than one planet in wild space before we either got too close or he got tired of us." Tolan looked away. "Lost most of them on Uru IV. Hastings checked out after that."

The spy cleared his throat.

"So there I was, no kidding, all alone in the *Joaquim*, when I considered my options. Follow Hastings' example, return to Albion with my tail between my legs with nothing to show for the loss of my team but a few interesting stories…or keep after Ja'war. I wasn't ready to give up."

"That's when you became a Faceless," Gage said.

Tolan narrowed his eyes at the Commodore. "Smart man, sir. Smart man. I knew Ja'war as well as anyone in wild space, so I scrounged up some—not some, a lot of—money and," he waved his fingers in a circle in front of his face, "made a change. I didn't have the coin to go the full Monty of DNA mimicry and bone replacement like Ja'war, but I could get work as a Faceless. And that's when I hung my shingle out to the criminal element as Ja'war. Funny thing, Faceless can be anyone they want, but if you've got the right set of attributes, you can pose as any Faceless you want."

"You became a terrorist," Thorvald said.

"For hire, but doing jobs as Ja'war wouldn't have helped me find him. Instead, I took a contract, got my half up front…and then managed to botch every job. Assassination targets got off with a good scare and a hint who hired me. Industrial espionage swipe? The employer got a data rod full of naughty comic strips. After a while…word got around that the good name and sterling reputation of Ja'war the Black had a few smudges."

"He came looking for you," Gage said.

"That he did." Tolan frowned slightly. "My faux Ja'war persona had built up a reputation for being sloppy and he was rather perturbed with the situation. He infiltrated a high-rise where I'd laid a trap and my crawfish nailed him. Rather embarrassing for someone like him to go down to something so elementary. If you've never seen ten taser drones mob a person before, I suggest you give it a watch, so satisfying."

"Then you brought him to Albion for trial and the Daegon found him in the Intelligence Ministry's holding cells." Gage leaned back from the table. "Now he's on this ship murdering my crew."

"Every department and section performed a head count," Price said. "No discrepancies reported. None of the dead or missing from the last Daegon attack have been seen either. The sailors that found the body in the lockers don't recognize the woman they saw after we had them go through head shots from personnel files."

"We call it a feint," Tolan said. "Human beings evolved to recognize faces. Change a few details here and there for a few minutes, then snap back to the set identity."

"How do we catch him?" Thorvald asked.

"What's more important right now is to figure out what he's already done." Tolan rubbed his chin. "Let's assume Prince Aidan is his target. Ja'war needs to get him off this ship and to the Daegon. Have separate crews go through key systems—engines, life support. Lock down the escape pods. Spike the shuttles and fighters."

"We might need the life pods and our void wing," Price said.

"You want a solution, I'll give you a solution. There's no sugarcoating or half-measuring out of this. Ja'war is as capable and as cunning as any Faceless that's ever lived," Tolan said.

"A DNA sweep?" Thorvald asked. "The ship's military police have crime-scene equipment. If we test every crewman against the medical database…"

"Sweepers read from skin cells and saliva," Tolan said. "Ja'war's body has had enough time to mimic his latest identity. He only needs," the spy glanced at a clock, "another twenty minutes before his blood morphs to match his last victim. The only medical way we'll find him is through vivisecting the crew one by one."

"This 'feint' you mentioned," Thorvald said, "how different could he look from his current identity? The information suggests he was caught off guard when the other sailors arrived in the locker room."

"Facial features…" Tolan's eyes lit up. "Not sex or height or skin color…you might be onto something."

"The two of you are in charge of finding

Ja'war," Gage said. "Price and I will work out how to get Prince Aidan off the ship safely."

"Salis and Bertram are with the Prince," Thorvald said. "No one else must come near them. The Genevan Houses are well versed in hunting down infiltrators, though Faceless rarely travel beyond wild space."

"Shell head and I will figure something out," Tolan said. "Just so you know, Commodore, if you lift the lockdown, Ja'war will use that as a chance to switch faces. At least, that's what I would do."

"The lockdown remains in effect," Gage said. "I don't like holding information back from the crew, but if we tell them there's a mimic on board, the paranoia will hurt us more than anything until we reach the nebula. Find him and destroy him."

CHAPTER 15

Hanging from the ceiling by a single arm, his feet barely able to touch the ground, Barlow drifted in and out of consciousness. Pain erupted across his body from time to time, emanating from the collar tight around his neck. Sometimes he felt knives skirt across his skin. Other times the band tightened to the point he couldn't breathe, then loosened just before he lost consciousness. His handless right arm hung slack against his side, the stump cauterized into an ugly black mass.

Time had lost any meaning. He existed only in

alternating periods of agony and dread.

The chain loosened and Barlow sank to the floor, a cold grate that reeked of old blood. He heard the door to his cell slide open but didn't bother to look up. The few seconds of rest were jewels beyond price.

A pair of ornate blue sabatons stopped in front of his face and then a hand gripped him by the elbow and sat him up against an ice-cold bulkhead.

Tiberian looked into Barlow's eyes. He snapped his fingers and a warm sensation flowed through Barlow's body, melting away the pain. Barlow's head lolled to one side and his eyes lost focus.

"We're going to play a game," the Daegon said. "The torque knows you. The torque knows when you lie, when you hold back. Speak wholly and truthfully and the torque will reward you.

Understand?"

Despite his brief foray into bliss, Barlow managed to look at the Daegon and spit on the floor.

A shock sent the Albian into convulsions. The assault ended and Barlow struggled to breathe.

"You have only a few seconds to answer any of my questions, or the torque will do that again. Do you understand the rules of our game?"

"Yes," Barlow said. He dug his chin against his chest, waiting for the next onslaught, but the band around his neck merely vibrated slightly.

"Good. Where is your fleet running to?"

Barlow's mind raced, thinking of an answer as the torque grew hot.

"Ceylon!" he spat. "We have a treaty with the—" His response ended in a gurgle as the torque sent a spike of pain down his back. He curled against the bulkhead, a scream trapped in his lungs.

Tiberian tapped a finger in the air and the pain ceased.

"This is not a game you can win, Commander Barlow. I will not let you die. I will rip your body apart until you are begging to tell me every last detail of your life. There is no escaping this. Now, I will ask again. You either answer truthfully or I will leave you to the torque for hours until I return to ask again. Where is your fleet going?"

Barlow began hyperventilating. Electricity arced from the collar and stung his cheek.

"The Kigeli Nebula," Barlow said quickly as tears rolled down his face and a deep feeling of shame settled onto his shoulders. "The Harlequins will lead us through to Indus space."

"How will they navigate the nebula?"

"I-I don't know." Barlow shrank back from his interrogator. "Loussan said he had the way. Gage never explained it. Just told us to hold a close formation once we came out of slip space."

Tiberian grabbed Barlow's right arm and lifted it up gently. The Daegon looked over Barlow's stump.

"Prince Aidan lives?" Tiberian asked.

"Yes." Pain twitched through Barlow's left arm as the torque sensed he was holding something back. "On the *Orion*. He's on the *Orion*."

"Have any of the other Albion royals survived?"

"No. Not that I know. The Genevans got Aidan off world. That's it."

"Good." Tiberian dropped Barlow's incomplete arm. "Now you will tell me everything you know about Commodore Thomas Gage."

CHAPTER 16

Gage looked at the Kigeli Nebula from the view screens on the *Orion*'s bridge. Vast bands of orange- and honey-colored gas filled the void. Tiny pinpricks of protostars shone like pearls through the nebula's fog and the horizon of an ice planet stretched across the bottom of the screen.

"Conn, what are we looking at?" Gage asked.

"We're at a nexus point over a rogue planet," the lieutenant said. "We're maybe a quarter light-year from nebula front. Sensors read a few nexi near gravity wells from planetoids with mass levels near

Mercury and Mars. Not that uncommon to find this sort of thing outside a stellar nursery. The bow wave from a supernova or passing micro-singularity can scatter a solar system to—"

"Thank you," Gage said, "but how do we get through the nebula?"

"We could do a hard bore, but all the gas will leach power from the drives. Doubt we could go more than a dozen AU at a time before we have to recharge. But it won't matter, as there's enough asteroids and comets in the nebula that we're almost guaranteed to hit something the drive shields can't mitigate and the impact will rip the ship to very small pieces and scatter us through the nebula…sir."

The lift opened, and Thorvald led a shackled Loussan out onto the bridge.

"Commodore Gage, I must say you are a poor host." Loussan tugged at the chains binding his wrists to his waist. "I am a fellow captain and not some common criminal. At least you allowed me some dignity and kept your crew from gawking at me as your hired gun waddled me up here from the brig—which I am not impressed with, I should add. I've been in better."

"The security lockdown remains in effect," Thorvald said.

Gage motioned to a pair of naval police and they removed Loussan's shackles.

"You have another matter to attend," Gage said to the Genevan.

Thorvald gave the pirate a look, then grabbed a disk off his belt and slapped it against Loussan's lower back.

"Crawfish," Thorvald said to one of the MPs. "Light him up if he steps out of line." He went back to the lift, pointed fingers at his eyes, then turned the fingertips to Loussan as the doors shut.

"He's fun," the pirate said, rubbing his wrists as the cuffs came off.

"This is the Anchor, I presume," Gage said. "What's the next step?"

Loussan hopped up on the command dais and tapped a panel. He tapped it a second time, then a third, and gave Gage a disappointed look.

Gage walked up next to Loussan, the corner of his mouth pulled into a half-sneer.

"Needs must," Gage said and put his palm against a panel. "Tank, set to general access. Command authority to biometric authorization."

"Now I'm at the helm of my very own Albion battleship." Loussan cracked his fingers and began typing.

"Don't push it," Gage said.

"There's more than one way through Kigeli.

Watch." The entire nebula, a segment several light-years in volume, appeared in the holo, the fleet's location pinging at the bottom. White lines bounced from the Anchor like cracks in a broken pane of glass up through the nebula to a point in open space. Additional routes appeared from the other rogue planets, some intersecting with the jagged path starting at the Anchor.

"The Harlequins have a grav-buoy network through the nebula. We'll make short slip jumps from one to the next. I have to access the buoys at each jump, so best get used to me being up here. Perhaps my own chair?" Loussan asked.

Gage stared at the man.

"Well, if I don't ask, the answer is definitely 'no.'" Loussan accessed the laser communication array and directed a beam down to a mountain range on Anchor. A connection established and Loussan typed out a long code. The connection flashed green and navigation data flooded into the holo tank.

Branches on the pathways from Anchor through the nebula fizzled out, stopping three-quarters of the way through at a dashed line connecting to a point with a solid path through the rest.

"That's...not as bad as I feared," Loussan said. "The buoy on terminus seventeen was always a little flaky. The problem's either in the relay or the buoy's readers. Either way, we can still make it through. Just have to do a bit of maintenance when we get there. Kick it a few times."

"What's the margin of error for transit?" Gage asked. "With all the stray rocks in there, my ships stand about as much chance as a bubble floating through a thorn bush."

"Tight, but not impossible." Loussan lifted

data from the holo and tossed it up. A mock-up of the 11th rearranged itself into an oblong formation, barely a few hundred meters between ships. "Your navigators can handle this?"

"That's well within minimum safe distance," Jellico said.

"But you can do it?" Gage asked her.

"It's iffy, sir," she said. "There's a risk of collision during slip transition. Push the formation out another ten percent and it's more manageable."

"You expand and the outer ships might smack into a rock," Loussan said. "The buoys can read a dangerous object on the ley lines—can give us a jump solution around it—but we're threading a needle tighter in some parts than others."

"We'll take the least risky option where and when we can," Gage said. "Plot our course."

****

"The *Ajax*, *Valiant*, and *Stiletto* need time to mitigate battle damage," Price said to Gage. The three ships floated in the holo tank, each with several systems highlighted in blinking amber. "We've been going essentially nonstop since Siam. The entire fleet could benefit from two or three days at anchor. Else we run the risk of…the *Retribution*."

"I'm aware," Gage said.

"I spoke with the *Hephaestus'* captain. She could have the void docks and factories set up within six hours. Repairs done in less than two days for the critical issues," Price said.

"Have you ever sent a ship to void dock and come out on schedule?" Gage asked.

"No, sir. The dock always finds something else that needs to be fixed or they break the rest of the ship in the process of fixing what's already offline."

"This nebula is a decent place to hide, but I'd rather have more distance between us and the Daegon than not."

"Commodore?" Ensign Clarke at the communications station stood up. Gage waved him over. He hurried, face pale, lips white.

"What is it?" Price asked.

"I went through our logs," he tapped a screen and a list scrolled through the holo tank, "checking to make sure our laser comms aren't back scattering off any of the receivers, and I found this."

He opened a single message and a jump equation came up.

"It's the same data Loussan gave us to leave Anchor," Clarke said, "but it didn't go to any of our ships. It went to the nexus points over the other rogue planets that side of the nebula, and according to the time stamp, it went out seconds before we entered slip space."

"Loussan was on his way back to the brig," Price said.

Gage felt dread build in the pit of his stomach and pulled up the map through the nebula. Three worlds near Anchor had routes to their first stop—much shorter routes.

"The Faceless," Gage said.

"Someone must have set up a splitter in the antennae array," Clarke said. "Recorded the information and sent it out manually. I never would have found it if I hadn't gone through the logs manually."

"He told the Daegon where we're going," Gage said. He looked over the map, then tapped his chin. "But this could be an opportunity. Get Thorvald and Tolan back up here."

****

Tolan rolled a crawfish tube around his hand and felt a tug on his mind. The urge was there, a scratch to return to his quarters and have another go at the Dizzy the Martian had given him. He grimaced, willing his face to hold steady for a bit longer.

He looked back at Thorvald and a trio of armed naval police. All had their backs to the bulkheads like Tolan.

The Genevan touched the side of his helm, and the armor closed around his face.

"Teams B and C are set," he said.

"You almost sound excited," Tolan said.

"The discovery of the lamprey device on the

antennae array was a clue to Ja'war's activity on board," the bodyguard said as he powered up his pistol. "That none of the crew with access to the antennae fit the general description of Ja'war when he left the locker room means he's assumed another identity."

"Kind of a rookie mistake," Tolan said. "A Faceless can be many people, but he can only be one place at a time." He raised a communicator to his ear. "Bridge, ambush element in place. Go for head count."

"Now hear this! Now hear this!" boomed through the ship's public-address system. "All section heads conduct immediate personnel accountability checks. I repeat…"

"Five minutes is the standard to send a thumbs-up or down?" Tolan leaned forward from the bulkhead and asked the armsmen.

"That's right," one said.

"This is the only passage open to the antennae array," the spy said. "Ja'war's going to be in a hurry to get back to the commo section to get counted or in a hurry to leave the commo section and get counted somewhere else."

Thorvald raised a stun pistol in his other hand. "You sure we can subdue him? I was taught the Faceless are more resilient than average people."

"I'm not so confident in this plan that we shoot anyone that comes down that passageway in the head without question or hesitation," Tolan said, "but a couple crawfish hits or stun bolts will put him down. He can't keep his face under that kind of trauma. *Then* we shoot him in the head with real bullets."

"Don't take him alive?" one of the armsmen asked.

"I made that mistake once," Tolan said. "I don't aim to repeat it."

"Movement in the passageway," an armsman said as he looked up from a handheld screen. "Coming right for us."

Tolan heard the thump of boots striking the deck at a run. The sound grew faster, almost discordant.

"Three personnel," the armsman said.

"Crap." Tolan looked down at his belt and drew his second—and last—crawfish. The sound of footfalls grew closer.

"We need to see which fits the description before we subdue Ja'war," Thorvald said.

"No, you imbecile, stun all three or he'll—"

Thorvald stepped around the corner and raised his pistols.

"Halt!" the Genevan shouted.

Tolan flipped the safety cap off a crawfish and joined the armsmen as they ran out and blocked the passageway.

Three crewmen in helmets and engineering coveralls stood in the passageway. All had their hands up, and one struggled to hold a case up by the handle.

"Commo just reported a power spike in their main conduit," said the female sailor with the case. "We were counted. Chief sent us over with the replacement part. You want to hurry up before the whole array gets fried?"

Tolan flicked the safety off his second crawfish.

"Helmets off," Thorvald ordered.

"I'll get left and middle," Tolan said. "You get right. On three."

"I have this under control," the Genevan said.

Two of the engineers popped off their

helmets. One was male, the other female and almost the same height and description as Ja'war when he left the locker room. The sailor with the case struggled to get her helmet off with only one hand.

"Has to be either middle or the other woman," Tolan whispered. "I'll take them both down." He shook the two crawfish and felt the drones inside hum to life.

"This thing's too heavy," the engineer with the case said. "Mind if I—"

The case emitted a high pitch.

"Down!" Tolan turned and leapt around the corner as the case exploded. A wave of overpressure smacked his head against the deck and sent stars blazing past his eyes. He rolled over onto his back, ears ringing.

The ship swirled around him and the smell of seared meat and copper wafted over him. He coughed and struggled to sit up. Two of the armsmen lay crumpled against the bulkhead, and he saw the feet of the third down the passageway. The bulkheads had a red tinge, and dark bits of sludge oozed to the deck.

Tolan saw one of his crawfish lying a few feet away. He crawled toward it, the sounds of emergency sirens and men groaning in pain growing louder as his ears recovered. He reached for the crawfish, and a boot slammed down onto his hand, pinning it to the deck.

Challons looked down at the spy with disgust, then his face morphed to obsidian.

"Pathetic," Ja'war said.

Tolan heard the rattle of Thorvald's armor from behind.

Ja'war picked up the crawfish and hurled it at the Genevan. The drone inside snapped from the case and latched on to Thorvald's chest. Electricity arced out of the drone and locked up Thorvald's armor, freezing him like a statue. He tilted forward and smashed the crawfish against the deck with his bulk.

The Genevan didn't move.

Ja'war grabbed Tolan by the throat and hoisted him into the air.

"You think you could catch me in something so simple? So basic?" Ja'war snapped.

"Sort of," Tolan gagged as Ja'war's grip tightened.

"*I* am the greatest assassin the galaxy's ever known. After this, no one will know what you did to me." Ja'war tossed Tolan to the deck and drew a pistol.

Behind Ja'war, the plates on Thorvald's armor shifted away from his spine, revealing bare flesh beneath.

"Whoa, whoa!" Tolan held his hands in front

of his face and shrank back like a hand-shy dog. "You think those Daegon give a crap about your reputation? They're not the covert-action types. We Faceless are for jobs without attribution, without any suspects. You think they need or want us in their world?"

"A contract must be carried out, and you are no Faceless," Ja'war said. "You are a poor imitation," Ja'war rolled his head in a circle, and his voice changed to match Tolan's, "but you'll do."

Tolan let half his face go slack, almost dropping from his skull. Ja'war's face mimicked Tolan's and the assassin growled.

"Want to imitate me to get around the ship now?" Tolan pulled the other side of his face into a rictus grin. He watched from the corner of his eye as Thorvald rose out of his armor, naked but for a skintight wrap around his waist. The Genevan picked up a pistol.

"Now who's the imitator?" Tolan asked.

Ja'war shifted back to his Challons guise.

"I was going to make it quick." Ja'war lowered his pistol to Tolan's stomach when a shot rang out and Ja'war stumbled forward. He half-turned and fired blind as he made for a turnout of the passageway.

Tolan heard a grunt of pain from Thorvald, then Ja'war swung his pistol toward the spy as he rounded the corner. Tolan rolled as Ja'war fired and fire erupted in his right thigh.

Tolan yelped and slammed his hands against the bullet wound while blood spurted from his fingers.

Thorvald, one hand against his own bullet wound on his side, lurched forward. The bodyguard looked all too vulnerable without his armor and blood trickling down his side.

"Help me," Tolan said. "I'm bleeding worse than you are."

The Genevan slowed to a stop, then turned back to his armor lying on the deck. He raised a hand and the armor reformed. The hollow suit crawled toward Thorvald, then froze solid.

"No. Don't abandon me…" Thorvald fell to a knee, then collapsed to the deck.

Tolan heard shouts and felt the vibration of more of the *Orion*'s crew coming for them. He felt a chill creep up his limbs and his mouth smacked with thirst.

"Not dying today," Tolan said. "Not today…"

****

Clarke braced himself against the casing of the

antennae array and shimmied up another foot. The inside of the array was not as tight as a coffin, he assured himself, but there sure wasn't room for anyone else in here.

The last time he'd done a chimney sweep, as commo sailors called any trip through the inner workings of the ship's array, he'd been a very junior sailor. He'd worked hard to get promoted away from jobs that involved very tight places and the risk of electrocution if all the systems weren't shut down properly. That he was doing this as the *Orion*'s senior communications tech would have irked him to no degree if the situation was different.

"Come on, where are you…" he said. He edged up again and found a black box bolted to one of the data lines.

"Bingo." He took a data slate from his belt and ran a line to the box. The slate lit up and text scrolled across. "Split command file...check. Looks like you've got multiple injects. Don't have to go back to the same place to send data. Smart. Decent setup. I'm almost impressed."

The bang of a wrench against the inside of the array carried through the metal.

"Yeah, short window of opportunity. Nice setup you've got here, Mr. Terrorist Guy. Sure would be a shame if someone were to...hack it."

CHAPTER 17

Gage gripped the railing around the command dais as the *Orion* came out of slip space.

The orange haze of the nebula surrounded the ship and slight waves of static floated across the shields. A dark, uneven circle loomed in the distance and a protostar lit up the far right of the screen like a spotlight in fog.

Loussan raised his arms and said, "Ladies and gentlemen, the Ring of Fire."

"Spare the theatrics and access the buoy," Gage said. "I don't like the look of this place."

"As you shouldn't." The pirate shook a finger.

"The Ring is a bit of a bastard. Might have become a planet, but some collision stopped that from happening. Now she takes that frustration out on passersby."

"Loussan…" Gage put a hand to his face.

"Set course through the Ring," the pirate said. "Straight down the middle. That's the only place we'll get line of sight to the buoy and get our next jump solution."

"Sir," Jellico said, looking up from her screens, "the radiation from the protostar's scattering through all the silicate near the toroid."

"Toroid?" Loussan asked.

"The Ring," Gage said quietly.

"Yes, I knew that."

"Sensors are useless beyond a few hundred meters, and from what little I can pick up, the risk of an asteroid strike is extremely high," Jellico said.

"We normally man point defense cannons and run shields through here," Loussan said. "And we always get a few dings, sometimes worse. Expect to lose ship-to-ship comms as well. We can regroup inside the Ring."

"Sir," Jellico said meekly, "would you like to know the odds of navigating through this without serious damage?"

"They don't matter." Gage ran his fingers down a screen and opened a channel to his fleet's ship commanders.

****

An asteroid the size of a city bus tumbled through the nebula, leaving a faint whirl in the thin gas as it arced toward the *Orion*. An energy bolt snapped past, leaving a streak of superheated plasma in its wake. A second bolt shattered the asteroid, blasting it across the heavens. Fragments rained down on the *Orion*'s shields, one hunk the size of a suitcase making it through the shields, which had been weakened by the deluge.

The hunk smacked against the hull, then bounced up and struck the bridge. Gage ducked aside as the asteroid broke against the view port, leaving a spider web of cracks behind.

"Another hit to starboard," Price said. "Hull buckling on decks seven and twelve."

The forward cannons fired, straight lines tracing out of the weapons and into the nebula, where twin explosions erupted deep within the haze. The lines dissipated, crumpling against the hull as the *Orion* advanced.

"We have a status update from the rest of the fleet yet?" Gage asked.

"Nothing," Jellico said.

"After point defense turrets report seeing shield strikes behind us," Price said. "All minor."

"Not a bad idea to lead with your largest ship," Loussan said. "Pushes the worst of the rocks out of the way of your smaller ships."

"That's not how the Harlequins came through here?" Gage asked.

"Oh no. Ships with the newest captain led the way, helped steel their nerves for a fight. Also helped us weed out the ships that didn't have their act together. You'd be surprised how hard crews would train when they heard they'd run the gauntlet through the Ring of Fire."

There was a bump as another asteroid struck the *Orion*.

"Flak's a bit heavier than I remember. For what it's worth," Loussan said.

CHAPTER 18

Thorvald sat up on his gurney, wearing nothing but his waist wrap, bags of fluid running into IVs on one arm. He felt an itch from the new tissue and skin filling his bullet wound. The injury had been easy enough to repair, but the pain was nothing compared to the sense of loss gnawing at his heart.

His armor lay on a surgical table next to him, the arms and legs straight, the whole thing flattened, like it had deflated.

A shadow limped toward the curtain hiding Thorvald from the rest of the med bay, and Tolan peeked around a corner, then let himself in with a swish of the curtains. The spy had a gel bandage over his thigh and munched on a ration stick.

"Well...shit," Tolan said.

"Are you really here to gloat?" Thorvald asked.

"I'm wondering when you'll stop moping around and get your stuff back on."

"It's not a matter of desire," the Genevan said. "Your crawfish disrupted my bond with the gestalt. It barely accepted me before. When I pulled myself out to try to kill Ja'war...the gestalt took it as a rejection."

"Awful moody for something designed to stop bullets." Tolan raised a hand to tap the armor on the foot, then reconsidered when Thorvald tensed up.

"I don't expect you to understand."

"We're not exactly back to square one on

Ja'war, but we're close," Tolan said, biting off a hunk of his ration bar. "Bullet wounds always make me hungry."

"If you were Ja'war, what would you do next?"

"I'd wait. He's not going to get to Aidan while we're in slip space. He needs the opportunity to get him off the ship and hand over the Prince…or he needs to get the Daegon onto this ship so they can take him." Tolan nodded his head slowly.

"You're coming up with something," Thorvald said. "The last idea you had cost six lives."

"Well, I'm not one to sit around feeling sorry for myself, especially when there's someone determined to kill me potentially around every corner," Tolan said. He gave the gurney with Thorvald's armor a quick shake, testing the weight.

"I will try to reconnect to my armor once the

system cycles down…which will be hours from now."

"No time to wait. How about we you find some clothes first?"

****

Thorvald, dressed in a crewman's overalls three sizes too small, pushed a covered food cart down a narrow passageway. An armsman followed close behind.

The Genevan stopped at a sealed air lock and waited as the door slid open. He rushed the cart through and the door shut right behind the armsman.

"Three seconds to get through," the guard said, "three different sets of doors. That other one of you doesn't fool around."

"She's being lenient," Thorvald said as he pushed the cart forward with a slight heave and stopped outside the Admiral's quarters.

"Thank you, sirs," Bertram said through a speaker over the door. "We do appreciate the fresh food."

"Get Salis." Thorvald looked up at the camera.

"You know the protocol," the woman said a moment later. "Leave so I can scan the—Thorvald?"

"*Bainvegna, Grisoni Salis,*" Thorvald said.

"*Tgau,* Thorvald."

"What the heck?" the armsman asked.

"While Ja'war could look like any of us, it's unlikely he can speak Genevan with my accent," Thorvald said.

The door to Aidan's quarters snapped open and Salis wrapped her arm around the door and aimed a pistol at the armsman's forehead.

"Prove yourself," she said.

"We met beneath the castle." Tolan let his guise slip just a tad. "Aidan had a teddy bear. We must have dropped it before we got onto my ship, the *Joaquim*."

Salis aimed her pistol toward the ceiling.

"Hurry in," she said.

****

A glut of cold air from the vent overhead washed over his shoulders. That Thorvald felt the temperature change through his borrowed coveralls made him feel even worse. He looked at the food cart covered with a tablecloth. His armor lay beneath.

For decades, he served the Albion royal family, wearing his old armor day in and day out, removing it only for maintenance to its systems and to the neuro-wire system beneath his skin that bonded him to the gestalt within the suit. His armor was taken from him when Captain Royce accused him of violating his oaths. Taking on the dead captain's armor during the Daegon assault on the palace had been an act of desperation, one the armor's gestalt barely agreed to.

Now, after the damage from the Faceless' ambush and Thorvald breaking out of the armor to save Tolan, the gestalt refused to acknowledge him.

He heard the heavy footfalls on carpet moving across the adjoining room, and Salis stopped in the doorway. That she, a neophyte guard that donned her armor for the first time days before the Daegon attack, bore her armor and he did not only strengthened his self-loathing.

"Anything?" she asked, nodding at the cart.

"The gestalt is off-line. It is still alive, but it will not speak to me. Older AIs grow temperamental.

That it was bonded to Royce the moment he died…rarely can a gestalt recover without going back to the forges on Geneva. How I bonded with it, severing to save that…spy. I've done everything wrong. It may never accept me again."

"None of your decisions were done for yourself," she said. "Each time you acted for the good of others, for your oaths. Regret is not for you."

"Look at this…" Thorvald held up his arms, then touched a hand to his chest. "Weakness. I am just a man now. The burden falls to you to protect the Prince and the Commodore."

"Did you forget what you learned at our House when you took off the armor? Did you not go through the years of unarmored training before you were bonded? All those years on Albion protecting our charges and now you're nothing? Nothing but an old fart with several million francs in cybernetics beneath his skin."

"Who are you calling 'old,' fish? But you have a point. My oath said nothing of serving with my gestalt and armor." He rapped knuckles against his chest. "I can still take *a* bullet."

The pitter-patter of little feet approached and Salis rolled her eyes.

"It is your turn to get him water, or tuck him in, or whatever he wants now," she whispered.

Aidan peeked around Salis' waist.

"What is that?" the boy asked.

"My armor is…resting," Thorvald said.

"You look funny in those clothes," Aidan said.

Thorvald huffed.

"I want to be a knight. Can I wear the helmet?" He tapped Salis on the side of her leg.

Thorvald slid the sheet off the cart. The body

of his armor was folded into a neat square, the gauntlets, boots, and helmet sitting on the second shelf.

Aidan maneuvered past Salis and knelt to examine the helmet. The face visor was in place, a dark line cutting across the eyes and down the center.

"Captain Royce never let me play with this. I told Mama to make him, but she said no." Aidan touched the visor and left a smudge. He grasped it with his tiny hands and tried to lift it, but dropped it with a clatter against the metal.

"So heavy." He looked at Salis.

"The armor carries itself," she said, "otherwise, Thorvald and I would become very tired."

"Why does Mr. Thorvald look so sad?" Aidan asked.

"A long day of…big person problems,"

Thorvald said. "Go back to bed, my lord. You need your sleep."

"But I'm scared. The silly man told Mr. Berty that there's someone without a face looking for me," Aidan said.

"You are perfectly safe while we're…" Thorvald felt a hum through his neuro-wires. A faint glow lit the inside of his helmet.

"*Prender el davent*," he said in Romanish.

Salis scooped Aidan up and carried him back to his room, the boy protesting loudly along the way.

The armor's torso lifted up. The arms rose, like it was a set of clothes worn by an invisible man, and plugged into the gauntlets. The armored fingers clicked as they opened and closed into fists. The armor lifted up one side and kicked out a leg that ended just below the knee, then the other. It snapped the boots on with a twist, then stood up.

It put its helmet back on, then went still, arms and legs locked tight at the position of attention. The hollow armor looked like it was meant for a man with a smaller frame, better matched to the dead Royce than Thorvald.

Thorvald put a hand to the armor's shoulder and pressed the neuro-wire port on his palm against the metal.

+Ticino?+ he sent.

+Stay...away.+

Thorvald let go.

"Now that's some old-fashioned nightmare fuel," Tolan said from the doorway. "Good call getting the kid out of here."

"This has nothing to do with you," Thorvald said. "Leave."

Tolan leaned against the doorframe and crossed his arms. "So what's...going on here?"

"The gestalt learns...very slowly. They develop personalities, quirks. But their core programming remains—to protect. Aidan expressed fear. The gestalt responded."

"Interesting." Tolan raised a crooked finger and moved to tap the helmet.

"Don't," Thorvald said.

"Why, will it break my finger?"

"No, but I will."

Tolan lowered his hand.

"Just how smart is the ghost haunting that shell of yours? I might have an idea."

CHAPTER 19

Gage watched his fleet creep closer to the ring of stone and ice. At several hundred miles in diameter, the celestial body struck him as a kind of a portal. Once he led the 11th through, they'd be one step closer to safety.

Icons for the rest of the fleet trailed behind the *Orion* as the flagship used her shields and massed forward firepower to plow a path through the asteroids. From what little the sensors could read, the debris thinned considerably closer to the Ring.

"I don't envy you," Loussan said from one

side of the holo tank.

"Something tells me you never wanted to be an officer in the Albion Space Navy," Gage said.

"Hardly." He flung a bit of his long hair over a shoulder and leaned into the holo tank. "Sure, you have all the nice new toys, but life in the clans means a responsibility to yourself first and foremost, as no one will take care of you. Then you see to your ship. Then the crew. You…you've taken it all on. A mantle for this whole fleet, regency for a world that's—"

Gage gave the pirate a hard look.

"—occupied. I never carry any responsibility I can't walk away from if things become a tad untenable."

"Then why do men and women sign up to fight for you?" Gage asked.

"Money, mostly. All crews share equally in the spoils and I have a reputation for success, all but for a certain incident that you well know. Plenty of disreputable scumbags in wild space that'll void their crews after a score. I remain the right kind of disreputable—I'm practically a saint."

"You need to go back to wild space and stay there," Gage said. "There's no place for you in the core worlds."

"Well, don't think I'd really fit in with the proper types like you. Not exactly sure how things will go for me back home. Sworn oaths before the table is one thing. Losing my ship is another. And you should hear my crew complaining in the brig. Nothing but 'are they going to let us go' and 'why don't they serve beer with meals' and 'soon as we get Loussan away from Ruprecht, he's a dead man.'"

Gage raised an eyebrow.

"I haven't actually heard them say that last one, but I know they're thinking it."

A flash of white light broke from behind the *Orion*, lighting up the nebula like a cloud directly beneath the sun, and an alert popped up in the holo, toward the tail end of the line of ships.

"Comms," Gage said, looking into the bridge's workstations.

"Got a fragmentary message from the *Mukhlos*," the ensign said. "She took an asteroid strike to the cargo hull…sending it to your tank."

The holo zoomed in on one of the two cargo ships, their web of interconnected cargo pods wrapping around the long spine of the ship's axis like cloth around a bolt. The *Mukhlos* flashed amber and fell back from beside her sister ship, the *Helga's Fury*. The warship on the fleet's rear guard, the *Valiant*, slowed.

"Damn it," Gage said. The two ships carried a mountain of supplies and were essential to tending his fleet—once they were finally able to stop for repairs and refit.

"I've got a video network established to Captain Ricci," Clarke said. "The interference has cleared just a bit, but it won't be perfect."

A grainy screen appeared in the holo, and a heavyset man with a week's worth of beard looked up at Gage.

"Commodore, I've only got bad news," Ricci said. "Something got past the *Valiant*'s and my pitiful point defense. Hit the struts between demolition charge containers and one of the pods blew, which cracked my girl's spine and killed my engines. All my crew are in the forward section, so no casualties."

Gage felt the bridge crew's eyes turn toward him. He looked through the damage report and knew the ship was dead in space.

"Can anything be salvaged?" Gage asked.

"My drones are locked for transit and the cargo pods are breaking loose. They'll scatter like billiards once the webbing finally tears." Ricci shook his head. "But my crew and I would appreciate a pickup. All sixty of us."

"I'll have the *Valiant* pick you up," Gage said.

"Sorry, boss," Ricci said and cut the channel.

"Commodore," Price said from her seat just below the command dais, "forward scopes are picking up something."

"This day just gets better and better," Loussan said.

"The second you stop being value-added on my bridge is the second you go back to the brig," Gage snapped. "Send it, Price."

The holo tank shifted to the Ring, and an inner ring of icons for unidentified objects appeared.

"That's…new," Loussan said.

Gage zoomed in on a live camera feed from one of the *Orion*'s forward batteries. A deep-blue diamond hung in space, the object tilted to one side, revealing linked segments of a Daegon warship.

"They beat us here," Gage said. There were fewer than two dozen Daegon ships, and none were the battleship-equivalent he'd encountered Tiberian on before.

"I'd say it's impossible, but I'll believe my own eyes. They must have hacked the buoy at Anchor. I knew I should have upgraded the self-destruct systems," Loussan said.

"We can lay blame later." Gage touched the holo and pulled up possible courses through the Ring. That their jump data made it to the Daegon through the Faceless somewhere on board was none of Loussan's business. "Where's the buoy? Can we still jump out of here?"

"There," Loussan said, touching the inner edge of the Ring at the five o'clock position. "Need line of sight to access the buoy and pull the jump data."

"The next stop—you called it Sanctuary? Is there anywhere else we can go?"

"There's Razor Fist. Do you want to know why we call it that and why the place called 'Sanctuary' is a better option?"

"Pull both jump solutions. Don't argue. I'll explain later." Gage opened a channel to his fleet captains.

"11th, we have a fight on our hands. Here's the plan."

CHAPTER 20

Tiberian leaned over the side of his throne and looked at Barlow. The Albion captain sat against the throne, his upper body bare and shivering. A chain ran from the throne to around his waist, neck, and wrists. The Daegon hammered a fist against his armrest and his prisoner jerked as the pain torque sent a pulse through his body.

Barlow stood up slowly, stooping against the weight from the chains. Tiberian tapped a command out on his armrest, activating translation software in the torque so the prisoner could understand his—and the rest of his crew's—words.

"Sire," Barlow said, his face downcast and eyes staring at the chain.

"Your fellows see my picket ships." Tiberian grabbed Barlow by the jaw and turned his head toward a 3-D display on the bridge's far wall. The view from within the Ring changed every few seconds to different Daegon ships arrayed within. Daegon script appeared next to each Albion ship as they emerged from the nebula.

"Tell me, what will Gage do?" Tiberian raked a sharp nail down the side of Barlow's face, leaving a thin line of blood behind.

"He means…" the torque tightened around his neck, sensing hesitation, "he means to escape. There's a slip nexus nearby, yes? He'll try for that."

Gustavus stepped around the throne and drew his sword, setting the flat of the blade on

Barlow's shoulder.

"This one is worthless," Gustavus said. "The nexus is well beyond the asteroid, yet Gage and his fleet are on course to skirt the outer edge where he'll come within range of our ships. He could avoid them entirely if he set course around incomplete moon. This is not the action of a man on the run. Let me throw this toy of yours into the pits for the thralls. Their aggression spikes are growing dull."

"His answer told me a great deal," Tiberian said. "Your fleet arrived at Anchor guided by a pirate?"

"Yes, sire, Loussan of the Harlequins."

"But we destroyed their ship," Gustavus said.

"Some, it seems, survived." Tiberian traced a circle on his armrest with a diamond-tipped nail on his gauntlet.

Barlow's spine felt like it was growing warmer,

growing into a red-hot poker. He gasped and fell to his knees.

"Hiding something?" Tiberian asked.

"A buoy!" Barlow spat. "There should be a grav buoy hidden somewhere. Loussan is the only one that can access it." The pain subsided and he collapsed to the cold deck.

"Order the ships to destroy the Ring," Gustavus said. "Trap them here and finish them."

"Gage will die before he lets us take the boy king, isn't that right, dog?" Tiberian jerked Barlow's chain and dragged him across the deck.

"That's correct, sire." Barlow stood up again. Tiberian turned off the translation device within the torque and Barlow winced in pain.

Tiberian turned a palm up and a straight line appeared. "All picket ships," he said, the line warbling with the inflections of his voice, "engage all Albion ships but do not destroy the *Orion*. Target her shields. Vessel Alpha one through three…bombard the inner ring. Split fire and converge at the six o'clock position."

"What about the rest of our ships? We're not far. We can destroy them in a few minutes," Gustavus said.

"We're not here to kill them all."

"I don't see how it matters if the boy lives or dies." Gustavus tapped his sword against his thigh in frustration.

"An insurrection rages on Albion." Tiberian leaned forward as the Albion fleet on the holo wall spread out and angled toward the bottom half of the ring. "The world is a jewel of natural beauty. The people, well educated and industrious. Baroness Asaria wants the world made compliant, not ground to dust. It takes a brute to destroy, young one. It takes a ruler to bend lesser to their will. We return with the boy, Albion's last hope will be lost. The planet will succumb to our rule and their compliance will be known through the rest of slave space.

"Albion will teach them that surrender is a better alternative than fighting to the bitter end. Then our crusade will accelerate as more worlds are taken whole, fewer ships lost, more thralls to the army. That is why the Baroness needs the boy. That is why we will not force Gage's hand into anything but surrender. Besides, we have another asset in play. Let's see if Ja'war is ready to deliver."

CHAPTER 21

Battle stations sounded around Ja'war as he ducked under a pipe. The explosive charge attached to his belt bumped against his thigh as he weaved through the cooling system servicing the main reactor.

The *Orion*'s engines and power plant were far better engineered than any other wild-space ship he'd ever been on. The redundancies built into the system were a challenge to understand, but once Ja'war realized the battleship was meant to withstand attack from without, not within, his task became easier.

He found a metal box nearly hidden between two wide pipes pulsing with heat. The fluid regulators controlled the flow of plasma around the fusion reactor. The loss of more than one sent the entire system into shutdown, and Ja'war had already rigged the other on this deck. He knelt and removed an explosive charge mixed from battery packs and grenade detonators he'd pilfered from an open arms room. He twisted the end cap once clockwise and a timer popped up on the tube. He twisted again and a red light pulsed.

"Foster!" someone called out. Ja'war heard footsteps pounding against the deck as the speaker ran toward him.

"Foster! They're calling us! Breach on deck four!"

"Be right there," Ja'war said, using the woman's voice. He slipped the charge behind the regulator and it mag-locked to the casing.

"What the hell are you doing?" Brown—that was his name—asked from the walkway at the end of the pipes.

"This regulator's reading a short and if I don't fix it, the whole thing will slag. You know how many man-hours that'll take to replace between these lava tubes?" Ja'war gave Brown an angry look.

"It *might* do that," Brown said and glanced at a screen on the back of his gauntlet. "And you haven't even cracked the case open to fix it." He tapped his forearm screen. "It's in the system. Meanwhile, we have actual problems to deal with. Let's go!"

Ja'war grumbled and squeezed past the pipes. His mind went through reasons to send Brown down here to repair the fault just before he blew it to hell.

****

Light flashed across the bridge as the shields took another hit.

"*Firebrand, Remorseless.*" Gage touched a Daegon ship moving toward the right of the inner ring. "This is your priority target. Stretch your legs and engage."

Loussan, who looked incredibly uncomfortable in an Albion vac-suit and helmet, leaned down to examine one of his screens.

"I need line of sight to the buoy hidden inside the Ring," the pirate said. "We're still too far away."

The Daegon ship that broke formation opened fire, bolts of energy streaking through space and crashing against the inside of the Ring. Boulders ejected from the impact and went hurtling through space.

"Guns, all forward firepower on the ship,"

Gage ordered.

In the holo tank, the two frigates raced ahead of the *Orion*. The spine lance on the *Firebrand* fired, and Gage shook his head. The shot streaked past the enemy ship assaulting the Ring, missing. The ship paused for a moment, then restarted the barrage, walking shots closer and closer to the hidden buoy.

"Conn, all ahead full. Take power from the shields if you have to, but we need to cross through the Ring," Gage said.

"Aye aye," Jellico said.

The *Remorseless* raced ahead of her sister ship and unleashed her own spine lance. The blast ripped down the side of the Daegon ship. The diamond points on the port side were shorn away and the ship bled air from a dozen cuts. The enemy vessel listed to the side, on a slow impact course with the Ring.

Torpedoes from the battle cruisers *Concordia*

and *Ajax* sailed over the *Orion* and activated. Laser warheads pounded a Daegon ship, which exploded in a flash of light. When the effects cleared away, the Daegon formation had broken apart.

Three ships headed toward the inner ring and opened fire. Gage looked at the distance his ship still had to cover to access the buoy and realized the Daegon would reach weapons' range well before he could get line of sight on the inner ring.

"*Remorseless*, *Firebrand*, engage those ships. We can't let them hit the buoy." Gage tapped the location within the ring and sent it to the frigate captains.

"Main gun's down for another ninety seconds," said the captain of the *Remorseless*. "But I think I can manage something."

"Thirty seconds," came from the *Firebrand*.

The *Remorseless* dove toward the inner ring, her ventral maneuver thrusters flaring and kicking her tail up and into her direction of travel. The engines fired and the ship came to a stop just over the buoy.

The three enemy ships opened fire, their shots converging on the *Remorseless*.

The *Firebrand*'s spine lance sent a searing green spear through one of the Daegon ships, piercing through the prow and exiting out the engines.

"Almost there," Loussan said.

The *Remorseless'* shields buckled under the onslaught. A hit broke through the hull over her forward point defense battery and blew out the bottom of the ship. The leading edge of the ship's prow broke away and went tumbling through the void.

"Conn, get us between the two enemy ships and the *Remorseless*," Gage ordered.

The *Orion* shifted beneath Gage's feet as the

battleship angled to one side.

The flagship's forward guns opened fire and pummeled one of the two Daegon ships. The shield popped with a flash of blue light and a pair of hits cracked the enemy ship in half.

The final ship lowered its shields and unleashed a torrent of fire at the *Remorseless*. The bolts left dying trails in their wake, then beat against the *Orion* as it took the punishment aimed at the badly damaged frigate.

Plasma bolts splashed against the *Orion*'s shields. An emitter buckled under the strain and a shot exploded against the hull. The *Orion* canted to one side as another shot came through the shield gap and annihilated a point defense turret in a brief fireball.

Gage's holo tank flickered.

A salvo from the *Renown* destroyed the final

Daegon ship, leaving nothing but an expanding cloud of gas and small fragments behind.

"My apologies." Captain Arlyss of the *Renown* came up in the holo tank. "Wanted a clean shot."

"Your judicious aim is appreciated," Gage said.

"Got it!" Loussan smacked a palm against the console. "Jump data going to your navigator now."

"And the second jump solution?" Gage asked. Loussan double-checked his screens and nodded. "Good. Send that to Clarke."

"Sir, more Daegon ships just appeared on the scope," Price said. "Moving to intercept."

"Never easy." Gage opened a channel to the stricken *Remorseless*. "Captain Bargia, what's your status?"

The frigate commander's profile picture came up on the console along with error messages from the damaged ship's communications systems.

"Engines are online, slip drive active." Bargia's words were muffled, his breathing labored. "Everything else is either on fire or off-line. We're conducting an emergency vent of the whole ship to get the fires under control."

"How long is the slip jump to the next waypoint?" Gage asked Loussan.

"Three hours," the pirate said.

"Bargia, complete your vent and enter slip space without delay," Gage said. "You'll have to make the whole trip without atmosphere, but your suits will last long enough. I'll have emergency crews standing by when you arrive."

"Aye aye," Bargia said, "my crew's tough. We'll manage just fine."

"Get into slip space. The fleet needs you and we are less without you."

"I'll pass that on. *Remorseless* out."

"Conn, how long until we can get out of here?" Gage asked.

"Two hundred eighty-five seconds until the jump solution is complete, sir."

Gage watched as more and more Daegon ships emerged from the nebula. None would enter weapons' range before his fleet could escape.

"They had us," Loussan said. "They could have packed their ships around the nexus point and we would've never stood a chance."

"Tiberian's not hunting for a trophy kill," Gage said. "He's after something more."

Ja'war, Gage thought. *The Daegon knows that monster's still in play. A poison on my ship that will bring us to our knees.*

"Tell me, Loussan," Gage said, "have you ever dealt with a Faceless before?"

****

Air rushed past Ja'war and through a rent just beyond a half-closed air lock. He could see the Ring as the *Orion* passed by, so close he could make out craters and a wrecked Daegon ship on the surface.

"Tell the team on deck six to shut their locks!" Ja'war shouted into his intercom as he and Brown heaved against a circular handle, moving the air lock shut inch by inch.

His intercom was a cacophony of conflicting commands from different deck bosses, none of whom seemed to have a fair grasp of what was happening to their ship or what it was doing.

"Are you actually trying?" Brown said as the flow of air lessened to a strong breeze.

Across the inside of her helmet, an emergency

message flashed across the glass.

PREPARE FOR SLIP JUMP

Ja'war gripped the wheel tighter and applied a good portion of the augmented strength that came with having an inhuman level of control over his musculature and shut the air lock door with a slam.

"Hot damn, must've been stuck," Brown said.

Ja'war ran toward a recessed control panel and pulled the trigger for his bombs off his belt. Dots ran in a circle on the touch screen, then flashed an error message. No connection to the bombs.

"All the blast doors," he said. The heavy doors were blocking his signal.

"What?"

"We need to report up that this door is sealed." Ja'war fought back anger. He had to keep his cover and composure for just a bit longer. He couldn't stop the *Orion* from leaving, yet, but he could keep the Daegon on their heels.

He entered an override command he learned from his time as Challons and accessed a hidden file that connected him to the splitter box hidden in the antennae array.

CHAPTER 22

"He's in!" Clarke shouted as Captain Price stalked toward his station.

"What part of 'keep this secret' didn't you understand?" the XO asked as she looked over Clarke's screen.

"Sorry, ma'am, just excited." Clarke watched as Ja'war, from his terminal within the ship, typed in commands. "He's sending it as a burst transmission. Wide spectrum. Guess he doesn't know where his spy master's hiding out there."

"Let it go through," Price said. "Just make

sure he's sending the wrong jump solution."

"Already got the bum data loaded…he's adding some free text. I don't know what it means," Clarke said. "Should I send it?"

"All of it."

Clarke tapped on his screen and a green TRANSMIT box appeared.

"Oh, I wish I could see their faces," Clarke said. "I'd just love to pop up and say 'Problem?'"

"You want to be on the Daegon ship when that happens?" Price asked.

"Well, no." The TRANSMIT box pulsed and Clarke touched it. "It's away."

"Commodore," Price called up to the command dais. Gage leaned around the holo tank to see her. "We've got our breathing room."

"Conn, engage the slip drives," Gage ordered.

****

Pins and needles traveled down Barlow's thigh as he huddled against Tiberian's throne. The Daegon crew ignored him completely while the ship traveled through slip space. Tiberian had remained on his throne, conversing with the other commander that enjoyed disturbing Barlow with his sword's edge.

Concentrate, Barlow told himself. *I'm an officer in the Albion Navy, the light against the darkness of wild space and beyond. I can still fight. Can still hurt them.*

He slowly raised his head. Tiberian's bridge was a circle, with workstations arrayed around the circumference. All the Daegon had the same eerie blue or green skin as Tiberian, but the bridge crew's armor was simpler. They each carried a helmet locked to their thighs when they walked around, which they snapped into a holder when they took their stations.

No unnecessary cross talk, no banter. Just focus.

Like a bloody Reich ship, Barlow thought. He tried to scratch his face…and waved the stump at the end of his right arm across his head. A bit of foil covered the end of his arm, applied by a Daegon after Tiberian had removed him from the torture chamber.

They'll keep me alive so long as I'm useful, he thought. *But this bastard gets his hands on Prince Aidan, I doubt they'll keep me around as a mascot.*

His ears rang and Barlow shrank into a fetal position.

"Dog," Gustavus kicked Barlow's bare feet, "I have questions."

"Sire." Barlow stood up, the chains around his neck and arms feeling heavier than ever.

"Do your ships have self-destruct protocols?" the Daegon asked.

"No, sire." The torque sent a lance of pain

through his stomach and Barlow doubled over. "Albion crews fight to the last. They do not take their own lives out of spite." The pain grew stronger, like a hot ingot was working through his gut. "We can overload the fusion cores. Burn out the engines."

Barlow took a ragged breath and lied, "The captains have no way of destroying their own ships." Sweat dripped down his face and he continued the lie. "Not unless they crash into something."

His ears rang and Gustavus moved away.

The pain subsided, and Barlow crumpled against the throne. Warmth spread from his heart to the rest of his body, and the constant pain of his injuries faded away.

He'd managed a half-truth through the torque's ministrations. While there was no command option from the captain to initiate self-destruct, a determined crew could flood their hull with oxygen and ignite the fusion reactors. The ensuing fireball would leave little of the ship behind. Or they could rig torpedo warheads to explode in their launch tubes.

Now. Now Barlow had a weapon he could use against the Daegon. A weapon he'd have to guard carefully.

The ship lurched as it dropped out of slip space and the bridge crew rattled off status reports, starting at the station just to the right of the holo wall and continuing from station to station clockwise.

Tiberian stood up, one hand on the hilt of the sword hanging from his belt, and walked down the steps circling his throne. In the holo wall, a small planetoid, volcanoes and molten rock active across its surface, hung in the distance. A ring of asteroids circled the moon. Dark spots speckled the orange nebula, and smaller rocks the size of destroyers danced around the planetoid.

One of the crew gave a terse warning, and an asteroid appeared as a holo projection overhead. It flashed several times and its projected course traced right through Tiberian's ship. The commander rattled off a series of orders, and the ship banked to one side and slid forward.

Slowly. Far too slowly.

Tiberian reached back, and a pack of escort ships appeared in the holo field. He grabbed one and hurled it at the incoming asteroid.

Barlow found a certain sense of tranquility as the escort ship raced to intercept the asteroid. His life was almost certainly forfeit no matter what happened in the next few minutes. That he could die along with so many Daegon was almost…quaint.

The escort ship didn't fire on the asteroid. Instead, she flared her engines and rammed into it, the ship crumpling like a cheap can as a fireball engulfed the asteroid. Large fragments of the broken asteroid emerged, still on a collision course with Tiberian's ship.

A hunk the size of a bomber crashed against the ship's port and shattered against the shields. The bridge jerked to one side, but Tiberian held his spot in front of the holo wall. More of the asteroid rained against the shields. A fragment of solid stone covered in steep spikes like a broken buzz-saw blade struck the prow of the ship and ripped through the shields.

The deck pitched up and sent Barlow flying. His chains went taut and he smacked against the deck. Pain, not from the torque, arced through his right shoulder. He rolled over and saw Tiberian next to a workstation. His ship hung in a holo field, a red pulsing gash along the prow.

His shoulder ached and Barlow winced as he looked at it and saw it was badly dislocated.

Tiberian stalked toward the prisoner, and Barlow tried to push himself away with his heels against the deck.

The Daegon slapped both hands against the injured shoulder, ignoring Barlow's pleading and snapping it back into place with a deft twist of his hands. Tiberian muttered a word and the pain torque grew warm as a wave of euphoria passed through Barlow's body.

"I don't…understand," he said.

"You serve. You are still useful," Tiberian said as he settled back into his throne. "This is our way. This is how it will be for your world, for all of humanity that submits to our rule."

Barlow didn't ask what the alternative was. He'd already had it in good measure.

****

Gage's arms tensed against his holo tank as the *Orion* emerged from slip space, the orange hues of the nebula filling the forward screens, a distant column of asteroids arrayed into a funnel stretching into the haze.

"Scope, any sign of the Daegon?" Gage asked.

"Negative, sir," Price said. "Sensors are still blunted by all the particles in the nebula, but the range here is better than our last stop. Ley line reads steady. If there was a fleet of Daegon on our tail, we'd see their bow wave in the nexus."

A message flashed on her screens.

"Captain Arlyss reports he's rescuing the crew of the *Remorseless*," she said. "He should have them all aboard the *Renown* in less than half an hour. We don't have the final damage report on her yet…that she managed to hold together through slip space is something of a miracle."

"Pull the fleet in close and put some distance between us and the nexus," Gage said. "Not a lot of room to maneuver here, but I don't want us in a knife fight the instant the Daegon come through. Speaking of which…" Gage turned to Loussan. "How long will it take them to double back?"

"Twelve, maybe sixteen hours if we're lucky," Loussan said. "Razor Fist isn't that far from the Ring. We can skip out of here before they catch up. Sanctuary is a bit easier going. We're two stops away from clearing this whole mess, but the slip transit to the next point is difficult. There's a dead star skirting the edge of the nebula a few light-years away eating up gas and playing hell with the jump calculations."

"He's right," Jellico said. "Kirkman's Star, we had a lecture on it at the academy. It might pull in enough mass to reignite in a few hundred thousand years. For now, it's causing turbulence on the ley lines."

"Care to explain the tunnel of loose asteroids? There's no way that's natural," Gage said.

"It isn't." Loussan chuckled. "Though it is fun to mess with the newbies and tell them we stumbled on an alien celestial temple and they might be sacrificed if the little green men catch us. It's a graviton lattice the first clans made to get through this place. Gravity emitters keep all the rocks in place, which smooths out the ley line for jumps."

"You don't say…" Gage stroked his chin.

Tolan stepped out of the elevator wearing a junior crewman's uniform.

"Ship's locked down tight," the spy said. "I tested ship's security just enough to get yelled at but not shot. Ja'war shouldn't have had a chance to change location, yet."

"Come read this," Gage said, pointing to a screen with the free text Ja'war sent to the Daegon along with his faux jump data.

"Looks like gibberish, which would mean he encrypted this part," Tolan said. He touched the screen and traced around the text. "Which would mean you sent this through the computers to brute force the message, but you got nowhere—stop me when I'm wrong." He lifted the text up and flicked it into the holo tank, flipping the message around, then inverting it.

"There we are," Tolan said. "Farsi-based language from a Podunk wild-space planet that went dark years ago. I've seen him use this before."

"Yes, you're very smart." Gage's hands balled into fists. "What. Does. It. Say?"

"It's a list. Ship's compartments and systems. More random words. Doesn't tell us anything by itself…let me look at the whole message he sent." Tolan scanned over the jump data and shook his head. "Jellico, I can't tell the signal from the noise here. Eliminate everything that's jump data for me."

Most of the text on Tolan's screen faded away, with the exception of several numbers at the beginning of the transmission.

"There we are," Tolan said. "Now we pick out the words. Fourth, nineteenth…" He tapped words in the holo tank. "Engines. Default. Daybreak. Shadow."

"He'll wreck our engines once the Daegon are within striking distance," Loussan said. "At least, that's what I'd do."

"I agree." Tolan erased the words with a wave of his hand.

"Then he's about to sabotage our engines, if he hasn't done it already," Gage said. The

Commodore double-tapped an icon on his screen to open a channel to the engine room.

"Hold on." Tolan raised a hand. "Ja'war's a blade of grass in an open field right now. We need to flush him out. We need to give him an opportunity."

"Yates," the chief engineer came up in the holo tank.

Gage gave Tolan a sideways glance.

"Status on jump drive?" Gage asked.

"Need three hours to recharge," Yates said. "No change from my last update."

"Thank you." Gage closed the channel, leaned back, and crossed his arms in front of his stomach.

"What do you suggest?" he asked Tolan.

CHAPTER 23

Seaver awoke to pain in his shoulders, the feel of his bare feet scraping against dirt and grass. He managed to open his eyes and look up. Two men in bodysuits the same blue as Daegon armor carried him by the armpits. His hands were bound behind his back.

Chain-link fences formed a narrow pathway for the three. The sound of sobbing and cries of pain came through the air.

One of his captors looked down at him with disinterest, then opened a flap on a tent made from dark fabric. They set him down on a patch of muddy grass inside the tent, the other side open to a long pit on the other side of a fence. Seaver knelt, the guards stayed within arm's reach.

Daegon soldiers dragged the bodies of Albion soldiers to the pit and tossed them in.

"No!" came from the other side of a tent wall. "I won't do it, you bastards! I'll—" the man's protest ended in a scream of pain. Two guards carried a struggling Albian Marine across the opening.

"What is this?" Seaver asked. "What're you going to do to me?"

One of the guards put a hand to his shoulder and shook his head.

On the other side of the fence, the guards carrying the protesting man dropped him at the side of the pit. He looked over the edge. He got to his feet slowly, never taking his eyes off the dead.

"Albion's light burns, you hear me?" He spun around to face one of the Daegon soldiers. "We will never—" He gagged as a metal band around his neck constricted. It broke the skin around his neck and blood gushed from severed arteries. The Marine collapsed to the ground and one of his guards kicked him into the pit.

Seaver bent his head to one side and felt the pinch of a band around his own neck.

A moment later, a Daegon in obsidian black armor swept into Seaver's small tent. The man wore no helmet. His hair was as dark as his armor, slicked back and long enough to almost touch his shoulders. His skin was sea green and utterly flawless.

Seaver looked at his two guards. One was pale with vaguely Asian features, the other dusky-skinned with a narrow face.

The Daegon reached towards Seaver's face.

He flinched back, but the guards held him steady. A thin nail snapped out of the black armored glove and pricked Seaver's cheek. The palm flashed, leaving a painful after image on Seaver's eyes.

"I am Syphax of the Inquisition. You are James Seaver...Youth Auxiliary...approved enlistment." One of the Daegon's eyes shined white. He spoke English without a hint of a foreign accent. "Your DNA was found and recorded on a rifle recovered in Ludlow."

"Seaver, James F. Serial number—" A shock went down his spine and the band around his neck tightened ever so slightly.

"You will speak when spoken to, thrall. Else I'll have your tongue," Syphax said. "Your mother is in the navy...likely dead. Your father...is in the processing facility outside of Camden."

Seaver's stomach twisted into a cold hard

lump.

"He suffers from Langfei syndrome," the Daegon said. "Low potential for service. He'll likely be culled in the next few days."

Seaver tried to stand up, but the band shocked him again.

"Your masters are merciful, young Mr. Seaver," Syphax said. "We do not waste potential, which you have. Even if you did blunder into my net outside of Ludlow. I will give you a choice; the last you will ever make. You may join a themata regiment. Do this, and your father will receive medical treatment and will be safe when we cull the herd of the less useful. Displease your officers and your father loses his protection. Choose. Now."

The inquisitor looked over his shoulder to the mass grave, then back at Seaver.

Seaver began breathing faster, his mind racing

as he tried to process the question. Did they really have his father? What did it mean to serve the invaders?

"Illi'ut auferad," Syphax said and the two guards grabbed Seaver by the arms.

"I'll do it," Seaver spat. "I'll do it; just don't hurt my father." The guards let go of him.

"Wise." The inquisitor hooked a finger into the band around Seaver's neck and broke it with a slight tug.

"Welcome to the new order. Serve well, thrall." Syphax turned and left the tent.

One of the guards slipped a hood over Seaver's head.

CHAPTER 24

Ja'war pulled off his gloves and leaned back against a bulkhead with the rest of his engineering team, brushing long strands of sweaty hair off his face. Assuming a female identity was always more trouble than he liked, but he knew he'd be stuck as Franks for a bit longer. At least nothing in her online files indicated she had any sort of romantic attachments on the ship. Trying to deceive a lover was almost impossible unless he'd had ample time to prepare.

The passageway stank of burnt wires and

body odor. A trace of smoke left dark smudges across the ceiling and dampened the brightness emanating from the light panels.

Brown passed him a water bottle swirling with electrolyte powder.

"Drink up," he said. "Who knows when we'll get a whole five minutes to rest again."

Ja'war mumbled thanks and took a sip.

"Wait, that's lemon, isn't it?" Brown asked. "Thought that made you puke."

"Amazing what you can get down when you're thirsty," he said, feigning disgust and passing the bottle back to Brown.

"Now hear this, now hear this," came over the PA system and the repair crew groaned. Ja'war pulled a glove back on and locked the cuff into his suit sleeve, anticipating yet another emergency that they'd have to deal with.

"*Renown*, arriving," came over the PA. "*Valiant*, arriving. *Concordia*, arriving."

"Thank God." Brown settled back against the wall. "Commodore's having a powwow with the other captains. Might mean we could actually get some shut-eye."

"*Ajax*, arriving. *Perilous*, arriving," the PA droned on.

"Gage brought all the captains over…" Ja'war wiped soot off his forearm screens and checked the ship's shuttle bays. Only the auxiliary bay beneath the ship was open, and a short line of skiffs from the rest of the fleet waited for their turn to land.

"Must be something important," Brown said. "Though I don't know why he wouldn't just give orders through the secure comms and holos. But officers. Got to feel important, right?"

"That they do." Ja'war pulled up the *Orion*'s

schematics and mentally traced a route from Prince Aidan's quarters to the auxiliary launch bay.

****

A tea set sat on a trolley against the back wall, locked to the floor. Gage kept glancing at it as the fleet's captains filed into his increasingly cramped ready room. To gather more than three Albion naval officers in a room and *not* provide tea was a faux pas of the highest order, but the last time the fleet's commanding officers were in a room together, a Daegon operative poisoned every last captain, with the exception of Admiral Sartorius, who was shot to death. So not serving tea seemed prudent. Gage made a mental note to never mention this to Bertram, who was still locked away in Prince Aidan's quarters.

Captain Arlyss came in, the coveralls over his skin suit almost immaculate. He looked at Gage and then the tea set and shook his head.

Bargia of the *Remorseless* was right behind Arlyss, whose *Renown* had pulled the crew from the *Remorseless* off their stricken ship. Bargia's face was gaunt, his uniform patched with emergency tape to repair cuts that would have leaked his suit's atmosphere into the void. His right arm was blackened by fire.

Gage waved Bargia over.

"Sir," Bargia said and handed over a data slate. "The *Remorseless* is dead in space. Reactors almost went critical when we came out of slip space. Had to do a hard shutdown or they would have lost containment. I have repair estimates. If the *Hephaestus* can—"

"What of your crew?" Gage asked.

Bargia swallowed hard.

"Lost nineteen sailors and three officers.

Another seven are in the *Renown*'s sick bay. Most…should pull through."

"If you hadn't put *Remorseless* between the grav buoy and the enemy, they'd have torn us all apart by now," Gage said. "You got us here, and we're almost free of this maze. Well done to you and your crew."

"What of my ship, sir?"

Gage glanced over the repair estimates.

"We can't stay here for four days," he said.

"That's worst case. My engineer is a miracle worker. Give him enough man power and—"

Gage reached out and grabbed Bargia by his singed sleeve.

"We're here to work out a plan." Gage raised his chin to the assembled captains in the crowded room.

"Of course." Bargia nodded and went back to the other side of the table between Gage and the rest of the room.

"Captains," Gage said, clasping his hands behind his back, "this isn't how I anticipated our first gathering after the tragedy that struck our fleet over Siam. We stand at a crossroads—"

"You've backed us into a corner, haven't you?" Arlyss asked. "You made the mistake of trusting a pirate, the very same pirate that wants you dead more than anything else in the galaxy, and now that trust has come to bite you—and all of us—in the backside, hasn't it? Don't hide behind some pretext of a gallant last stand. Show some honor and admit we're trapped here because of your mistakes."

More than a few captains nodded in agreement with Arlyss.

"Admiral Sartorius was a fool to have you in the chain of command." Arlyss shook his head slowly. "Why he thought some lowborn officer that graduated from a second-rate school and with only a smidge of aptitude could command anything but an ore freighter is beyond me. How badly have you fouled this up, Gage? How many lives are we going to lose because we've our backs to the wall with no way out?"

A text message scrolled across a data slate on the desk.

"I daresay everything's going according to plan," Gage said.

"Commodore," Captain Erskine of the *Valiant* rubbed her face, "would you please enlighten us to this plan?"

Gage rapped his knuckles against the desk twice, and Loussan stepped through a doorway that opened behind the Commodore. Several captains grumbled and more than one put a hand to their side arms.

"I'll let you all guess how happy I am about this too," the pirate said.

"This is treason," Arlyss said. "To have a wanted criminal directly—"

"This is surviving," Gage said firmly. "We've been on the run, barely a step ahead of the Daegon, for weeks. You know your crews, your ships, no fleet has been under such a sustained threat since the final days of the Reach War when the Reich attacked Albion. There is no surrendering to this enemy. There is no glory in a last stand. We carry the only hope our people have—Prince Aidan and our fighting spirit. What must we sacrifice to keep that hope alive?"

Gage looked at Bargia and the *Remorseless'* captain's gaze fell to the floor.

"This fleet left sailors and soldiers behind on Siam," Gage said. "I have no misconceptions about what happened to them because of my decision. I ordered the *Retribution* to buy the rest of us time to escape. Captain Barlow...was an old and true friend."

He pointed at Loussan. "While I have more reason to despise this man than any of you, he has dealt true with us up until now. And the only reason I haven't thrown this sack of pirate filth out of an air lock is that he knows the only way out of this place."

Loussan shrugged his shoulders.

"Just admit you're in over your head." Arlyss levelled a finger at Gage. "You're drowning. Step aside and one of your betters can take over."

"No, Captain Arlyss." Gage ground his knuckles against the table. "I have a plan, and bringing you all here was part of it."

The deck rocked and the lights cut out, replaced moments later by red emergency lights.

"All part of the plan?" Arlyss asked.

"Actually," Gage said, "it is."

****

Ja'war—as Franks—felt a wave of satisfaction pass through him as the *Orion* shut down. The first of his bombs had knocked out the ship's power. While the crew scrambled about to mitigate the damage, Ja'war slipped away from his engineering team and climbed up into an air duct.

As he hurried through the duct, the panicked shouts of crew were music to his ears. Confusion was his ally, one he'd leverage to the hilt for the next few minutes.

Ja'war felt a vibration on his forearm. He glanced down at a snippet from a security camera at a hallway junction near Prince Aidan's quarters. An infrared image of a full team of armsmen and both Genevan guards formed a circle around a short figure and turned a corner, heading for a lift.

While the security around the Prince's

quarters was too strong for him to get close, he'd tapped into the ship's firefighting systems and set up motion alerts. He didn't have close surveillance on his target, but he knew any time someone came or went from the secure area.

Ja'war came to a join in the ductwork, where a small pile of clothes, badges, and an armsman's shotgun waited for him. He'd found the armsman separated from the rest of his team in an air-locked segment of a damaged deck a few hours ago. Killing him and stripping him of all his possessions had taken less than two minutes, and the nihilum had removed all evidence of the body.

Armsman Second Class Horace had been listed MIA and assumed lost to the void during the last battle. Ja'war slipped on the armsman's flak jacket and armored pads and scooped up his shotgun. Ja'war concentrated on the dead man's baby face and his body morphed to match.

Swiping through the camera feeds around the Prince's deck, Ja'war ignored the pack of security as it slowly made its way down the hallway.

There…a stout man pushed a covered food cart out of the other end of the corridor leading to the Prince's quarters. Ja'war zoomed in on the cart, adjusted the infrared sensitivity on the camera, and found the blur of a small child crouched within the food cart.

"There you are," Ja'war said. He bent an ear to a nearby grate, heard no footsteps or voices in the passageway, and dropped down with the bang of his heel against the metal. He pushed the grate closed with the muzzle of his shotgun and ran to a lift that serviced both the Prince's deck and the auxiliary flight bay.

Touching a palm to the lift door, he waited

for a vibration to hum through the metal, then removed an override fob Franks had and pressed it against the reader. The doors opened a second later and a rather surprised Bertram looked from Ja'war to the deck number on the lift's control panel.

The steward gripped the food cart's handle bar tightly.

"This lift is in use, sailor." Bertram puffed his chest out and shooed the armsman away.

"Security emergency." Ja'war stepped in and hit a deck number between their floor and the flight deck. He waited until the doors shut, then Ja'war racked the shotgun and aimed it at Bertram's face.

"The food's not that good," Bertram squeaked. "Better in the mess…I swear—"

"Don't. I know you've got the Prince in there." Ja'war kicked the cart. "You want the boy to live? You tell me what ship you're taking him to."

Bertram put his hands up and backed away.

"No ship, just a brief walkabout. Kick the footy ball around on—"

Ja'war swung the butt of his shotgun around and smacked it against Bertram's shoulder. The steward yelped in pain as the Faceless pointed the muzzle at the cart.

"The *Orion* is dead in space," Ja'war said. "The Daegon will be here soon. Your miserable leader won't let the brat die here, so he's sending him to another ship. Tell me which one or you'll both die right here, right now. The boy first, so you can hear that scream."

Bertram was nearly hyperventilating with fear. Sweat poured down his forehead.

"You-you promise he'll live?" Bertram asked.

"Of course." Ja'war took in the steward's features. His look wasn't too far off the armsman's, easy to adopt. His face began reforming.

"He's going to the *Gudar*," the steward said.

Ja'war stopped his transformation and brought the weapon up to Bertram's face.

"There's no ship in this fleet named the *Gudar*," Ja'war said.

"Of course the *Gudar* is real. I was just on the *Gudar* when I *Gudar*. *Gudar!*"

A small hand snapped out from under the tablecloth that covered the cart and grabbed Ja'war by the shin. He looked down and saw an armored gantlet and felt the impossibly strong hold. Then the gauntlet grew larger as fingertips slid around his leg.

Bertram knocked the shotgun up as Ja'war pulled the trigger. The blast tore through the ceiling and set the Faceless' ears ringing. The grip on his leg jerked him aside and sent the shotgun flying out of his hands.

Ja'war's head bounced off the side of the lift and he crashed to the floor.

There was a groan of metal as Thorvald's armor stood up, armor plates unfurling as it reshaped itself from a child's size to adult dimensions. The light beneath the visor lit up an angry red as the armor slammed Ja'war against the elevator walls with a bang of metal.

Ja'war reached for a knife on his belt, but the armor grabbed him by both shoulders and pinned his arms to his side. Ja'war felt crushing pressure against his sides, then the bones in his upper arms broke with wet snaps.

The Faceless fought against a scream as the armor grabbed him by the throat and pinned him against the wall. With two quick blows, the empty suit shattered both of Ja'war's knees.

Now he screamed, his voice modulating as he

lost control of his voice box, his cry echoing victims from decades of assassinations across the stars. He tried to struggle, but his limbs were useless. His face reverted to its base form—pitch-black.

"I honestly expected better," Bertram said, but not with his own voice. He buried his face in his hands for a moment, gave his face a twist, and Tolan looked up. "That's twice, Ja'war. Twice I've beat you."

Ja'war growled and spat at Tolan.

"You give me some useful information, this golem here will kill you quickly," Tolan said. "Otherwise, it's the void. The thing about getting spaced is that you know there's no chance to survive. You just suffocate and wonder if any random ship will ever bump into your corpse. Wonder what they'll think when they find you…"

"You're a fake!" Ja'war hissed. "An insult to

the craft. You think you have a chance against them? I've seen their fleets. Their armies. They'll take every star and there's nothing you can do to stop them. Better to serve…than die."

The elevator came to a stop.

"Here comes my cavalry," Tolan said. "Before you do it, know that as an enemy, as an opponent, I found you…wanting."

The doors opened, and a team of armsmen and Thorvald raced down the passageway towards them.

"You became me. You got exactly what you wanted." Ja'war cocked his jaw to one side, then slammed his chin against the armor's grip around his neck. He locked eyes with Tolan and laughed—slowly and deliberately. Smoke rose off his skin and his body began disintegrating. Black skin flaked off his face and the rest of his body ripped away from his neck.

Within seconds, a soot-stained skull lay atop the armor's grip, then that collapsed into dust and evaporated.

Tolan stepped back from Ja'war's remains and stomped his boots against the deck.

"You think Bertram will still want these clothes? The smell might never go away," he said to Thorvald.

"You were supposed to take him alive," the Genevan said. He removed his helmet and tossed it to the deck, where the cheap molded plastic bounced away.

"I believe we said 'if possible.'" Tolan brushed dust off his sleeves. "I always suspected Ja'war had a nihilum tooth. They're terribly expensive and have fail-safes out the wazoo. They're impossible to extract."

"You could have mentioned this when we

were planning this operation," Thorvald said, stripping off the fake armor on his arms and chest.

"Well, I didn't think your shell could handle emergency dental work." Tolan stepped around the suit of armor. "Dead is dead. Our problem is solved. Mission accomplished. Now, if you don't mind, I'd like to retire to my quarters and celebrate my own way. Give Gage the good news—take all the credit you want."

Tolan slapped Thorvald on the shoulder and made his way past the horrified armsmen as they watched the last of Ja'war dissipate.

"Impossible man," Thorvald said. He placed a palm on the armor's chest. +Ticino,+ he sent to the armor's gestalt. +The Prince is safe. Well done.+

The armor's helm snapped up.

+Threat eliminated,+ the gestalt replied.

+Yes. Follow me to Salis and Morgaten.+

Thorvald pulled his hand back, but the armor reached out and grabbed him by the forearm. The plates folded over Thorvald's skin and the suit stepped toward the bodyguard. The armor flowed over him, twisting itself inside out and shredding his clothes.

The gestalt touched his mind, and he felt the AI's true spirit—stoic and resolute.

+You will serve to your last dying breath. Your oath is true. I will have you,+ the gestalt said.

+Thorvald.+ The bodyguard gave his name.

+Grynau.+

CHAPTER 25

Wyman slapped his hands together, then pounded them against his thighs. His breath fogged inside his cockpit as a wan orange light crept through the stealth sheet over his fighter. The glow reminded him of a childhood vacation to Albion's Sheppey Isles, where the sunsets seemed to last forever. The cold, cramped confines of his cockpit and the pinch of his flight suit told him he was anywhere but a vacation destination.

Only one screen on his control panel had power: his connection to an external wired communication network linking him to the rest of his squadron. He checked that he was indeed still connected to the antenna pointed at the fleet, then double-tapped Ivor's icon.

"Briar...I've got a bad feeling about this," he said.

Static hissed over the open line.

"Briar. Wake up!"

"Huh?"

Wyman heard Ivor slapping at her control panel and the rustle of her moving around her cockpit.

"I wasn't sleeping. Is it go time?" she asked.

"Bullshit you weren't sleeping. How the hell can you even manage to zonk out? I'm freezing my ass off over here."

"Practice. God knows how long we'll sit on this rock before something happens. Brass want us to hurry up and wait; least I can do something productive."

"You're the only person I know that thinks sleep is productive."

"Maybe this'll be nothing but a snipe hunt. Maybe we'll end up fighting a running battle that lasts for days on end. Welcome to the war. If I give my brain a rest, I'll be that much more alert when the balloon goes up." The click of popping joints came over the line as she stretched. "I take it you have a damn good reason for waking me up."

"I have a bad feeling about this," he said.

"What part? The Daegon fleet hunting us or that to stay hidden, our thermal signature has to be so low that our cockpits are leaching the life out of us?"

"I hadn't thought about that last part…What I'm worried about is if the *Orion* jumps out and doesn't bother to tell us. We're under commo blackout, no wireless transmissions. Got the one antennae pointed at the fleet. If the fleet goes bye-bye, how long are we supposed to sit here? In the dark. Freezing. Waiting for a message that will never come."

"I'm sure the boss has a contingency plan. Our batteries will only last so long. Gage sent us out to lay an ambush, not to fulfill a suicide pact. This whole thing is weird. You saw him on Sicani. Gage seem okay when you left?"

"He got cut up pretty good by that pirate."

"One of the techs said the primary flight deck did an emergency vent of its entire atmosphere on Gage's order. Why? Would've hit the ship like an explosion. Old girl's taken enough of a beating as it is," Ivor said.

"Yeah, didn't make any sense to me either. You think the stress is getting to him?"

"I bet he's held it together better than any of the blue-blood officers. But the lockdown during slip transit, doing God knows how much damage to the deck with that emergency blowout, sticking us out here on a hope and a prayer…if this was peacetime, I'd be a bit skeptical."

"It's hard to make sense of anything. My grandpa told stories about the Reich assault on Albion back during the last war…this is different."

"Hold up—Gage really got marked up by an actual sword? Tell me more, because I thought my last shore leave was out of control," Ivor said.

CHAPTER 26

Barlow felt the deck shift as the Daegon battleship left slip space. He heard Tiberian bark off orders and the curt replies of the bridge crew. He'd listened to their language while huddled against the side of Tiberian's throne but had picked up little. The words were long, convoluted. Some reminded him of the local dialects he'd heard around Nyarit worlds during a midshipman cruise many years ago. That Daegon and the Latin vulgate of Nyarit would be at all similar was a surprise to him.

"Dog," Tiberian said, jerking Barlow's chain.

The prisoner stood up, his head slung low. The pain torque sent a tiny shock around his neck, reminding Barlow that it was still there.

"Sire."

"What is Gage doing?" Tiberian waved his hand toward the front of the bridge.

Within the holo wall, the *Orion* floated inside the long tunnel of asteroids, her hull canted to one side, a cloud of frozen water vapor trailing behind her, engines cold and silent. The fleet's cruisers and battle cruisers accelerated down the tunnel and away from the flagship.

"The *Orion* looks dead in space," Barlow said. "The damage is recent—very recent. Hull integrity is the highest priority for repairs." The torque sent a jolt up the side of his face, but Barlow accepted the pain instead of providing more information. The torque's effects were just as strong as ever, but Barlow had become more accustomed to its administrations.

"Which ship has the boy?" Tiberian asked.

"There is a code." Barlow's jaw clenched as the torque sent his left arm into a painful spasm. "We call it vermillion. Look for it in the telemetry data between the ships. Text is V-N-4-2-1-5."

One of the bridge crew called out and a ring appeared around the *Orion*.

"The boy is still on Gage's ship. Curious." Tiberian rose to his feet, raised a hand over his head, then pointed to the *Orion*. The Daegon fleet shot forward, racing toward the Albion warship.

Barlow's ears rang.

"Why keep the boy on a dead ship?" Gustavus asked.

"If Gage didn't trust the other captains…but watch. A ship will double back and—" A frigate looped around and made for the *Orion*.

Tiberian traced a symbol in the air and lines appeared connecting the returning frigate to the Albion flagship and from the closing Daegon packs to the *Orion*. Barlow didn't need to read their language to see the Daegon would be well within firing range before the frigate could flee with the Prince.

Pulses emitted from the asteroids forming the tunnel just ahead of the lead Daegon ships…and they began moving inwards, accelerating faster by the second. The cruisers altered their course, threading around the projected pathways as the asteroids closed in on them.

The bridge crew remained deathly silent as explosives cracked the rocks into pieces, turning the crushing objects into a rain of fragments ranging from the size of fighters to small buildings. There would be no escape for the forward ships.

"You led us into a trap." Gustavus drew his

sword and struck at Barlow's neck.

Tiberian jerked the chain and yanked the prisoner away from the blade's edge as it whistled through the air. Barlow's head bounced off the side of the throne and he raised his hand to ward off the next blow.

"Shortsighted as ever, child," Tiberian said. "Sheath your blade or I'll bury it inside you. This is my bridge, not yours."

Gustavus flipped the sword around and slid it back into its scabbard.

"My regret to you, Uncle." The younger man raised his chin slightly, baring his throat.

Asteroids crashed into the lead Daegon ships. Their shields held as the impacts knocked them off course. Explosions erupted within the avalanche and broken hull fragments joined the slew as the ships died.

Barlow considered how many men and women crewed those ships. Albion vessels of the same size carried nearly a thousand souls apiece. Tiberian remained impassive, almost contemplative, as a quarter of his force and tens of thousands died.

The ambush of asteroids ground to a halt between the *Minotaur* and the *Orion*, a scrum of broken rock and warships that meshed together in a roiling mass.

The *Minotaur*'s prow raised slightly, carrying it over the blockage and toward the still-motionless *Orion*.

"Too soon," Tiberian said. "Gage sprung the trap too soon."

"Why didn't he wait for the *Minotaur* to enter his kill zone?" Gustavus asked. "He must know this ship carries high born."

Tiberian's eyes went to Barlow.

"The Commodore doesn't care about this ship or you, sire, just the Prince. He activated the trap to buy time to get the boy away, not to hurt you for the sake of winning a battle," Barlow said. He looked up at the holo wall and examined the situation as an officer and a commander.

The tunnel of asteroids was by no means natural. Such constructs weren't unheard of across settled space, but they required massive graviton emitters and a fair amount of computing power to set up. To launch that kind of an attack, Gage must have sent engineers to the asteroids to reconfigure the emitters. If he had the time to do that, then…

Barlow quickly counted the Albion ships on the scope and he came up short by almost a dozen ships.

Gage, you never cease to amaze me, Barlow thought.

The *Minotaur* plowed through the outer edge of the mass of loose rocks and dead ships, her shields lighting up like a thunderstorm as objects bounced off the energy walls. At one workstation, a diagram of the ship came up over the sailor, wedges on the forward and port shields flashing orange.

Tiberian gave the alert a quick glance, then turned his attention back to the *Orion*. One of the Albion frigates was mere minutes away.

"Forward lances, prepare a volley," he said. "Destroy the smaller ship on my order."

A ring appeared over the frigate, the center point pulsating in and out as the gun crews worked to find the range.

Barlow wasn't sure of the name of the frigate, but it was the same class and crew complement as his beloved *Retribution*. A welter of emotion formed in his chest as the dying screams of his crew returned to him.

"Sire?" Barlow hunched forward and meekly raised a hand. "Let me speak to Gage. I can convince him—" he forced a smile as the torque forced his heart to flutter "—to surrender. Give up the boy. He must know there's no escape by now."

"The smaller ship is nearly there," Gustavus said. "He still has a viable option."

"Then we destroy the frigate." Tiberian raised a finger.

"If I may, sire, destroying the ship will force Gage into a corner. He'll do something stupid and reckless then. Fire a warning shot. It will confuse him, give you time to get closer, make your victory inevitable." The torque forced Barlow's left foot to contract so hard he felt a toe break, but he kept his composure.

Tiberian moved his hand to the left and cast

his fingers forward. A lance fired from the forward batteries and cut through the void between the frigate and the *Orion*, just ahead of the smaller ship's course.

The frigate banked away.

"If he surrenders the boy," Tiberian said, "I will spare his crew."

"And Gage?" Barlow asked.

"Officers make poor thralls," Tiberian said, "but you were weaker than I expected. Deliver on your promise and you'll live out your days on a labor camp." He snapped his fingers and a holographic line appeared over his palm.

"This broadcasts across all your channels," Tiberian said. "Speak."

"I am Captain Michael Barlow of the Albion Royal Navy ship…*Retribution*. Commodore Gage, please respond." There was a pause as Barlow felt his every heartbeat, the bite of cold air along the rim of his ears.

Tiberian huffed and gestured at the frigate, now moving slower as it closed on the *Orion*. A target reticule appeared on top of the ship's bridge.

"This is Captain Barlow for Commodore Gage. You prefer your scotch neat and aged at least fifteen years in Albion oak barrels, not proper Kentucky wood because you're a filthy heathen. You would have failed out of slip-stream physics had I not tutored you—"

Gage appeared in the holo floating over Tiberian's palm. The Daegon tossed the image toward Barlow and it grew to life-size, hanging in the air. Barlow stared face-to-face with his old friend and commander.

The Commodore looked over Barlow, his gaze lingering on the chains and bruises.

"What have they done to you?" Gage asked.

"The *Retribution* is lost with all hands," Barlow said.

Tiberian scratched the claw tips on his armored glove down the side of his throne.

"I must tell you…" The feel of knife points pricked down his back as the torque goaded him toward following Tiberian's instructions. "That Prince Aidan will be…" Barlow coughed, then a slight half-smile appeared on his face as the pain melted away and he felt a small bit of pride with his next words.

"This ship's forward shield emitters are damaged." He ducked a swipe from Tiberian. "Starboard! Three o'clock are weak—" Gustavus kicked him in the small of the back and sent him crashing to the deck. Blood poured down the side of his nose and he spat blood as he laughed.

Tiberian scooped him up by the neck and held him in front of the holo for Gage to see.

Barlow felt his feet swinging in the air, his lungs burning from lack of oxygen. He locked eyes with a furious Tiberian…and smiled.

Tiberian snapped his neck with a twist of his hand and tossed the body aside. The Daegon commander slowly turned his head toward Gage.

Gage, his face alive with fury, stared at Tiberian, then the transmission cut out.

****

Loussan lifted his finger off the communications panel and backed away from Gage.

"No words." Loussan shook his head, then motioned toward Price just below the command dais.

"Commodore, enemy flagship charging another shot," she said.

"Break off," Gage half-choked. "Have the *Perilous* break off. Time for phase three of this operation." Gage straightened up, his countenance changing to a mask of command.

"Helm, take the engines off standby and give me best speed through route alpha. Price, pass on Captain Barlow's information to the fighters. Tiberian's ship is the primary target. Tell the assault element that I expect them to catch up with empty magazines and bare tubes."

"Aye aye, doubt they need much encouragement to put the hurt on these bastards," Price said.

A lance from the *Minotaur* ripped through the debris field and glanced off the *Orion*'s shields.

"Port emitters holding," Vashon said, "for once. The beam suffered significant degradation through that mess."

"Hot damn, you were right," Loussan said. "Right that they'd believe we were sitting ducks. Right that they'd charge right into your trap. How?"

The *Orion*'s engines flared and the ship rumbled toward a group of asteroids making up the wall of the funnel.

"Would you be so kind as to clear our path?" Gage asked Loussan.

The pirate tapped out a quick series of commands and the asteroids parted, leaving just enough space for the *Orion* to slip through.

"Victory after victory can poison the mind of any commander," Gage said. "When every battle goes as planned, when you have every advantage, the mind looks for the easy path to the next victory. It doesn't see your downfall around every corner. Tiberian had his saboteur aboard my ship, and we played right into his expectation of finding us crippled and helpless."

"Then why did you practically wreck one of your launch bays *before* the Daegon even showed up? I thought this ship would crack in half when you ordered that emergency vent," Loussan said.

"Tolan found Ja'war's bombs. We set up the opportunity for him to get the Prince off this ship when I brought the other captains aboard. He triggered an explosion to get the Prince out of his quarters and to another vessel, which we provided with the emergency venting. All the debris and air sucked out of the hangar made us look even more damaged to the Daegon."

The *Orion* skirted past the asteroid wall just as another lance shot glanced off their shields and annihilated a hunk of ice and rock.

"Enemy vectoring to port," Price said. In the holo tank, the Daegon fleet angled toward the same side the *Orion* had just escaped through, opening fire, blasting the asteroids apart.

"Too bad we didn't have time to booby-trap every graviton emitter," Gage said.

"You know how much those things cost? Know how hard it will be to ever reconstruct this place?" Loussan asked.

"You mean after this, neither pirates or the Daegon will be able to cut through the Kigeli Nebula and attack the core worlds?" Gage said evenly. "Such a shame."

"Assault element reports ready," Price said.

"Cry havoc, XO. Show the Daegon as much mercy as they've given."

****

A buzzer snapped Wyman out of a daydream.

"About damn time," Ivor said through his

helmet.

Wyman slapped his visor down and sealed it shut with a press. Air—blessedly warmer air—filled his helmet and he brought his fighter online. He felt the thrum of engines through his seat and grabbed the throttle and control stick.

"Cobras, the *Orion* has a critical task for us," Commander Stannis—call sign Marksman—sent over the squadron frequency. "Daegon capital ship has a known vulnerability. We're to do a shield emitter strafe and open her up for the torps."

"This is your fault," Ivor said to Wyman.

"What?" he asked as he angled his main engines perpendicular to the asteroid surface and waited as they charged up.

"If you hadn't wrecked that Daegon interdictor ship back on Siam, we wouldn't have drawn the short straw. You remember how much flak the larger ships can put up?"

"You think there's some safe assignment for us out here?"

"I'm just saying that if you screw up once in a while, we won't keep getting thrown into the fire…engines to power. Waiting on Marksman," she said.

"Sounds like you want to take the shot that earns the laurels. Is that the case, Briar? I'm green across the board."

"A little."

"Just fly. So long as we put the hurt on the bastards, doesn't matter who gets the credit."

"All craft," Stannis sent, "lift on my mark."

Wyman stretched out his fingers and drew in a deep breath.

"Three."

He gripped the control stick and throttle

control, wrapping one finger around at a time.

"Two."

His mind went to the dancer that died in his arms, the look of shock and denial on her face. The Daegon killed her; now was his chance to avenge that death.

"Mark."

Wyman pushed the throttle control forward and his Typhoon ripped through the stealth sheet and rose over the asteroid he'd been tucked into for the last several hours. Ivor and the rest of his squadron pulled away with him. He looked up and found the Daegon fleet, their guns blasting away at the rocks to one side. A target icon appeared on the *Minotaur*, sections of her shields flashing amber.

He angled his fighter toward the enemy ship and locked his vectored engines back into place. Flicking a cover off a switch on his throttle control, he fired the afterburners. The acceleration pressed him against his seat and darkness crept around the edges of his vision. Pads around his legs and abdomen squeezed blood back into his head as he rocketed forward.

Wyman struggled to press a hand forward and jabbed at his fire control panel, activating the rocket pods slung beneath his wings.

His afterburners cut out as the *Minotaur* loomed ahead. Almost all the escort cruisers had maneuvered between the battleship and the asteroids, leaving her port flank exposed.

Icons from three other squadrons came up on his HUD. Most of the 11th's fighters had been dedicated to the ambush, a decision on Gage and Stannis' part that would either carry the day or leave the fleet vulnerable to Daegon fighters if the Typhoons fell to the enemy's guns.

"Do this in one pass, Cobras," Stannis said. "Won't be as easy the second time around."

Wyman banked to a side as bolts from the *Minotaur*'s flak cannons opened fire. A yellow flash cut across the side of his canopy and he jinked, sending his fighter into a slalom. He dove, the explosions from Albion fighters flashing across his cockpit.

He kicked his tail down and hooked back toward the enemy ship, the rapid change in acceleration pressing down on his head and making his shoulders ache. From this angle of attack, he made out wide cracks along the *Minotaur*'s segmented hull and several turrets…none of which were shooting.

"Marksman, think I've found a way in," Wyman called out to the commander. "Starting my attack run."

"I'm on your wing," Ivor said. "Smooth

maneuver back there. Looked kind of like a happy accident to me."

"Less talking. More shooting." Wyman felt a rumble as his fighter passed through the *Minotaur*'s shields. He flew down and along the slope of a hull segment, the reflection of his fighter nearly perfect against the mirrored hull. He soared over the crest and spotted an open fighter bay, dozens of the enemy's spear-tip-shaped fighters inside. Pilots and crew swarmed over the void craft.

Wyman rolled his Typhoon over and let off a barrage of rockets. Two landed inside the open hangar, destroying a fighter and blasting it into the one next to it. A flurry of explosions erupted on the upper edge of the hangar, and the force field holding all the air inside flickered.

The hangar decompressed, hurling bodies and everything else not bolted down out into the void.

The dark-suited crew stuck out against the orange tones of the Kigeli Nebula as they tumbled through the void.

"Not our target," Ivor said.

"You want to wait until they're flying around and shooting at us? Find the shield emitters!" he said as flak shot across his nose. One bolt struck just ahead of his cockpit and knocked his fighter into a roll.

The side of the ship and the nebula alternated through his cockpit, and the ship grew larger with each pass as he fought to regain control of his fighter. He changed the vector on his engines to counter the spin and let off a quick burst from the afterburners.

His fighter stabilized, then smacked—belly down—against the hull. It skidded along, the screech of metal against the Daegon alloy carrying into Wyman's helmet. His control panels flickered on and off.

"Not good. At all."

Looking to his right, he found he was a few yards away from a flak turret. A quad-barreled cannon fired into the void, covered by a clear dome. Daegon crew in full bodysuits manned the weapon. One did a double take at Wyman, then pointed at him excitedly.

The flak cannon slewed toward him.

Wyman flipped the reset switch on his controls, and the whole thing died.

The cannon lowered…and came to a stop too high to engage him.

"Come on!" Wyman bashed a hand against his control panel and his fighter roared back to life. He rose a few feet off the hull and swung his nose toward the flak turret. The crew ducked away just as a quick burst from his forward cannons broke the dome and destroyed the weapon inside.

"Freak Show? You okay down there?" Ivor's voice came through his helmet laced with static.

"Sort of," he said, nudging his fighter forward.

"There's a shield emitter just over the bend in the hull ahead of you. We're dealing—son of a bitch, that was close—with fighters. You want to hurry up?"

"Moving." Wyman gradually increased his speed and his fighter's nose cracked. He looked behind and saw his forward landing gear tumbling across the hull.

"Probably don't need that anyway," he said. Flying over the bend of the diamond-shaped hull, he saw a glowing circle wider than his fighter along the spine of the ship. The shield emitter fluctuated as gossamer-thin lines appeared just over it, wavering like auroras.

Wyman activated his rocket pod and fired

twice. The shots hit the semi-opaque energy field and ripped apart. Fragments spread throughout the shield just around the emitter, then were cast up and away.

With that, Wyman knew exactly the limits of the shield. He aimed just below the edge of the emitter and let off a half-dozen rockets. They exploded against the hull, cracking the blue-tinted surface. The emitter powered down, exposing the inner workings to the void.

"Not giving you the chance to fix this." Wyman unleashed the last of his rockets into the *Minotaur*. The hull danced as explosions racked the interior of the ship. The emitter shot off the hull and went tumbling end over end through the void.

"Marksman, mission accomplished!" Wyman shouted.

"All fighters, break off and make for your anchor points," Stannis said. "Torps will impact in less than two minutes and we do not want a front-row seat for that."

Blasts from Daegon fighters ripped down the hull near Wyman. He punched his Typhoon forward and banked to one side, dodging a shot that would've hit his center axis. His engines were almost sluggish as they fought to propel him forward.

A fireball erupted behind him, then another a few seconds later. He caught movement out of the corner of his eye and jerked his control stick to the side.

"Easy, Freak," Ivor said as she flew alongside him. "Think we're in the clear now."

Warning icons popped onto his HUD. Icons for the 11th's destroyers appeared around asteroids on the far side of the tunnel. Torpedo salvoes flew from the ships, their projected paths leading through Wyman and toward the *Minotaur*.

He changed the vector on his engines…and they didn't respond. His maneuver thrusters sputtered. The torpedoes sprinted across the void, hell-bent on their targets.

"Hold on." Ivor flew just over Wyman and pressed the bottom of her ship against the top of his. A shudder went through both fighters as Ivor pushed their fighters out of the line of fire.

A torpedo raced overhead, the blaze from the engine leaving an afterimage in Wyman's vision.

A second volley roared by.

"You're welcome," Ivor said as she nudged away from Wyman.

"She's holding together with hope and fairy dust right now," he said. "Don't jinx it."

"Ah…shit, look behind you."

Wyman felt a cold patch form in the pit of his stomach. He twisted around, half-expecting to see a hundred Daegon fighters bearing down on him. The *Minotaur*'s shields were alive, pulsing with energy as the last effects of the first volley of torpedoes died away. Where Wyman had destroyed the emitter, the neighboring shields had extended out, covering the gap.

The second volley changed formation into a V, the point aligned with the destroyed emitter. The leading torpedoes struck the shields, exploding against the energy walls. The next pair hit with the same results. The third strike sent a ripple through the shields, like twin rocks dropped into a still pond. The shields retracted, and the next five torpedoes struck home.

Two of the *Minotaur*'s diamond segments exploded, hurling shards of the hull into the void. The ship slid to the right, crushing a pair of escort cruisers. The battleship lumbered forward and into an asteroid. The rock rolled up the shields, then a spiked outcrop pierced the shields and ripped across the prow of the ship.

The *Minotaur*'s engines flickered and died.

Wyman cheered and punched a fist up and into the canopy. The strained glass cracked and he jerked his hand back down.

"Not to ruin your mood," Ivor said, "but can you mag-lock to our destroyer?"

Ivor's question did indeed drive away his elation as he checked his control panel. His mag locks, even the auxiliary docking claw, read as off-line or destroyed.

Just ahead, the destroyer *Epee* slowed to a stop. The plan was for the Typhoons to latch on to the destroyer's hulls for the slip transit away from Sanctuary—a plan that his damaged fighter couldn't fulfill.

"*Epee,* this is Freak Show in Cobra One-Niner. Can you take on an EVA?" Wyman asked.

"Negative," replied the captain of the destroyer. "We're buttoned up for combat conditions. Enemy escorts are closing fast. We've got a two-minute window to boost out of here before they reach weapons' range. Figure something out, Freak Show."

Wyman caught the underlying message that the captain wouldn't doom her entire crew and her ship for his sake.

"I've got it," Ivor said. She banked next to the *Epee* and locked her fighter against the hull, then raised her canopy and waved to Wyman. "Get in here!"

The *Epee* accelerated and Wyman's damaged fighter trembled as it fought to keep up.

"Bad idea's better than anything I can think

of," he said as he pulled the emergency release on his canopy and it ripped away. He maneuvered his fighter onto one side, facing his cockpit toward Ivor's, and edged his throttle forward, trying to eye the *Epee*'s speed as he unsnapped his seat belts with his other hand.

"Thirty seconds to afterburners," came from the *Epee*.

Wyman pushed his fighter just ahead of Ivor and stood up on his seat. He knelt slightly, then jumped toward the destroyer. That he'd mistimed the jump became apparent halfway across the gap. He hit just ahead of Ivor's cockpit, doubling over the nose, the ship and the fighter's joined momentum sending him tumbling up the fighter. He bounced off its hull and crashed into Ivor and against her open canopy.

The *Epee* accelerated forward, and Wyman slid away from the canopy. He bent at the waist, reached for the edge of the glass…and missed by a half inch.

Ivor grabbed him by the wrist and heaved back, pulling her wingman into her cockpit.

The canopy closed over them both, a tangle of limbs in a space that was barely big enough for Wyman on his own.

"You…big…dumb…animal," Ivor said as she struggled to extricate herself from Wyman.

"Sorry. And thank you," Wyman said, trying to wiggle around and making slow progress. "Briar, where's your left hand right now?"

"We will never speak of this again!"

****

Flames licked at the edges of Tiberian's bridge as he knelt beside an unconscious Gustavus. Half the man's face was blackened, seeping blood, his armor dented and scorched, but he lived.

Tiberian pressed a thumb against Gustavus' neck and extended a razor-tipped nail. One deft motion would end his nephew and free him to continue his hunt. Tiberian could recount this battle in more favorable light; the truth of this defeat would be his alone. If Gustavus lived, the Baroness would know what transpired in this nebula. She could lose the last of her faith in him, exile him to the lower castes forever. Eubulus, his brother, could be told some fantastic tale of his son's final brave moments…

He retracted the claw.

No, the bonds of family still meant something to him, even in the midst of the Daegon's ultimate purpose—their grand crusade to unite all of humanity beneath their rule. The authority to rule came from birthright, and from just action.

"Sire," one of his sub-lieutenants called to him from a control station, "the Albians are nearly to the nexus point. Shall the escorts give chase?"

"No." Tiberian stood and looked to the flickering holo wall. "Bring us about and get us out of this nebula. I know where the Albians are running to." He looked at Barlow's corpse. "They'll find no escape there. Then this hunt will end."

CHAPTER 27

Seaver, still trapped in silence and blindness by the odd hood over his head, felt one of his guards press down on his shoulder. He went to his knees and the cuffs locking his wrists together pulled his forearms down and locked against a metal plate, pinning him into a submissive posture.

A guard pulled the hood away, and Seaver turned his face away from lights glaring from the ceiling. It had been hours since the inquisitor had spoken with him. Hours spent waiting in darkness before he walked up a ramp and felt the acceleration of a shuttle leaving orbit.

He looked around and found that he was one of ten individuals arrayed in a circle, all in the remnants of Albion uniforms and all with their wrists locked to a metal plate near the center of a round room. Several tiers of seats surrounded them, like they were in the middle of an arena. Dark chambers blocked off by metal bars were at the four compass points of the arena floor.

"Hey, Seaver," a man hissed. Inez and Powell were in the circle with him. "Who do you think sold us out? Smith or the navy guy?"

"Had to be O'Reilly," Powell said.

"Shut up!" someone hissed from across the circle.

The bars on one of the chambers slid open, half going up and the other going down, mimicking a mouth. A man in cut-down Daegon armor walked into the arena. He had a shaved head, his skin a light tan. A spiked truncheon hung from his belt. On his face, just below his right eye, was a black symbol a few inches tall in the shape of an hourglass.

"Oss," he intoned as he walked into the circle. "Inquisition sends Lord Erebus thralls for his themata. Lord Erebus tells me he no trust. He say...Albion fight, but not fight well. He say inquisition no know if thralls can fight. He say...take half for themata. So I take half. I take half that fight."

The man pointed to the middle of the circle and a hatch slid aside. A round weapons rack rose out of the floor, bearing blunt and chipped short swords, spears with slightly bent shafts, and maces missing several spikes.

"Figure out which half I take. Quick quick. Or the wolves choose." He turned and walked back to the open chamber and disappeared into the darkness.

The manacles around Seaver's wrists released from the metal plate and he stood up, rubbing his sore knees. He looked at the pile of weapons, then to the equally confused others around the room.

"He can't be serious," Powell said. "Does he...want us to kill each other?"

"What did he mean by 'wolves'?" someone asked.

Inez hurried toward Seaver. Seaver brought his hands up, ready to fight.

"No, no way, man," Inez said. "I know you, Powell. None of these others."

"Little early to form a prison gang, don't you think?" Powell half whispered as she joined Seaver and Inez. The others coalesced into two groups, leaving two standing all by themselves.

"Look," Seaver eyed the pile of weapons, "there's got to be a way out of here. We can get a weapon now."

"We are on a Daegon spaceship," Powell said. "Have to be. You think we're going to break out of here, fight through them when they're in armor, and then we'll just magically find a shuttle?"

"They got my sister," Inez said. "They said if I don't fight for them she'll be killed." He looked at a sword and his hands opened and closed several times.

"My mother," Powell added. "She's in a home for disabled vets. They pull her life support and…"

Inez sprinted for the weapons rack, and two from other groups ran in.

One of the prisoners snatched up a war hammer and made a quick swipe at Inez, more to scare him off than to try and hurt him. Inez sidestepped the blow, then grabbed a sword and swung it at the man with the hammer, missing by a mile. He jabbed the sword at the third man, warding him away from the pile of weapons.

Inez grabbed a short spear and tossed it at Seaver. He picked it up. The wood was rough and splintered to his touch, the metal tip rusted, but sharp at the edges. Inez grabbed a second sword and backed away toward Seaver and Powell. He handed the weapon off to her and the three stood shoulder to shoulder.

"Okay, now what?" Seaver asked.

One of the lone prisoners thrust his arm into the rack, reaching for a metal glove tipped with a wide punching dagger. The man with the hammer attacked and hit the other in the shoulder. There was a crunch of bone and the lone prisoner fell back, clutching his arm.

"All of you listen to me!" the hammer bearer shouted. "I am Staff Sergeant Rollins, Albion Marine Corps. This is how it's going to be…"

There was a whine of machinery and the four chambers opened. Seaver swung to one side, forming a triangle with the other two. Sets of three red dots appeared in the darkness. High-pitched growls sounded across the arena.

Powell began sobbing.

"Come on," Seaver said. "Stay strong."

From the darkness, an animal leapt into the arena. It resembled a wolf, but hairless from snout to hind quarters. A cybernetic crown covered the wolf's eyes and top of its head. Its shoulder came up to Seaver's chest, ivory teeth glistening with saliva.

The wolf jumped onto a woman and bit down on her shoulder. It shook her back and forth, snapping her neck from side to side, then ran back into a chamber, carrying the body in its jaws.

A second wolf stalked out of the darkness. It snarled and lowered its head almost to the ground, ready to pounce.

Rollins put a boot to the back of one of the people in his initial group and kicked him towards the wolf. The man's screams ended abruptly as the wolf ripped his head away with a single bite.

Snarls rose from the other two chambers. Seaver and his two friends inched back towards the middle of the arena.

"Three more." Rollins brought his hammer back and swung at another prisoner. His target dove away and scrambled for the weapon rack, where he picked up a mace.

A scream broke out behind Seaver as a wolf dragged another into the darkness.

One of the wolves loped towards the center, and Seaver felt a sense of atavistic dread as the predator closed on him. The wolf suddenly stopped, as if hitting an invisible wall, diodes on the cyborg crown flashing. It retreated to a chamber, tail tucked between its legs.

"What gives?" Inez asked.

"I think...they want us to do the rest," Powell said.

Two prisoners armed with hand-held axes charged at Seaver. Powell backed away, her sword held high, chopping at the air to ward off the rushers.

Seaver backpedaled, then stopped when he heard the growl of a wolf behind him. He tightened his grip on his spear, then lunged forward and thrust it at the nearest attacker. The spear ripped across the man's flank, drawing blood and a cry of pain. Seaver swiped the spear at the other man just as he swung. The haft hit his arm, the impact knocking the spear out of Seaver's grip and sending it clattering to the floor.

The axe man's weapon sliced down, narrowly

missing Seaver's face. The attacker was so focused on his next strike that he didn't see Inez as the man plowed into him with a shoulder bash.

The attacker stumbled to the side and fell into a roll. Seaver picked up his spear and found the man he'd injured. He lay on the ground, head at an ugly angle, with Rollins standing over the body.

"Good." Rollins nodded emphatically and lifted his bloody hammer up next to his face. "One more." He pointed to Seaver's side.

The other attacker with the axe lay in a pool of spreading blood, half of his weapon sticking out from beneath his body, the blade of his own weapon buried in his chest.

"Just one more." Rollins' eyes were wide, his mouth half open.

The first person the Marine attacked, the one with the broken shoulder, crept up behind Rollins, a dagger in his hand.

"We kill the weak ones." Rollins pointed at Powell.

Seaver kept his mouth shut as the man with the knife raised the weapon up and plunged it into the base of Rollins' neck. Rollins barely managed a grunt as the other man wrenched the knife out. A spurt of blood spilled down Rollins' chest and he fell on his face.

The cuffs around Seaver's wrists hummed and a shock went through the back of his hands, forcing them to open and drop the spear. The clatter of fallen weapons echoed through the arena as the prisoners all suffered at the same time.

He felt a pull on his arms like there was a rope dragging him by the wrists towards one of the plates in the floor. Seaver tried to pull back, but the pull grew so strong, it took him off his feet. He slid across the floor until his wrists locked against a plate.

The other four prisoners were all locked in to his immediate left and right. The dead lay where they fell.

From a dark chamber, a tall, straight-backed woman in Daegon armor marched towards them, the bald man from earlier two steps behind her. She stopped in front of Inez and touched him gently just below the chin, lifting it up to look at her. Her helmet visor lifted up and shifted to the top of her hair. She had deep blue skin and sapphire colored eyes.

The Daegon turned her head to speak with the other man, who answered with a nod.

She moved to Powell next. Tears had cut through some of the grime smeared to her face. The Daegon put two fingers next to Powell's' throat and inch-long blades snapped from the tip of her gloves. Powell closed her eyes.

"You there, spear," the other man said to Seaver. "You want this one fight beside you? She worth the trouble?"

"Yes! Yes, you said you wanted five. You got your five. Leave her alone." Seaver tugged at his restraints.

The blades snapped back into the Daegon's gloves and she came to Seaver. He looked up at her, taking in her strange appearance and a thin scar that ran below one eye, branching along its path like a lightning bolt.

She reached across her waist, then backhanded Seaver so hard he saw stars.

"Head down, mouth shut when you're around the masters," the other man said. "They lift your chin only if they think you serve well."

Blood dripped from a split lip and fell onto his restraints.

She grabbed Seaver by the back of the head and pressed her other palm against the Albian's face. There was an instant of excruciating pain on his face and the smell of burnt meat.

Seaver pulled back, his eyes twitching with pain.

The Daegon moved away. He sat with his chin against his chest, the pain in his face receding slowly. He heard muffled screams from the others, then his restraints unlocked from the floor.

The woman was gone, the man remained. The other prisoners all had brands on their face, an angular hourglass, the same as the man's.

"I am your legio. Name Keoni. Don't say so before culling, bad luck for a ghost to have your name on their lips," he said. "I no master. I thrall like you, but still a legio." He gave the truncheon hanging from his belt a touch.

"Can talk to me. Can ask question. You get

the whip for failure, *I* get the whip too," Keoni said. "Centurion Juliae hard, but she fair. We lucky. Some centurions use thralls to stop bullets, then just get more thralls. Our Centurion won't get us killed for nothing."

"You're not...one of them?" Seaver asked.

Keoni rubbed his face, then looked at his fingers. "Not blue, eh? I born on Papa'apoho. Then masters come lead us. I join themata and be thrall like you. Come. You need armor. Weapon." He sniffed the air. "Bath."

Seaver stood up and touched the brand on his face. The raw nerves still stung.

"So what're we going to do in this...themata?" he asked.

"Fight." Keoni pounded a fist into his palm twice. "I no fight on Albion, bad if we take in new thralls. You no fight here either. Masters not stupid.

Come. Stay with me. You get lost, other legio find you." He tapped his truncheon.

Seaver spat out a glob of blood.

Keoni motioned to a chamber with a jerk of his head, then walked towards it. The other two Albion thralls followed, one cradling a broken shoulder. Powell hurried after them. Inez shrugged at Seaver.

Seaver's cheek spasmed as he was the last to join the procession out of the arena.

"My father is alive," he whispered. "Prince Aidan lives. Albion…her light still burns through me."

CHAPTER 28

Eubulus walked across the wide bridge of his dreadnought, the *Medusa*, the holo emitters in the deck giving him a semi-opaque view of the desert world beneath his feet. Malout was a fringe Indus world, its strategic value lying in the nexus connections to other systems, not in the population eking out a miserable existence. Black smoke carried away from burning cities. Streaks of fire from dying starships cut across the sky. Tiny pinpricks of explosions marked the edge of the world's last organized resistance.

A sphere appeared next to his head and a text message spun across the surface. In the distance, Daegon ships emerged from slip space.

"Well, well. Look who's back." Eubulus snapped his fingers and the sphere expanded and reformed into a holo of Tiberian.

"Where are the rest of my ships, brother?" Eubulus asked.

"Lost to the crusade. Their skills were found wanting," Tiberian said.

"I have more faith in their training and discipline than your leadership," Eubulus said, looking up from the destruction below and eyeing his fellow commander. "And my son?"

Gustavus stepped into the holo, the left half of his face a mess of fresh scar tissue.

Eubulus snarled at Tiberian.

"Uncle's search continues, Father," Gustavus

said. "I've learned much from him...and this," he waved fingertips over his ruined face, "I might keep."

"If you think I will waste more resources for your task, you are a fool, Tiberian," Eubulus said.

"The Albians fled to New Madras." Tiberian touched the slate-gray box hanging from his neck, reminding Eubulus just where Tiberian's authority came from. Baroness Asaria set Tiberian to capture the last of Albion's royal family, and her authority came with Tiberian. "That is your next objective, correct?"

"A more difficult world to conquer than this." Eubulus scraped his heel over the projection from Malout. "New Madras promises some sport. Our specters have destroyed the slip network. The Albians will be there when we attack."

"Then take your ships and your son back," Tiberian said. "I and the *Minotaur* will join your assault."

"You will *serve* under my command and follow my orders," Eubulus said. "You are under my leash until I choose to set you loose. Is that understood?"

The two brothers stared each other down, then Tiberian lifted his chin slightly, signaling his submission by offering a bare throat to cut.

"Too much has been lost trying to capture the Prince," Eubulus said. "We will destroy every Albion ship we find. If the boy dies, he dies."

CHAPTER 29

Gage watched a timer in his holo tank count down to zero, then the *Orion* shifted out of slip space.

"Time to see if you're right, Loussan," Gage said.

"This is not my first rodeo. I know how to get into a system without being noticed," the pirate said.

Data poured into the tank and the New Madras system unfolded. The system's only inhabitable world, just on the outer edge of the Goldilocks Zone from the star, appeared. Large polar ice caps extended almost a quarter of the way to the equator. The *Orion* had emerged several hundred thousand kilometers away, between the orbits of Madras' two large moons.

Star forts popped up around the planet. Icons for civilian ships and Indus naval vessels sprang up over the poles and in high orbit over New Madras City.

"XO?" Gage asked.

"System's communication network is still intact. No unusual radiation in the atmosphere or sign of widespread fires," Price said. "Looks like we got here before the Daegon."

An error message beeped on her screens.

"Odd. No reading from the grav buoy," she said.

"We're being hailed," Clarke said. "A Fleet Admiral Chadda."

"Send it through." Gage straightened his

uniform.

"A hail, much better greeting than I ever got here," Loussan said.

"Given your assistance, I'm willing to overlook your many Albion arrest warrants," Gage said. "You have no such arrangement with New Madras, and if Admiral Chadda demands you and your crew, I'm hardly in a position to refuse."

"You son of a...you brought me all this way just to throw me to the wolves now?"

"No, Loussan. I'm telling you to keep your damn mouth shut while I'm speaking with the Indus. I won't advertise that you're aboard if you don't." Gage hovered a finger over an icon to open the channel to Chadda.

Loussan ducked beneath the holo tank.

A dark-skinned man in a white turban and high-necked tunic with gold cord and braids appeared in the tank. The exhaustion in his eyes made Gage question if the gray hairs in the man's beard were a recent occurrence.

"*Sat sri akaal,*" Admiral Chadda said as he pressed his hands together, his fingertips just ahead of his chin.

Gage nodded back.

"Admiral, I am Commodore Gage of the Albion 11th Fleet. The rest of my ships will exit slip space shortly. Please forgive our abrupt and…unusual arrival," he said.

"A battleship appearing on our scopes through a nexus point leading to dead space…you gave me and my staff quite a stir. So long as you're not Daegon, you're most welcome here." Chadda glanced to one side. "By the condition of your ship, I'd say you've dealt with the invaders…I do hope you burned all the bridges you took to get here. I barely have enough ships to cover the slip routes from known Daegon incursions."

"We destroyed the grav buoys at our last three jumps. The path through the Kigeli Nebula is difficult enough, and we gave them a decent beating the last time we saw them."

"Kigeli…the old pirate route?" Chadda raised an eyebrow.

"Needs must, Admiral. How far have the Daegon advanced?"

"Bengal fell two days ago. Tsing Yi is under siege. My scouts have seen Daegon in three neighboring systems…it is only a matter of time before they come to New Madras."

"What of the League? Have they responded yet? The Reich, Cathay, even the Mechanix must respond to this," Gage said.

Price sent a star map to the side of Chadda,

showing the stars the Daegon now occupied. Gage swallowed hard. No belligerent had ever advanced so far and so fast in the history of interstellar warfare.

"The League meets on Vishuddha," Chadda said. "Let us hope they move with unprecedented speed or the Daegon will reach Earth before the first meeting is finished."

"We've fought them," Gage said. "We've beaten them. I will take my ships to Vishuddha and share what we've learned to—"

"I'm afraid that won't be possible." Chadda shook his head. "Not for some time. Our grav buoys—and every single backup—were sabotaged. We tracked down the spies responsible, but that was a small victory. It will take weeks to replace the lost data."

Gage's jaw clenched. He'd led his fleet into an imminent war zone. The shadow of the Daegon still loomed over him and Prince Aidan.

"Albion and Indus are allies. We welcome your ships to join our line until you're able to leave," the admiral said. "Only a few ships have ever escaped the Daegon. Anything you can share will be most helpful."

"We stand shoulder to shoulder. We threw back the Reich the last time our nations fought together. The Daegon will do no better."

"We shall see…" Chadda's face fell slightly and Gage's hand clenched into a fist. This admiral did not carry himself with confidence. The air of defeat in a commander could poison any fighting force. The Indus military normally picked the best qualified men for key positions, and Gage began to wonder just how Chadda ended up as an admiral.

"You are our guests. Bring your ships into New Madras orbit," Chadda said. "Albion vessels will receive the highest priority for repairs. I hope you and your staff will join me for a meal once conditions allow."

"The Indus are gracious hosts as ever," Gage said and the channel closed.

Loussan peeked over the side of the tank.

"Well, that's that." He stood up and brushed himself off. "I promised to get you here. Don't blame me that you've come to a dead end—wait. Poor choice of words. Now, if you'll be so kind as to loan me a slip-capable ship, I'll be—"

"You think we have a spare warship just lying around to give you, pirate?" Price marched up the stairs to the command dais.

"Would you really miss one destroyer all that much? Let's not pretend you want me around. That Genevan guard back there is constantly giving me the look. I'm not sure if he wants to kill me or buy me a drink," Loussan said.

"I can answer that right now," Thorvald said as his armor slid over his bare face and solidified into a visor.

"I may have a ship for you," Gage said.

"Wait—what?" Price went pale.

"Tolan." Gage waved the spy over from his spot next to the lift doors. "We—and every nation fighting the Daegon—are at a distinct disadvantage. We don't know this enemy—what they want, the extent of their combat power...Where they even came from. You found us a clue from that Martian on Sicani, but it isn't enough by far."

"You're the regent." Tolan gave Gage a mock bow. "What would you ask of me?"

"Take your ship, the *Joaquim*, back to wild space. Then slip into occupied territory and learn what you can. Given your...unique capabilities, you stand a good chance of success," Gage said.

Tolan tugged at his bottom lip, then looked at Loussan.

"Is there another way back through the nebula?" the spy asked.

"Naturally," said Loussan. "One more suited to a smaller ship than an entire damn fleet. Can you fit thirty of my crew into this *Joaquim* of yours? They're rather anxious to get out of the brig."

"No chance," Tolan said.

"Who in your crew do you absolutely trust?" Gage asked.

"Besides Ruprecht, my Katar that's hard wired to protect my life at all costs? Maybe Tatiana. She's the only one that hasn't been whispering for my blood. The rest are a bunch of ingrates. Sure, we lost our ship, but they're all still alive, aren't they?"

"Get Tolan back to Albion space," Gage said.

"Then bring him back to me once he's gathered enough intelligence and you can have his ship."

"That's...that's..."

"The only deal I will give you. I'll hand over the rest of your crew to the Indus. Any *not* wanted by local law enforcement will go free. You go with Tolan or you take your chances with the Indus. Choose. Now."

"Did I spy some Reich tech on that ship of yours?" Loussan asked Tolan.

"You can do this?" Gage asked his spy.

"Infiltrate into occupied territory and get back to you without being captured and tortured to death?" Tolan's face fluttered, then went all black like Ja'war's. "Challenge accepted."

****

Prince Aidan held on to Gage's hand as they watched crewmen load supplies and finish repairs on the *Joaquim*. Salis and Thorvald stood to either side of them. Through the open bay door, most of what was in view of New Madras was bathed in twilight.

"But I want to go back home," Aidan said.

"Mr. Tolan has a special job to do there," Gage said. "One not for young princes."

"When can I go?" Aidan looked up at Gage. "I don't like this place anymore."

"Do you know what a consulate is, my Prince?" Gage asked.

Aidan shook his head.

"It's a part of Albion on other planets. We have a consulate on New Madras City. It's very well protected and the woman in charge, Lady Carruthers, is very excited to have you stay with her." Gage forced a smile. The consulate was in the center of the planet's largest city, which would be the focus of any Daegon attack. Still, it had a bomb shelter and an entire corps of Indus troops in and around the city, offering a better chance of survival than being aboard the *Orion* in a ship-to-ship fight.

"Will you come with me?" Aidan asked.

"No, I have to stay here. But Salis will go with you," Gage said.

The Prince pouted.

"I want Mr. Bertram." Aidan's lip began quivering and he pointed to the steward standing behind them.

"Prince Aidan, I do need—"

"I want Mr. Bertram!" Aidan stomped a foot and began whining. Bertram stood stock-still, his eyes darting to the exit.

"Fine, he'll go with you." Gage took a deep breath as crew glanced over at the crying Prince. Salis slowly turned her head to Gage. "Until such time as the Prince is comfortable with the local staff," he said to the Genevan.

Aidan's sniffling subsided.

"How long?" Aidan asked.

"No more than—" Alert sirens cut Gage off as Prince Aidan hugged the side of Gage's leg.

"Commodore," Price sent through Gage's earpiece, *"Daegon ships just emerged from slip space. They came in just over the horizon and are attacking the star fort above Theni City."*

"Any instruction from Admiral Chadda?" Gage asked.

"Nothing yet. At least nothing coherent. The Indus command channels are chaos right now. The attacking force is anywhere from a dozen ships to fifty, might just be a reconnaissance in force."

"Might be the beginning of a full-scale

invasion," Gage said. "Salis, take Prince Aidan and Bertram to the consulate. The alert fighters will escort you down to the spaceport."

"Understood," she said, reaching for the boy.

"No! I want to stay!" Aidan yelled.

Gage bent to one knee and looked the Prince in the eye.

"Prince Aidan," the Commodore said evenly, "you are the light and the hope of Albion. I must keep you safe, and I can't do that while you're aboard the *Orion*. Will you be brave for me, for everyone on this ship, and go with Ms. Salis to the consulate?"

Aidan shook his head rapidly.

"My Prince," Bertram said as he shuffled over, "I'm dreadfully scared. Would you protect me down there on the new planet?"

Aidan let go of his hold on Gage's leg.

"For a grown-up, you aren't very brave,"

Aidan said.

"Well, the Commodore's brave enough for me and everyone else," Bertram said. "I just have to make sure he eats his dinner and washes up from time to time. Can we go now?"

"Yes, we can." Aidan looked up at Gage with wide eyes. "Will you be okay?"

"The *Orion* is a strong ship. We'll be fine." Gage forced a smile, not knowing if that second part was a lie.

"Bay seven has a shuttle ready for us," Salis said. She picked Aidan up and hurried away as Bertram followed.

The steward pointed at Thorvald and said, "Anything happens to the Commodore, you'll answer to me. And don't you dare shine his boots with the generic polish!"

Gage looked out beyond New Madras as

explosions flashed over the horizon.

THE END

The story continues in *Their Finest Hour*!

ABOUT THE AUTHOR

Richard Fox is the author of The Ember War Saga, and several other military history, thriller and space opera novels.

He lives in fabulous Las Vegas with his incredible wife and two boys, amazing children bent on anarchy.

He graduated from the United States Military Academy (West Point) much to his surprise and spent ten years on active duty in the United States Army. He deployed on two combat tours to Iraq and received the Combat Action Badge, Bronze Star and Presidential Unit Citation.

Sign up for his mailing list over at www.richardfoxauthor.com to stay up to date on new releases and get exclusive Ember War short stories.

The Ember War Saga:

1.) The Ember War
2.) The Ruins of Anthalas
3.) Blood of Heroes
4.) Earth Defiant
5.) The Gardens of Nibiru
6.) Battle of the Void
7.) The Siege of Earth
8.) The Crucible
9.) The Xaros Reckoning

Printed in Great Britain
by Amazon